PATRICIA WENTWORTH
HOLE AND CORNER

PATRICIA WENTWORTH was born Dora Amy Elles in India in 1877 (not 1878 as has sometimes been stated). She was first educated privately in India, and later at Blackheath School for Girls. Her first husband was George Dillon, with whom she had her only child, a daughter. She also had two stepsons from her first marriage, one of whom died in the Somme during World War I.

Her first novel was published in 1910, but it wasn't until the 1920's that she embarked on her long career as a writer of mysteries. Her most famous creation was Miss Maud Silver, who appeared in 32 novels, though there were a further 33 full-length mysteries not featuring Miss Silver—the entire run of these is now reissued by Dean Street Press.

Patricia Wentworth died in 1961. She is recognized today as one of the pre-eminent exponents of the classic British golden age mystery novel.

By Patricia Wentworth

PATRICIA WENTWORTH

HOLE AND CORNER

With an introduction by
Curtis Evans

DEAN STREET PRESS

Published by Dean Street Press 2016

Copyright © 1936 Patricia Wentworth

Introduction copyright © 2016 Curtis Evans

All Rights Reserved

Cover by DSP

First published in 1936 by Hodder & Stoughton

ISBN 978 1 911413 27 1

www.deanstreetpress.co.uk

Introduction

BRITISH AUTHOR Patricia Wentworth published her first novel, a gripping tale of desperate love during the French Revolution entitled *A Marriage under the Terror*, a little over a century ago, in 1910. The book won first prize in the Melrose Novel Competition and was a popular success in both the United States and the United Kingdom. Over the next five years Wentworth published five additional novels, the majority of them historical fiction, the best-known of which today is *The Devil's Wind* (1912), another sweeping period romance, this one set during the Sepoy Mutiny (1857-58) in India, a region with which the author, as we shall see, had extensive familiarity. Like *A Marriage under the Terror*, *The Devil's Wind* received much praise from reviewers for its sheer storytelling élan. One notice, for example, pronounced the novel "an achievement of some magnitude" on account of "the extraordinary vividness...the reality of the atmosphere...the scenes that shift and move with the swiftness of a moving picture...." (*The Bookman*, August 1912) With her knack for spinning a yarn, it perhaps should come as no surprise that Patricia Wentworth during the early years of the Golden Age of mystery fiction (roughly from 1920 into the 1940s) launched upon her own mystery-writing career, a course charted most successfully for nearly four decades by the prolific author, right up to the year of her death in 1961.

Considering that Patricia Wentworth belongs to the select company of Golden Age mystery writers with books which have remained in print in every decade for nearly a century now (the centenary of Agatha Christie's first mystery, *The Mysterious Affair at Styles*, is in 2020; the centenary of Wentworth's first mystery, *The Astonishing Adventure of Jane Smith*, follows merely three years later, in 2023), relatively little is known about the author herself. It appears, for example, that even the widely given year of Wentworth's birth, 1878, is incorrect. Yet it is sufficiently clear that Wentworth lived a varied and intriguing life that provided her ample inspiration for a writing career devoted to imaginative fiction.

It is usually stated that Patricia Wentworth was born Dora Amy Elles on 10 November 1878 in Mussoorie, India, during the heyday of the British Raj; however, her Indian birth and baptismal record states that she in fact was born on 15 October 1877 and was baptized on 26 November of that same year in Gwalior. Whatever doubts surround her actual birth year, however, unquestionably the future author came from a prominent Anglo-Indian military family. Her father, Edmond Roche Elles, a son of Malcolm Jamieson Elles, a Porto, Portugal wine merchant originally from Ardrossan, Scotland, entered the British Royal Artillery in 1867, a decade before Wentworth's birth, and first saw service in India during the Lushai Expedition of 1871-72. The next year Elles in India wed Clara Gertrude Rothney, daughter of Brigadier-General Octavius Edward Rothney, commander of the Gwalior District, and Maria (Dempster) Rothney, daughter of a surgeon in the Bengal Medical Service. Four children were born of the union of Edmond and Clara Elles, Wentworth being the only daughter.

Before his retirement from the army in 1908, Edmond Elles rose to the rank of lieutenant-general and was awarded the KCB (Knight Commander of the Order of Bath), as was the case with his elder brother, Wentworth's uncle, Lieutenant-General Sir William Kidston Elles, of the Bengal Command. Edmond Elles also served as Military Member to the Council of the Governor-General of India from 1901 to 1905. Two of Wentworth's brothers, Malcolm Rothney Elles and Edmond Claude Elles, served in the Indian Army as well, though both of them died young (Malcolm in 1906 drowned in the Ganges Canal while attempting to rescue his orderly, who had fallen into the water), while her youngest brother, Hugh Jamieson Elles, achieved great distinction in the British Army. During the First World War he catapulted, at the relatively youthful age of 37, to the rank of brigadier-general and the command of the British Tank Corps, at the Battle of Cambrai personally leading the advance of more than 350 tanks against the German line. Years later Hugh Elles also played a major role in British civil defense during the Second World War. In the event of a German invasion of Great Britain, something which seemed all too possible in 1940, he was tasked with leading the defense of southwestern England. Like Sir Edmond and Sir William, Hugh Elles attained the rank of lieutenant-general and was awarded the KCB.

Although she was born in India, Patricia Wentworth spent much of her childhood in England. In 1881 she with her mother and two younger brothers was at Tunbridge Wells, Kent, on what appears to have been a rather extended visit in her ancestral country; while a decade later the same family group resided at Blackheath, London at Lennox House, domicile of Wentworth's widowed maternal grandmother, Maria Rothney. (Her eldest brother, Malcolm, was in Bristol attending Clifton College.) During her years at Lennox House, Wentworth attended Blackheath High School for Girls, then only recently founded as "one of the first schools in the country to give girls a proper education" (*The London Encyclopaedia*, 3rd ed., p. 74). Lennox House was an ample Victorian villa with a great glassed-in conservatory running all along the back and a substantial garden-- most happily, one presumes, for Wentworth, who resided there not only with her grandmother, mother and two brothers, but also five aunts (Maria Rothney's unmarried daughters, aged 26 to 42), one adult first cousin once removed and nine first cousins, adolescents like Wentworth herself, from no less than three different families (one Barrow, three Masons and five Dempsters); their parents, like Wentworth's father, presumably were living many miles away in various far-flung British dominions. Three servants--a cook, parlourmaid and housemaid--were tasked with serving this full score of individuals.

Sometime after graduating from Blackheath High School in the mid-1890s, Wentworth returned to India, where in a local British newspaper she is said to have published her first fiction. In 1901 the 23-year-old Wentworth married widower George Fredrick Horace Dillon, a 41-year-old lieutenant-colonel in the Indian Army with three sons from his prior marriage. Two years later Wentworth gave birth to her only child, a daughter named Clare Roche Dillon. (In some sources it is erroneously stated that Clare was the offspring of Wentworth's second marriage.) However in 1906, after just five years of marriage, George Dillon died suddenly on a sea voyage, leaving Wentworth with sole responsibility for her three teenaged stepsons and baby daughter. A very short span of years, 1904 to 1907, saw the deaths of Wentworth's husband, mother, grandmother and brothers Malcolm and Edmond, removing much of her support network. In 1908, however, her father, who was now sixty years old, retired from the army and returned to England, settling at Guildford, Surrey with an older unmarried sister named Dora (for whom his daughter presumably had been named). Wentworth joined this household as well, along with her daughter and her youngest stepson. Here in Surrey Wentworth, presumably with the goal of making herself financially independent for the first time in her life (she was now in her early thirties), wrote the novel that changed the course of her life, *A Marriage under the Terror*, for the first time we know of utilizing her famous *nom de plume*.

The burst of creative energy that resulted in Wentworth's publication of six novels in six years suddenly halted after the appearance of *Queen Anne Is Dead* in 1915. It seems not unlikely that the Great War impinged in various ways on her writing. One tragic episode was the death on the western front of one of her stepsons, George Charles Tracey Dillon. Mining in Colorado when war was declared, young Dillon worked his passage from Galveston, Texas to Bristol, England as a shipboard muleteer (mule-tender) and joined the Gloucestershire Regiment. In 1916 he died at the Somme at the age of 29 (about the age of Wentworth's two brothers when they had passed away in India).

A couple of years after the conflict's cessation in 1918, a happy event occurred in Wentworth's life when at Frimley, Surrey she wed George Oliver Turnbull, up to this time a lifelong bachelor who like the author's first husband was a lieutenant-colonel in the Indian Army. Like his bride now forty-two years old, George Turnbull as a younger man had distinguished himself for his athletic prowess, playing forward for eight years for the Scottish rugby team and while a student at the Royal Military Academy winning the medal awarded the best athlete of his term. It seems not unlikely that Turnbull played a role in his wife's turn toward writing mystery fiction, for he is said to have strongly supported Wentworth's career, even assisting her in preparing manuscripts for publication. In 1936 the couple in Camberley, Surrey built Heatherglade House, a large two-story structure on substantial grounds, where they resided until Wentworth's death a quarter of a century later. (George Turnbull survived his wife by nearly a decade, passing away in 1970 at the age of 92.) This highly successful middle-aged companionate marriage contrasts sharply with the more youthful yet rocky union of Agatha and Archie Christie, which was three years away from sundering when Wentworth published *The Astonishing Adventure of Jane Smith* (1923), the first of her sixty-five mystery novels.

Although Patricia Wentworth became best-known for her cozy tales of the criminal investigations of consulting detective Miss Maud Silver, one of the mystery genre's most prominent spinster sleuths, in truth the Miss Silver tales account for just under half of Wentworth's 65 mystery novels. Miss Silver did not make her debut until 1928 and she did not come to predominate in Wentworth's fictional criminous output until the 1940s. Between 1923 and 1945 Wentworth published 33 mystery novels without Miss Silver, a handsome and substantial legacy in and of itself to vintage crime fiction fans. Many of these books are standalone tales of mystery, but nine of them have series characters. Debuting in the novel *Fool Errant* in 1929, a year after Miss Silver first appeared in print, was the enigmatic, nautically-named *eminence grise* Benbow Collingwood Horatio Smith, owner of a most expressively opinionated parrot named Ananias (and quite a colorful character in his own right). Benbow Smith went on to appear in three additional Wentworth mysteries: *Danger Calling* (1931), *Walk with Care* (1933) and *Down Under* (1937). Working in tandem with Smith in the investigation of sinister affairs threatening the security of Great Britain in *Danger Calling* and *Walk with Care* is Frank Garrett, Head of Intelligence for the Foreign Office, who also appears solo in *Dead or Alive* (1936) and *Rolling Stone* (1940) and collaborates with additional series characters, Scotland Yard's Inspector Ernest Lamb and Sergeant Frank Abbott, in *Pursuit of a Parcel* (1942). Inspector Lamb and Sergeant Abbott headlined a further pair of mysteries, *The Blind Side* (1939) and *Who Pays the Piper?* (1940), before they became absorbed, beginning with *Miss Silver Deals with Death* (1943), into the burgeoning Miss Silver canon. Lamb would make his farewell appearance in 1955 in *The Listening Eye*, while Abbott would take his final bow in mystery fiction with Wentworth's last published novel, *The Girl in the Cellar* (1961), which went into print the year of the author's death at the age of 83.

The remaining two dozen Wentworth mysteries, from the fantastical *The Astonishing Adventure of Jane Smith* in 1923 to the intense legal drama *Silence in Court* in 1945, are, like the author's series novels, highly imaginative and entertaining tales of mystery and adventure, told by a writer gifted with a consummate flair for storytelling. As one confirmed Patricia Wentworth mystery fiction addict, American Golden Age mystery writer Todd Downing, admiringly declared in the 1930s, "There's something about Miss Wentworth's yarns that is contagious." This attractive new series of Patricia Wentworth reissues by Dean Street Press provides modern fans of vintage mystery a splendid opportunity to catch the Wentworth fever.

Curtis Evans

Chapter One

WILLIAM AMBROSE MEREWETHER was altering his will. This was his most constant recreation. It was also a steady source of income to the lawyers who managed his affairs. Whenever he had an ailment which confined him to the house, it was his practice to send for Mr Van Leiten or for his son Schuyler and play the fascinating game of curtailing legacies here and doubling them there, striking out a New York hospital and substituting one in Washington, deciding to give a year's wages to all his employees, or to found a magnificently endowed retreat for superannuated members of the teaching profession, then doubling this with a stroke of the pen so as to provide two establishments, one male, one female, and finally sweeping the whole thing away in favour of hostels for sales-ladies. At one time or another he had bequeathed magnificent sums to practically every scientific, philanthropic, and educational body in the United States. High-sounding titles decorated a page of Mr Van Leiten's foolscap for a brief space, and then gave way to other titles, other names.

To-day it was Schuyler Van Leiten who was in attendance, a man of about forty with a shrewd, pleasant face and a figure already tending to heaviness. He sat in one of Mr Merewether's excellent and expensive chairs, and William Ambrose Merewether, wrapped in a dressing-gown of scarlet and blue silk, sat in another. Beneath the dressing-gown he was fully dressed. It served merely to advertise the fact that he was, officially, indisposed, as did the scarlet leather bedroom slippers which replaced his ordinary footwear. He sat forward in his chair with his very thick white hair standing up like the crest of a cockatoo and a bright dancing gleam in his pale blue eyes. His thin old face wore an expression of lively interest, and when he wished to make a point his forefinger shot out at Schuyler Van Leiten in a curious stabbing motion.

"The West Central Hospital comes out?"

William Ambrose nodded.

"They don't get a cent," he said. "No more do the whole lot of these," He whisked a paper out of his dressing-gown pocket, leaned forward, and shot it at Schuyler, "Take 'em all out—the whole darned lot of 'em! They don't get a cent, none of 'em—not a cent!"

Schuylet Van Leiten was well trained. He made a note, and waited. This was all in the day's work. "Presently," he thought, "when the old man's run through all the lot of them, he'll have to make a fresh start and work through again. When he dies, some will be lucky and some won't. It's a gamble, like roulette." He looked up, pleasantly inquiring, and saw old William Ambrose sitting very taut, a hand on either knee and the oddest flicker of a smile about his thin lips.

"Ready, Schuyler?"

"Oh quite."

"What we've just knocked off totals up to a million dollars, and I'm putting that into a trust. You'll be one of the trustees, and your father'll be another, and J. J. Wilson'll be the third. Have you got that? A million in trust for the descendants, if any, of my cousin Jane Lorimer."

"One r or two?" said Schuyler. His face remained impassive, but he raised a mental eyebrow. Never before had any relative figured in the long procession of William Ambrose Merewether's legatees. Servants, employees, business associates, and institutions had passed, repassed, and jostled one another upon the pages of his will, but this was the first mention of any warmer claim.

Schuyler, an easy-going man with a wife as pleasant as himself and a cheerful, affectionate family of boys and girls growing up, had a momentary feeling of pity. If the only folks you could rake together were the hypothetical descendants of a cousin whom no one had ever heard of, it was a shade bleaker than having no folks at all.

He looked up, and found William Ambrose regarding him with amusement.

"One r—but you don't need to trouble too much about it, because if she didn't quit being Lorimer a good long time ago, there won't be any descendants."

"You don't know if she was married?"

William Ambrose shook his head and emitted a short cackling laugh.

"She wasn't the sort to stay single, but I don't know anything. It's fifty years since I saw her—fifty years since I've heard from her—fifty years since I heard of her. And what do you think was the last thing she said to me? 'I should hate to marry you,' she said, 'but when you've made that fortune you've been bragging about you can send me some of it for a Christmas present.' And she threw a rosebud at me, hard as a bullet, and hit me in the eye, and no thanks to her that I wasn't blinded. And then she ran away, laughing at me, and if I could have killed her without getting hanged for it, I'd have done it then and there. And I cleared out and came over here and made the fortune I'd set out to make—and I'd had enough of asking young women to marry me, so I've managed to keep what I made. So now Jane's going to get her Christmas present—she or her descendants. Better make it two million in case there are a lot of them. Yes, two million—and that'll mean knocking it off somewhere else. Got a list of the legacies there? Just hand 'em over and let me see where we can get the other million.... Here we are!" He ran a pencil down the list of names, bending over it agog with interest.

The legacies began as it were to slide, to mingle, to interlace. Some disappeared altogether, others emerged like frail ghosts without weight or substance. In the end William Ambrose had collected his second million. He pushed the list back to Schuyler with a triumphant "There!" Then, hands on knees again, he said in his thin, dry voice,

"Two million dollars in trust for my cousin Jane Lorimer or her descendants—"

"One moment, Mr Merewether—do they share equally?"

William Ambrose considered this. The fingers of his right hand played a tune upon his knee, a slow tune which changed suddenly into a quick-step. He gave his cackling laugh again, stopped the dancing fingers, and said in a pleased voice,

"Equal shares—equal shares all round. No, no—wait a minute, Schuyler—cross that out. I can do better than that. Yes, yes, I can do a whole lot better than that. If Jane's alive she can have the lot—but she isn't alive."

Schuyler Van Leiten preserved his patience.

"Don't you know whether she's alive, Mr Merewether?"

"I told you I didn't, didn't I? Told you I hadn't heard of her in fifty years. You don't attend—that's what's the matter with you, Schuyler. Now you sit right up and take notice, because I don't expect to say everything twice! If Jane's alive she can have the lot, but I'm pretty well sure she's dead—I've got that kind of feeling about her." The quick gleam danced in his eyes. "Jane's gone, and if I'm wrong she can have the laugh of me."

"Well, Mr Merewether?"

"Then we come to the next generation. If there are half a dozen sons and daughters, they get equal shares all round. If there's only one, that one'll take the lot. If there's been half a dozen of 'em, the survivor gets it all. Have you got that?"

Schuyler nodded,

"You're not putting in the grandchildren?"

"Not if there's a son or daughter of Jane's alive—unless—but we'll come to that presently. And if there isn't a surviving child, then the grandchildren divide, whether there's two of 'em, or five, or fifty. And whether it's Jane herself, or her children, or her grandchildren, they'll all be under the same condition. If Jane breaks it, the whole goes down to the children. If one of 'em breaks it, that one loses his share to the rest. If there's no one in that generation that complies with the condition, then the grandchildren come in." He lifted up his hands and let them drop again upon his knees with a resounding smack. "I'd like to see Jane's face when she hears about the condition! Pity I can't! And a pity if she's dead, because I'd like to get a bit of my own back on Jane—after fifty years."

"What's eating the old man now?" said Schuyler to himself. But aloud he said, "Oh—there's a condition?"

"There's a very important condition," said William Ambrose Merewether.

Chapter Two

SHIRLEY DALE made a face at the London fog. It was a face which had had an immense vogue in her school, where it was known as a Woggy Doodle. The eyes bulged and squinted, the nose appeared to curve downwards, and the lips widened into a grin of almost unbelievable idiocy. It is said to have been inspired by the picture of the Jabberwock in *Through the Looking-Glass*. The whole school had laboured and panted in imitation, but Shirley's preeminence had never been seriously questioned. The perfect Woggy Doodle was hers, and hers alone. She made it now at the fog, and felt a good deal relieved. When a fog has gone on for three days, you have to do something to show it how poisonously loathsome it is.

Having shown it, she whisked round to look in the glass and make sure that her face hadn't lost its cunning. It hadn't. The Woggy Doodle was distinctly a good Woggy Doodle—one of the best. And then, even as she caught sight of it, it broke up in a burst of laughter. You couldn't really look at a Woggy Doodle and hold it at the same time—your nose began to twitch, and then you were lost.

Shirley's features resumed their normal appearance. Her nose had a slight upward tilt really. A pleasant little nose, soft and very lightly powdered with freckles. It wrinkled when she laughed, and it went very well with her rather thick, smudgy eyebrows and her very thick, soft lashes. Between the lashes she had grey eyes—very clear and very grey, without the slightest tinge of green or blue—and the clear, rather bright grey iris was encircled by a ring as black as her lashes. Except when she was making a Woggy Doodle, these rather noticeable eyes had the straightest look in the world. They were the first thing anyone noticed about Shirley, and the last that anyone forgot. She had very dark hair which curled and matched her lashes, and a warm, wide mouth with a further sprinkling of freckles at each corner. The lips were very red, and the teeth inside them very white.

She frowned at herself in the glass and wished for the nine hundred and ninety-ninth time that she was very tall, and willowy, and exotic, with red hair and green eyes, or else the sort of pale gold hair which goes with ice-blue eyes … and she wouldn't walk, she would just undulate … and she would either have a very deep husky voice to go with the red hair and green eyes, or the silvery, mellifluous sort which sounds as if it would break if you tried to say ordinary, sordid words with it—words like rent, job, landlady, and lodger.

Her nose wrinkled at her in the glass, and she laughed. If she couldn't willow or look exotic, she had at least managed to get a job, and that was more than some people did. It wasn't a very exciting job—not in the least what she thought she was going to get when she came up to town. If she had been really willowy, she might have been taken on as a mannequin. She thought it would be too marvellous to trail round wearing Paris models—only perhaps you'd get bored with it after a bit, and it would be dreadfully difficult not to laugh when fat old women bought heavenly slinky clothes which they couldn't possibly get into. But if you laughed, it would be all *up*.

Perhaps it was really better to go and read to Mrs Huddleston, and write her letters, and run her errands. And thank heaven she didn't live in, so she had her evenings, even though they were generally as dull as ditchwater. When you live in a village, you think London is going to be very exciting, but when you live there on two pounds a week London is often very dull indeed.

Shirley paid Mrs Camber twenty-five shillings a week for bed and breakfast. Sometimes she paid her something for lunch, and sometimes she didn't have lunch at all, only a cup of tea and a bun, and that left her about fourteen shillings a week for her supper, her laundry, and her bus fares, to say nothing of clothes, shoes, and amusements. It was very difficult to know what to do about bus fares. They ran away with a most frightful lot of money, but if you walked you got hungry and your shoes wore out. Shirley had only been in town six months, but she was already a little scared about the shoe problem. Clothes could be made to last almost indefinitely, but shoes simply wouldn't.

She switched her thoughts firmly away from shoes. This was one of the days Mrs Camber had given her lunch, and it was time to think about going back to Revelston Crescent. If the fog was going to get any worse, it might take longer than usual. She put on a dark grey coat with a black collar, pulled a black beret over her curls, grabbed a pair of gloves, and took another look out of the window. Her room was on the top floor of a house which was rather taller than its neighbours. She looked down at a foreshortened pillar-box, and the pavement, and the street, and the roofs and windows of other houses, and they all swam in the fog like bits of toast in a plate of lentil soup. *Disgusting.* But it was going to be worse before it was better. She banged her door behind her and ran downstairs, quite regardless of the fact that Miss Maltby would probably seize the opportunity of complaining to Mrs Camber about Noise, Total Lack of Consideration, and The Manners of the Present Generation.

Miss Maltby had two rooms on the next floor. To have a bedroom and a sitting-room naturally placed you in a position to complain about someone who only had a bed-sitting-room, and attic at that.

Shirley stopped for a moment on the landing to put out the tip of her tongue at the nearer of Miss Maltby's doors. She had a front room and a back room, and on the other side of the landing there was Jasper Wrenn's room, and the shabbier of the two bathrooms.

She was in the middle of putting out her tongue, when Jasper Wrenn opened his door. As this happened nearly every time she came downstairs, it caused her neither surprise nor embarrassment. She drew in her tongue, turned round with a casual nod, and exclaimed,

"Glory, Jas! What *have* you been doing?"

Mr Wrenn's scowl deepened perceptibly. He was a dark and ferociously untidy young man. His right hand was imbrued to the knuckles in ink. He passed it over an already murky brow and said crossly,

"What have I been doing about what?"

Shirley put out the tip of her tongue again. It really only just showed and went back, but the intention was clear.

"Ink," she said. "Seas of it. You know—not the multitudinous sort that was encarnadined, but just common or garden black ink all over you like Struwwelpeter—'Eyes, and nose, and face, and hair. Trousers, pinafores and toys—'"

Jasper removed the hand from his brow and gazed at her.

"I've been writing."

Shirley giggled.

"I'm so frightfully clever, I guessed that." She came a little nearer. "Where have you got to in the book? Are they still having nothing to eat? I do wish you'd feed your people. I've got a feeling that they wouldn't make such an awful muck of everything if you'd let them have a proper meal sometimes."

Jasper ran his inky fingers through his hair. A slightly sheepish expression struggled through the frown.

"As a matter of fact it wasn't the book. It ought to have been, but it wasn't. I got an idea for a poem. It isn't worked out or anything, but it's an idea." His hand came down from his hair, fished in a gaping pocket, and produced a smeared and crumpled piece of paper. "I could read it to you if you've time."

Shirley said, "'M—not more than five minutes. Mustn't be late, because I was late yesterday, and she said everything you *can* say then. If she had to think of some more to-day, something might go pop, and then I'd be out of a job. I suppose you know you've got a button just hanging."

"It doesn't matter."

"It does. You'll lose it, and then you'll have to buy another. Wait a sec and I'll sew it on while you read me your stuff."

She ran upstairs with even less regard for Miss Maltby's nerves than she had shown when coming down, and was back in a minute with a threaded needle.

"What does it matter about the button?" said Jasper. He gloomed self-consciously at the smudged sheet in his hand, and added with impatience, "Come in and shut the door."

Shirley made a very fine Woggy Doodle at Miss Maltby's doors. Then she skipped into the room, left the door ostentatiously open, and said in a reproving voice,

"Jas, I'm surprised at you! Just think what the Maltby would say! I've got a character if you haven't. Now hurry up with the poem, because I'm not going to be late even for you."

He shrugged a pettish shoulder.

"How can I read anything with the whole house listening?"

Shirley pricked him sharply on the arm with her needle.

"Darling Jas, I shall probably stab you to the heart if you do that again. Nobody's listening, but if they *were*, you ought to be *pleased*. Don't you want to have a public? Come on—get it off your chest!" She bent to the button.

Over her head Mr Wrenn declaimed in tones rendered hoarse by emotion:

> "Wake in the night and find
> That you are blind.
> No left, no right,
> No up, no down,
> No shape or form—
> And there you drown
> In a despair
> That says *'You are not,'*
> And, *'You never were.'*
> Wake in the night and find

That you are blind.
Nothing is real at all,
Nothing is true.
There never was a day,
There is no you.
Wake in the night and find
That you are blind!"

"Glory!" said Shirley. "How *damp!*"

He pulled furiously away from her, and the cotton broke.

"How do you mean *damp*?"

"Now look what you've done! As a matter of fact I'd just finished, so it doesn't matter, except that I might have pricked you to the bone. When people are kindly sewing buttons on for you, you ought to stand still."

"What do you mean by *damp*? That's what I want to know!"

Shirley wrinkled her nose at him.

"Well, it gave me a sort of creep down the middle of my spine—like getting into a wet bathing-dress."

Jasper scowled.

"If it gave you a creep, that's what it was meant to do. Why drag in bathing-dresses?"

Shirley gurgled.

"I didn't drag them in—they came. That's the way my mind works—if I don't think of something practical at once it just goes floating up in the air like a balloon, and then I feel giddy." She darned the needle in behind the revers of her coat and kissed her finger-tips to the frown. "*Some* day the wind will change and you'll get stuck like that. And nobody'll *ever* fall in love with you. Must fly—I'm a wage-slave." She ran down the remaining stairs and all the way to the end of the street, where she scrambled breathless upon a bus. She was in far too great a hurry to notice that the nearer of Miss Maltby's doors was ajar.

Through the crack Miss Maltby watched her go, her little sharp eyes intent behind scant sandy lashes, her long pale nose quivering slightly at the tip, her thin lips folded in and very tightly compressed. She was a tall, bony woman with a forward stoop and a faint habitual cough which was a constant source of annoyance to Jasper Wrenn, who contended that she could control it if she wanted to and only coughed because she liked the sound of her own voice. It was certainly true that she had made no sound all the time she stood spying through the crack. Not a stitch of Shirley's needle, not a frown of Jasper Wrenn's, not a word of their nonsensical talk had escaped her. She now saw Jasper bang his door, and opined that he had plunged again into inky meditation.

She waited five minutes, then opened her door a little wider, and came furtively out upon the landing, an odd figure in a long old-fashioned dress of black cashmere with a tucked silk front, and a sagging coat of faded purple wool. Long, long ago, when Miss Maltby was young, she may have believed, or someone may have told her, that violet and purple shades were flattering to her hair and to a skin which was now colourless but had perhaps once been fair. The hair must certainly have been bright in those far off days. Even now, brushed thinly back and screwed into a scanty knob, gold gleamed unexpectedly here and there from the prevailing sandy grey.

She looked down over the stairs, and then turned her head sharply as if she expected to find someone behind her.

There was no one there. There might have been no one but herself in all the house. Mr and Mrs Monk who had the drawing-room floor were out all day. They had an antique shop. Miss Pym who had the dining-room and the bedroom behind it was a buyer at Madeline's. At the moment she was in Paris choosing spring models, Mrs Camber in the basement was taking what she described as a bit of a set down, Mabel, the cheerful Salvationist help, was washing up to the hearty strains of *Pull for the Shore, Sailor, pull for the Shore*. To all intents and purposes Miss Maltby had the house to herself. She listened nevertheless for three or four minutes, her head poked forward, the skin straining over her cheek-bones.

At last she drew back, turned round, and went noiselessly upstairs to the top floor. Here she stopped and listened again. Only the higher notes of Mabel's cheerful soprano reached her now, as faint and thin as a bat's cry. Miss Maltby nodded approvingly. Then she opened the door of Shirley's room and went in.

Chapter Three

SHIRLEY WOULD HAVE GONE on the top of the bus if it hadn't been foggy. As it was, she squeezed in between a lady with a string shopping-bag whose clothes flowed and billowed over the most astonishingly ample contours and a little man with a billycock hat on the top of his head and longish hair which smelt of moth-ball. At least that is where the smell seemed to be coming from. Perhaps he had just got his hat out of cold storage, or perhaps he really was afraid of getting moth in his hair. It was the sort of hair that looked as if it might get moth in it rather easily. Shirley looked at it, and at the large lady's profusely patterned scarf, and at the contents of her shopping-bag alternately disclosed and hidden by the meshes of coffee-coloured string, all with the deepest interest. She was often dull when she was indoors by herself, and she was continuously bored with Mrs Huddleston, but the streets, the buses, the trains, and the shops were a lively and perpetual source of interest.

She looked out on the fog, and the shop windows, and a poster which said, "American Millionaire Dead." It seemed funny to think of anyone having millions. She looked at the people opposite, and read all the advertisements. The conductor was a nice young man with a merry eye. There were a lot of nice people in the world, but it was a pity that most of them had so little money. Some of the people who had a lot weren't half so nice. Perhaps Mrs Huddleston would have been nicer if she had been poor and had to do things for herself instead of ordering other people about. Miss Maltby on the other hand was poor, and she was easily the nastiest person Shirley knew.

The bus stopped with a jerk at Acland Road and Shirley jumped off. Revelston Crescent was the first turning on the right out of Acland Road. A newsboy stood there, thrusting out his papers at the passers-by. Shirley shook her head. She hadn't any coppers to spare, but the poster news was free. She could amuse herself as she went along trying to piece the headlines together like a jigsaw puzzle. This boy's poster was quite a new one, fresh and hot from the press. It said in big letters of staring black:

"Death of William Ambrose Merewether."

The name did not stir her memory in even the slightest degree. It meant nothing to her except that in a faint, uninterested way she linked it with the other poster she had seen, and supposed that William Ambrose Merewether was the Dead American Millionaire. That the death of this unknown person would affect her, her life, and her safety would have seemed an impossibility, yet at that very moment a train of events had been set in motion which were to change the whole course of her life and endanger all its hopes and prospects.

She cast only one glance at the poster and ran as far as the fifth house of Revelston Crescent, where she pulled up, because Mrs Huddleston lived at No 15 and she certainly wouldn't approve of a secretary who added to the misdemeanour of being late the solecism of running in a public street.

As a matter of fact, the solecism had practically cancelled the misdemeanour. Shirley arrived only one minute late by the ormolu clock on the drawing-room mantelpiece. It was the most hideous clock in the world, and it was three minutes fast by Big Ben, so she wasn't really late at all—only it wasn't any use saying so.

Mrs Huddleston lay on a rose-coloured couch by the fire with a piece of old Italian brocade drawn up to her waist and a bottle of smelling-salts in one long pale hand. She wore a trailing garment of sky-blue satin profusely trimmed with lace after the manner of a tea-gown of the nineties. In the nineties she had been a beauty of the Burne Jones type. It was her misfortune that she had been born too late to be painted by him or by Rossetti. She had had the long, full throat, the free contours, and the immense bush of hair which those artists regarded with idolatry. She had them still. The hair cascaded to her eyebrows in a sort of tangled fringe and hung upon her neck in an immense loose knot. It was still black, with no more than a thread or two of grey in it. Her really enormous eyes were as dark and languishing as they had been when she was twenty-five, but she had rather the look of something preserved very carefully under a glass case and belonging quite unmistakeably to a previous generation, like paper flowers or fruits modelled in wax. The diamonds in the brooch which flashed among her laces seemed more alive than she herself.

Shirley closed the door behind her, Mrs Huddleston lifted the smelling-salts to her nose.

"It is past the half-hour, Miss Dale."

Shirley said nothing. She had had six months to discover that even Mrs Huddleston found it difficult to nag a secretary who didn't say anything at all.

The aggrieved lady took another sniff.

"I suppose it is too much to expect punctuality, but if you could be here by the half-hour, Miss Dale—"

Shirley smiled, still without speaking. She meant the smile to say, "I'm not sulky. Do come off it and be human!"—things like that.

Mrs Huddleston showed no sign of becoming human.

"To lie here hour after hour and listen to the feet going by in the street—happy, hurrying feet of happy, hurrying people! Ah well, you're too young to understand—but your time will come. *Si jeunesse savait!*" She inhaled deeply, and rather spoilt the die-away effect by a loud resounding sneeze.

Shirley stood by the foot of the sofa and waited until Mrs Huddleston had finished patting her nose and dabbing her eyes. Then she said,

"What would you like me to do this afternoon? Shall I read to you?"

"No," said Mrs Huddleston—"no, I don't think I feel equal to being read to. There is something exhausting about another person's voice—I have always found it so. Even when I was a girl I used to find society exhausting. Other people's voices, other people's thoughts, other people's ideas—I found them terribly depleting. I have, of course, a peculiarly sensitive nature—easily jarred, easily bruised. I remember my mother taking me to see Sir Sefton Carlisle when I first came out— he was the great nerve specialist in those days—and I remember so well his saying to my mother, 'There is no disease, no actual weak spot, but she is fragile, madam, fragile. There must be no strain, nothing to jar the sensitive nerves, or I cannot answer for the consequences'."

Shirley listened to this, her smile decorously modified into an expression of sympathetic attention. Once off, Mrs Huddleston would go on happily relating apocryphal interviews with the leading lights of the medical profession for hours, and hours, and hours. You didn't have to listen, thank goodness—you only had to look as if you were listening. You could plan a frock, or write a letter in your head, or make up stories about the people in the bus. At intervals such phrases as "He said I had the lowest pulse he had ever felt", or, "No one could imagine how I survived," or, "Five doctors, and four nurses," might impinge upon your ear, but you didn't have to do anything about them.

Mrs Huddleston flowed on. If the voices of other people exhausted her, the prolonged exercise of her own had no such effect.

When Shirley got tired of standing she let herself down into a little armless chair in the gap between the sofa end and the chimney corner. The day was cold, and it was a good opportunity of getting really warm through and through before she had to go back to her fire-less room. This was one of the weeks that she couldn't afford a fire. It had started very mild, and she had blued her fire money on a cinema with jasper Wrenn. Cinemas with Jas were always strictly on a fifty-fifty basis, because he had even less money than she had, whereas when she went out with Anthony it was dinner at the Luxe, and stalls, and the very best chocolates. Only in a way it was more expensive than sharing with Jas, because it meant decent stockings and shoes, and things like that—and what on earth she was going to do when her one and only evening dress gave out she couldn't imagine. Like Mrs Huddleston it was no longer young, and like Mrs Huddleston it had been a beauty in its day. Shirley had had it for two years, and it had come to her from Alice Carlton, who had swopped a rather hideous hat for it and then found it was too tight for her, its original owner having been Selma Van Troyte, a fabulously rich American girl who bought all her clothes in Paris. It was in fact a pedigree garment—black georgette, and practically indestructible. Alice had been a school friend and was now in China. Selma was merely a legend, but the black georgette endured. Anthony liked it—men always did like black. Anthony—

With a start she heard Mrs Huddleston say like an echo,

"Anthony—" And then, sharply. "Dear me, Miss Dale, are you listening? You look half asleep."

Shirley felt the fire hot on her cheek. She said quickly,

"Oh no, Mrs Huddleston. You said—Anthony—"

"I said my nephew Anthony Leigh would be coming in presently. Perhaps I had better rest. He has been away, you know. He had a case somewhere—about a will, I believe—I forget where. So terribly sordid, but I suppose barristers have to do these things, and I'm sure he looks very handsome in his wig and gown. I remember when my sister-in-law, Anthony's mother, used to come and ask my husband's advice about a profession for him—she was left a widow when Anthony was only ten—I used to say, 'My dear Edith, how can you possibly hesitate? With that profile! Only think how well he would look in a wig—a kind of fascinating irregularity.' Oh no, he couldn't really have been anything but a barrister, and though my husband always said 'Nonsense!' a barrister he is. And at barely thirty, I am told, he is beginning to make quite a name for himself."

"Would you like the blinds down, Mrs Huddleston?" said Shirley.

"No—yes—I don't know. If I don't rest I shall be a wreck. Dr Monsell is most particular about my resting before I see a visitor—before and after. But on the other hand, if I fall asleep I ought not to be roused. 'Wake naturally,' Dr Monsell says. 'Let the exhaustion pass off in sleep, and then wake naturally.' So I really don't know what to do. I think perhaps I ought to have my rest. And if Anthony comes early, you can explain to him—and give him the *Times*. There's a very good fire in the study, and I'm sure he will understand. I'm sure he wouldn't want me to miss my rest."

Shirley said nothing. A dance of imps was going on in her eyes, so she kept her lids down. The imps were quite sure that Mr Anthony Leigh wouldn't wish his aunt to curtail her rest. They preferred the study to the drawing-room. They liked Anthony Leigh a great deal better than they liked their revered employer.

Shirley pulled down the blinds, made up the fire, drew the Italian brocade an inch or two higher, flattened the rose-coloured cushions a little, and tiptoed noiselessly out of the room. With any luck Mrs Huddleston would sleep till tea-time.

Chapter Four

ANTHONY LEIGH ARRIVED at a little before half-past three. He was shown into the study, and made himself excessively comfortable in the largest chair. He refused the *Times*, and expressed the pious hope that his aunt's slumbers would be long and deep. With his head against the back of the chair, the profile commended by Mrs Huddleston relieved against a background of orange wall-paper, and his legs stretched out upon the hearth-rug, he surveyed Shirley with pleasure and inquired,

"How's everything?"

Shirley sat on the arm of the opposite chair and swung her feet. She had taken off her coat and hat when she came into the house. She had on a dark grey jumper suit with a scarlet belt. She hated the jumper suit, which she had had for two years, and which would probably never wear out. Alice Carlton had mourned an aunt in it and then passed it on. It would be heavenly to buy your own clothes—*new*—in a shop. She swung her feet and said,

"Much of a muchness."

Anthony stretched, which had the effect of making him seem even longer than before.

"You can't have been as bored as I've been," he said.

Shirley giggled.

"I've been hearing all about it. A will case, wasn't it? Mrs Huddleston said it was all terribly sordid, but she seemed to think that the fascinating irregularity of your profile might just manage to buoy you up, and anyhow it would be nice for everyone else. She thinks you must look lovely in a wig."

"I do," said Anthony—"too, too heart-smiting. You must come and see me. But you're getting a private view of the profile now. Is it very fascinating?"

"It's a profile," said Shirley in non-committal tones.

"Doesn't it fascinate you?"

"I don't think so—it's too wavy."

"Don't you like them wavy?"

"Not a bit. Profiles ought to be quite straight. I used to draw them on my blotting-paper at school. Just one lovely straight line from the top of the forehead to the tip of the nose—that's what I call a profile."

"All right," said Anthony—"then you shan't come and see me. How is the Blessed Damozel?"

"Frightfully trying," said Shirley with frankness. "And some day she'll hear you call her that, and then—"

"She'll be tickled to death," said Anthony. He hitched himself up an inch or two, looked at her with lazy admiration, and inquired,

"Doing anything to-night?"

"Why?"

"I thought perhaps we could dine and do a show."

Shirley kicked her heels. If Anthony thought he'd only got to ask her to something and she'd jump at it, he could think again—*lots* of times.

"I'm probably going to a flicker with Jas."

A gleam came into Anthony's eye.

"Does he know?"

"Of course he does."

"Liar!" said Anthony. "You made it up—I saw you." He sat up suddenly and shook a forensic forefinger at her. "I put it to you that the accused had no previous knowledge of this alleged engagement. Remember—you are on oath."

"Idiot!"

"There—you can't deny it—the accused doesn't know anything about it."

Shirley tried not to laugh, and failed.

"Why do you call him the accused?"

"It sounds better than Jasper—anything would sound better than Jasper. You know, you absolutely can't go about with a fellow called Jasper—it's simply asking to get into a melodrama, and be drugged, and kidnapped, and married against your will, and fished up out of the Thames, a demd damp, moist, unpleasant body. Much better dine with me."

"Had I?"

"I shan't kidnap you," said Anthony. He looked at her teasingly—disturbingly.

Shirley began to invent excuses for saying yes. It would save getting anything for supper, and she was really terribly hard up. This was a *good* excuse. She leaded to produce it to Anthony.

"Did you say dinner?"

"At the Luxe."

She stuck her chin in the air.

"Well, I'm out of cheese, and I do hate dry bread, so I don't mind if I do."

"Honoured!" said Anthony. His voice changed in the middle of the word. He leaned back again and frowned at the ceiling. After a moment he said, "Is that true, or are you having me on?"

"Gospel," said Shirley with a little colour in her cheeks.

"You really have bread and cheese for supper?"

"When I can afford it. Why not? It's cheap, and it's filling."

"And you only dine with me because of the flesh-pots?"

Shirley looked at him with an imp in either eye.

"Very good flesh-pots at the Luxe," she said.

Anthony went on looking at the ceiling. Presently he said,

"Why do you go on doing this?"

"Because I've got to." Her voice had changed too.

"There must be lots of better jobs."

"I'm not trained for anything."

"Then why not train?"

"No money."

He leaned forward suddenly and sat with his elbows on his knees looking at her.

"Haven't you got any people?"

She met his eyes quite frankly.

"No, I haven't. I was a sort of after-thought in my family. My brothers were grown up when I was born, and they were both killed in the war. And then my father and mother died. They lived in New Zealand, and I was sent home when I was sis years old to an aunt in Devonshire. She was my father's sister, and she brought me up and sent me to school, and when she died I found she was living on an annuity, and that there wasn't any money at all, which was pretty fierce."

"No other relations?"

She gave a funny little gurgling laugh.

"I've got a half-sister called Rigg. Sounds grim, doesn't it?"

"Is she grim?"

"I should think so—I've never seen her. It sounds odd, but you see it's like this. My mother married a man called Augustus Rigg when she was seventeen, and she had twins on her eighteenth birthday, and they called them John and Jane. And then Augustus took a toss in the hunting-field and died, and about a year later a French artist called Pierre Levaux came along and married my mother and took her away to France. She left the twins with the Rigg relations, and two years later she was a widow again with a French baby called Perrine, and she left it with Monsieur Levaux's mother and married my father and went out to New Zealand."

"Then you've got two sisters and a brother?"

She shook her head.

"No—the John twin was killed in the war like my two real brothers. And Perrine's dead too, a long time ago, but Jane's alive. She wrote when old Aunt Emily died about eight months ago."

"But you've never seen her?"

Shirley shook her head. Her eyes sparkled.

"It wasn't the sort of letter that makes you want to rush into the arms of the person who wrote it. She must be thirty years older than I am, and I thought she was most horribly afraid I'd want to come and settle on her. It was a sort of 'Shoo, fly!' kind of letter, if you know what I mean. Of course I don't suppose the Riggs liked my mother going off and leaving them like that, but Jane wrote a lot about not having a spare room in her cottage, and what a dull place Emshot was for a young girl, and all that sort of thing."

"Emshot?" said Anthony. "That's funny."

"Why is it funny?"

"Because I'm week-ending at Emshot House. Shall I go and call on your sister Jane?"

"You can if you like. Oh, Anthony, *do*! And then you can tell me what she's like. Acacia Cottage, The Green, Emshot—that's her address. Be an angel pioneer and find out just how grim she is!"

"Perhaps she isn't grim at all."

"Sure to be. I've always meant to go and see her some day, but whenever I've felt brave enough I haven't had the money, and whenever I've had the money I haven't felt nearly brave enough."

"I think you ought to go and see her."

"'M—" said Shirley. Her eyes sparkled again. "Do you know, Anthony, it's about forty-six years since my father and mother went out to New Zealand, and I wasn't born or thought of for another twenty-six years, and Jane's been going all that time and a good bit longer. You can't really bridge over a gap like that—can you?"

"It's a bit difficult. Is there no one on your father's side?"

"Only the aunt who brought me up. She was awfully old too. My father would be eighty if he was alive, and she was five years older. I'm not really in my right generation. I ought to have been a grand-daughter—I might have been one quite easily. Hugh was twenty-three when he was killed in 1914, and Ambrose was twenty-two. They were my brothers, but they ought to have been uncles or something like that really." The colour ran up bright and clear into her cheeks, and she jumped down from the arm of the chair. "I'm talking the most frightful nonsense, but you led me on. Anthony, the oddest thing happened to me yesterday. I'd like to tell you about it."

She knelt down by the hearth and began to put coal on the fire, a piece at a time, with an aggravating pair of brass tongs which could not be stretched to take a large piece and invariably dropped a small one.

He watched her, and said presently,

"What happened?"

"Well, I thought it was an odd thing. It was when I was coming away from here last night. I struck the rush hour, and there were a lot of people waiting for the bus at the end of the road. Everyone was pushing and jostling when it came up—you know how they do. And when I got near the bus I caught hold of the rail to pull myself up—and there was somebody else's handbag on my wrist."

"Somebody else's handbag?"

"Yes—wasn't it frightful? I hadn't got my own bag with me, only a little purse in my pocket, and anyhow this was a complete and absolute stranger of a bag."

"What did you do?"

"I had got on to the step, so I gripped the conductor by the arm, and I said, 'Look here, this isn't my bag.' And he said, 'I don't know nothing about that.' And I said, 'Well, I don't either,' and I held it right up and called out, 'Is this anyone's bag?—because it isn't mine.' And a woman with a red nose and a vinegar eye says yes, it was hers, and it had got a crocodile purse with seven and elevenpence half-penny in it, and a paper of peppermints, and a letter addressed to Mrs Heycock. And so it had. And she sat opposite me all the way in the bus eating peppermints and looking as if she thought I had stolen her bag."

Anthony laughed.

"If you're going to take to crime, I should pinch something better worth having than seven and elevenpence halfpenny and a paper of peppermints."

"You forget the crocodile purse," said Shirley over her shoulder. "If I get taken up for stealing something really worth having, will you defend me, and make a lovely speech, and get me off in the teeth of the evidence with the jury wringing out their pocket handkerchiefs and reporters sobbing on each other's shoulders?"

"You'll have to pay me a fee."

She laughed too, and cocked an impudent eyebrow.

"Twopence halfpenny's about my limit."

"What about a kiss on account?" said Anthony in a soft, lazy voice.

He was still leaning forward, and she had turned round from the fire and was half sitting, half kneeling on the hearth-rug no more than a yard away. Their eyes met, and a little disturbing spark leapt between them. Shirley, still laughing, had begun to shake her head, when without warning Anthony reached out, caught her by the shoulders, and pulled her hard up against the chair.

The laughter went out of her with the most extraordinary suddenness. One moment it was a game, and the next moment it wasn't. Anthony had kissed her before, once when they had been dancing, and twice on the doorstep when he had seen her home, and she hadn't minded a bit. They had been light, cheerful kisses that meant nothing at all. She had laughed, and he had laughed. But now the laughter was gone out of her. For a second there was a frightening emptiness.

Anthony was still laughing. His lips were very near.

And then into the emptiness there poured a boiling torrent of anger. She struck him hard across the mouth, and twisted free, and got to her feet, shaking with rage.

Anthony let go of her at once. Then he pushed back his chair and got up, and there they were with about the width of the hearth-rug between them.

Shirley's heart had begun to bang against her side. It wasn't fair of him to be so tall, and to keep his temper. She wanted to go on being furious, but she could feel the anger simply leaking away and leaving her quite horribly frightened. She wished he had shaken her, she wished he had kissed her by force, because then she would have stayed at boiling-point and not minded, and now she was beginning to mind horribly. If Anthony didn't say something in a minute—

From the drawing-room Mrs Huddleston's bell rang sharp and clear. Shirley had never been so glad to hear it in her life. She put up a shaking hand and smoothed her hair. Anthony walked to the door and opened it. Perhaps he would go away. She hoped with all her heart that he would go away. But then perhaps she wouldn't ever see him again. He would never want to see her again. She ought to feel glad about this. She didn't feel glad. She felt utterly desolate and miserable.

Mrs Huddleston's bell rang again, more sharply than before, and just as Shirley ran past him out of the room, Anthony said,

"I'm sorry."

He said it with the cold politeness of the total stranger who has trodden on your foot or bumped into you in a crowd.

It was ten minutes before Mrs Huddleston was ready for her nephew. She didn't use lipstick, but she put on a little rouge. And the cushions had to be beaten up, the lights switched on, and the curtains drawn.

The room was in a rosy glow when Anthony was admitted. It smelled of scented pastilles, and eau-de-cologne, and the forced white lilac which stood in a tall iridescent jar on the piano. He reflected that there were far too many things in the room, and that he was one of them. Shirley perhaps was another. She had retreated to the window, and stood there until he had embraced his aunt and seated himself, when she took a chair behind him. As he talked, he could catch teasing glimpses of her in the Venetian mirror which hung above the piano. It reflected the white lilac, and it reflected Shirley, who was very nearly as pale. He had stopped feeling angry, but he was still feeling very much surprised, and under the surprise there was a hint of amusement and a hint of compunction. And were they dining together to-night. Or weren't they? He thought they were, but he didn't think Shirley thought so.

The amusement quickened. He smiled amiably at Mrs Huddleston, who was encouraged to expand an already diffuse narrative—"Quite a new treatment and very expensive, as all these things are. And I asked him most pressingly whether the waters have a very disagreeable taste, and he said he was afraid they had, only I mustn't mind that. And the baths aren't exactly mud-baths, but a sort of special stuff that they pack you in right up to the chin, and you do it for one hour the first day, and two the second, and three the third, and then you stop for three days, and when you start again you begin with two hours the first day, and three the second, and four the third, and then you stop again...."

Mrs Huddleston, however, did not stop. She was still talking when the tea came in, and Shirley was still sitting on her stiff little chair by the window. She had tried to get away, but Mrs Huddleston wouldn't let her go. Now she had to pour out the tea, and when Anthony took his cup he looked at her with laughing eyes that asked a question. He had his back to Mrs Huddleston, so he could look as he pleased. His eyes said, "You're not going to go on being angry, are you?" But hers couldn't say anything at all. They had to be the eyes of a perfectly correct secretary who was only pouring out the tea because her employer was an interesting invalid, and she never stopped watching her and Anthony for a single second, so that it was quite impossible to frown at him or to look repressive.

Mrs Huddleston had a most excellent appetite. She could not, naturally, admit this, and ate merely to keep up her strength, and under pressure from her medical advisers. Having provided her with a good-sized piece of cake, Anthony wandered round the room, cup in hand, fetching up presently by the piano, where he was quite out of Mrs Huddleston's sight. Putting down his cup, he proceeded to make peace overtures to Shirley in pantomime. He stretched out his hands in an imploring gesture. He clutched his heart, smote his brow, and went down upon his knees.

Shirley ought, of course, to have looked away. Unfortunately, however, she hesitated, and was lost. She tried for a politely indifferent gaze, felt it slipping, and was torn by an awful inward desire to laugh. Anthony was a *devil*—he really was. If she laughed, she would lose her job. She jerked her cup to her lips just in time to hide them, and choked realistically over a sip which she had not swallowed.

Mrs Huddleston was annoyed, and showed her annoyance. She said, "Really, Miss Dale!" several times, and then asked for another slice of cake—"Just the merest shaving. Because Dr Monsell does so insist that I should eat. And I'm sure I always say to him that I have no appetite—no appetite whatever, but he *insists*. No, not you, Miss Dale—my nephew will cut it for me.... My dear Anthony, what *are* you doing? Nothing makes me so nervous as feeling that there is someone just behind me. If you have recovered yourself Miss Dale, I should be glad of another cup of tea."

Shirley *had* recovered herself. She filled up Mrs Huddleston's cup, and saw Anthony make a final despairing gesture as he came forward to cut the cake. She was quite determined not to look at him, but out of the tail of her eye she could see him wringing his hands in most dangerous proximity to the sofa. If his aunt turned her head she would see him too. Even as the thought went through Shirley's mind, Mrs Huddleston did turn her head, but all she saw was a debonair nephew hastening in the direction of the cake-stand.

"Isn't that a new maid you've got—the one that brought in the tea?" he said.

Shirley choked down an unwilling giggle. Anthony was a devil, but he was quick.

Mrs Huddleston could talk for hours about her servants. She began to talk about them now. Yes, the maid was a new one. She had replaced Annie Mossop, who had behaved with a total lack of consideration in rushing off at a moment's notice because some relation was ill—"At least that is what she *said*, but the postman told Possett—my maid Possett—that he had seen Annie since she left me, and she was looking as pleased as could be and told him she had got a better place and a rise in wages, which is just what I should have expected, and I'm thankful to be rid of her and to have someone a little older and more responsible."

"What's this one's name?" said Anthony idly.

"Bessie Wood—and she's over thirty and seems to know her work. She heard about Annie going off like that from one of the tradespeople and came and offered herself, and she had very good references, so I engaged her."

Anthony felt that he had heard as much as he could bear about Bessie—a thin, plain person with cold eyes and tucked-in lips. He came and sat down by Mrs Huddleston and laid himself out to be charming. Next to conversation about her health and her servants, Mrs Huddleston loved anecdotes about the Royal Family, and the decadence of modern youth. Anthony obligingly produced three stories all equally apocryphal, and two that might possibly be true, after which, having finished her tea, she was ready to moralize.

Anthony moralized too. He did it very well. His dark blue eyes gazed with unwinking solemnity at his Aunt Agnes whilst she reprehended the manners of the modern girl. There was manly emotion in his voice as he agreed with her.

"You wouldn't believe it," he said, "but a friend of mine had a most painful experience the other day. He is a very tender-hearted man, and it upset him very much when a girl he was being kind to suddenly took offence and struck him in the face."

Mrs Huddleston made a shocked sound.

It was no part of Shirley's duty to thrust herself into a conversation between her employer and that employer's favourite nephew, but she could not contain herself. She said, "Why?" in a tone that made Mrs Huddleston start.

Anthony turned a little, gazed with a kind of mild sadness, and said in a tone of courteous surprise,

"I beg your pardon, Miss Dale?"

The tone rejoiced Mrs Huddleston's heart. How *right* of him to put that girl in her place.

Shirley's colour had risen brightly.

"Why did she hit him, Mr Leigh?"

The colour was very becoming. Since his aunt could not see his eyes, Anthony permitted them to admire, whilst he replied with the distant politeness which had pleased Mrs Huddleston.

"I think he had planned some little pleasure for her, and she did not appreciate it." He turned again to the sofa. "So few girls seem to appreciate simple pleasures nowadays."

It was at this moment that Shirley decided that she would after all keep her engagement with Mr Anthony Leigh. If she couldn't put it across him now, she could at least deal faithfully with him to-night. Little simple pleasures indeed! All right, Anthony, *you just wait*!

Mrs Huddleston was speaking.

"It ought to be a lesson to your friend not to mix himself up with that sort of girl."

"It *ought*," said Anthony in heart-felt tones. "But will it?"

Mrs Huddleston sniffed.

"She sounds *utterly* brazen!"

"Well, he's very kind-hearted."

"Kind-hearted!" The sniff became a snort. "My *dear* Anthony!"

"I believe he's dining with her to-night," said Anthony mournfully.

"Then he knows what to expect," said Miss Shirley Dale.

Chapter Five

Shirley dressed as carefully as if she were going to Buckingham Palace. If she had had a new and frightfully expensive dress she would have worn it, but as she only had the black georgette she had to fall back on its really dazzling original cost as reported by Selma Van Troyte to Alice Carlton, and by Alice Carlton to its present Cinderella of an owner who had never paid five pounds for a frock in her life—let alone fifty.

Shirley looked well in black. It made her hair darker, her eyes greyer, and her skin whiter. It enhanced the red of her lips. Only she wasn't taking any chances about that. If she could keep absolutely at boiling-point she wouldn't need any more colour—but that was the worst of your own colour, it had a nasty way of going back on you, and when you got home you found you were looking like something that's run in the wash, which is very embittering. No, she was really going to make up to-night—not much rouge, but very red lips. Her stockings were all light, thank goodness, but her shoes gave her a pang. Once black satin begins to rub you can't do anything, and if the toe of the right shoe wasn't rubbed yet, it was going to be the very first time it got a chance. Now if she had a silver dress, and silver shoes, and a lovely silver wrap, all absolutely brand new, it would be a great help in putting Anthony in his place. An odd little surge of pride rose up in Shirley. She didn't want a silver dress, or new shoes, or a shimmery wrap. That is, she wanted them all right, but she didn't *need* them to help her to wipe the floor with Anthony. And a four years old georgette was *quite* good enough for him to dine with.

She cast a final glance at this sparkling, confident Shirley, and ran downstairs past Jasper's door, which was open because he always opened it when he heard her come out of her room, and Miss Maltby's door, which was ajar with Miss Maltby's eye at the crack, and so to the street door where Mr Leigh waited politely upon the topmost step.

Shirley got into the taxi and settled herself well in the corner. Anthony got in, banged the door, sat down, and remarked with cheerful bonhomie, "And here we are again!"

Shirley said nothing. She was waiting for the taxi to start. It started. Anthony said,

"Aren't we on speaking terms? It'll be an awfully dull evening if we're not."

A street-lamp shone into Shirley's corner and showed her sitting up very straight, her lips very red with lipstick, and a bright natural carnation in her cheeks which completely swamped the rouge. The light shone right into her eyes and made them look very bright and very angry. She folded her hands on her knee and said with great distinctness,

"I wonder you had the nerve to come."

"My nerve is very good."

"*I* only came because I wanted to tell you exactly what I thought about you."

"But not till after dinner. Keep it for dessert. Look here, we'll have a truce till we've fed. We can be polite strangers if you like—just met for the first time. But don't let's have a dog-fight over the food."

"I'm simply boiling with rage," said Shirley.

"I can't think why."

"I suppose you know I'd have lost my job if Mrs Huddleston had looked round when you were playing the fool this afternoon?"

"You drove me to it," said Anthony.

"*I* did?"

"With your harshness. You've no idea how harsh you were. Besides I had a bet on with myself about making you laugh, so I had to try and win it."

Shirley looked coldly at him in the light of another lamp.

"Well, you didn't win it."

"I didn't? You mean I did."

"I didn't laugh."

Anthony said "Liar!" and at the same moment the taxi drew up at the Luxe.

The Gold Room was tolerably full. They had a table at one end of it, which pleased Shirley very much. She liked to see everyone who came in, to watch the way they walked, to try and guess what sort of people they were when they weren't dining at the Luxe. It was like a game, and it was one that amused her very much to play.

They had *hors d'œuvres*, and she was wondering why anyone liked olives, when Anthony asked her in an interested voice,

"Are you still boiling?"

She decided to leave the olive alone. That was one point about dining at an hotel, it didn't matter what you left on your plate. She looked severely at Anthony and said,

"I could have murdered you this afternoon."

He smiled seductively.

"Better not. I couldn't defend you for my own murder. You're not going to put strychnine into the soup or anything like that, are you? I'd hate you to go to prison."

A little shiver went down Shirley's back. She said, "So should I," and the waiter changed their plates and brought them fish because neither of them wanted soup.

He said, "Fish isn't so easily poisoned. But you're not absolutely at murder point now, are you?"

That was the worst of Anthony, he got round you. She was finding it very difficult to go on being as angry as she had meant to be.

"I'm not very far off it."

"But why? What made you go off the deep end like you did? Have you joined an anti-kissing league? Because if you have, I think you ought to have given me fair warning. You might have it on your cards—'*Miss Shirley Dale. A.A.K.L.*' And then in brackets, '*Associate Anti-kissing League.*' Or simply, '*A.K.A.—Anti Kissing Association.*' I think that's snappier on the whole. If you'd handed me something of that sort, I should have known just where I was, instead of which you struck me with unwomanly violence, and if you'd had on a diamond ring I might have had a split lip for life, and then I'd have had to address a jury like this—" He proceeded to address an imaginary jury in a speech without any consonants.

The little freckles at the corners of Shirley's lips trembled dangerously. She tried to stop her eyes dancing, but without any marked success.

"The people at the next table will think you're mad," she said in rather a shaky voice.

"Not mad—only afflicted," said Anthony, still without consonants. Then, returning to ordinary speech, "That's what you might have done to me. I hope remorse is gnawing at your vitals."

Shirley shook her head. Then the corners of her mouth gave way.

"Anthony, you're a *devil*, and some day you'll get paid out. Mrs Huddleston will look round and see you, or you'll slip up and call her the Blessed Damozel to her face, and then you'll be in the soup."

Anthony looked up with a gleam in his eye.

"What'll you bet I don't call her the Blessed Damozel and get away with it?"

Shirley met the gleam with a very dancing one of her own.

"You wouldn't dare."

"Bet on it?"

"You *wouldn't* dare."

"What'll you bet?"

"Tuppence," said Shirley.

"My good girl, I don't take my life in my hand for tuppence!" He leaned across the table, gazed at her tenderly, and said in his softest voice, "Resign from the A.K.A. and make it a kiss."

To her intense annoyance Shirley blushed. She felt the colour run hot and quick to the very roots of her hair. She felt it at her temples, and even round at the back of her neck. She could have stamped with rage, and the angrier she felt, the more she blushed.

Anthony leaned back in his chair and surveyed her with pleasure. It amused him very much to make her angry, and to see how easily she blushed. Under the amusement there was something else.

"Well?" he said. "What about it? Is it a bet?"

"No, it isn't."

"Well, I won't do it for tuppence. Have you ever been in for a blushing prize? I should think you would win hands down. But of course there wouldn't be many entries. It's almost a lost art—girls don't do it now."

"Village maidens do. I was brought up in a village, so I blush frightfully easily, and it's absolutely pig-mean of you to make me do it in front of hundreds of people."

"I shouldn't worry—you looked very nice."

"I couldn't have! It's all very well to get pink in the right place, but it's frightful to turn puce all over."

"I shouldn't have called it exactly puce," said Anthony kindly.

The couple at the next table had observed Shirley's change of colour with interest. They did not stare, but anyone watching them might have thought them a little too consciously discreet. The man wore his evening clothes rather as if he did not wear them very often. He might have been an old thirty-five or a young forty. He had a long pale nose in a long pale face. The nose was sharp at the tip, and the face was sharp at the chin. The eyes were sharp all over. They never rested long on anyone. When they had looked they looked away again. There was too much pomade on the rather sparse reddish hair. The woman was younger, taller, plumper. She filled a shiny red sequined dress. She had more bust than is the fashion. She had a trick of wriggling her shoulders and using her hands that was not quite English. She had fine dark eyes and fine dark hair, a sallow skin, and a very good conceit of herself. She used scarlet lipstick. Her name was Ettie Miller. She was a typist in a private inquiry agency, and she was dining, not by any means for the first time, with Alfred Phillips, clerk in the firm of Schuyler and Van Leiten of New York. English by birth, American by choice, he was at present in London on his firm's business, and Miss Ettie Miller was part of that business. Shirley Dale was part of it too, but neither she nor Anthony Leigh were to know that. They went on talking nonsense in a cheerful, light-hearted manner.

Alfred Phillips and Ettie Miller did not talk nonsense. They leaned to one another across the table and kept their voices low. The tables were rather close together. If Miss Miller had pushed back her chair six inches, her arm would have touched Shirley's shoulder. She had brought with her into the dining-room a large white fox fur which kept slipping from her shoulders as she shrugged them. The waiter picked it up twice, and she herself made constant play with it, hitching it up, pushing it back, letting it slip down upon the floor, and snatching it again, all these movements being made more noticeable by the flashing of the small *diamanté* bag which she wore suspended from her right wrist. Anthony was rather amused by her antics. He guessed the fur and the horrible little shiny bag to be new acquisitions—gifts, perhaps, of the foxy gentleman. The lady was obviously throwing her weight about. The Luxe was new ground to her. He wondered if they would get through the evening without Shirley coming in for a swish from the white fox tail or a bang from the little gleaming purse. Then the lady seemed to quieten down. The fox subsided between her and the back of her chair, and the *diamanté* bag worried his eyes no more.

He and Shirley were going to dance presently. He stopped teasing her, and they talked about everything and nothing, with the little thrill running through it all which comes when talk is just a way of exploring another mind. You never know what you are going to find— you've never been that way before, so you have to walk warily and look where you are going. There is danger, adventure, charm. There may be anything round the next corner from Bluebeard's Chamber to the Garden of Eden. At any moment a cavern may open at your feet or a river come rushing out of nowhere to carry you away. The air is quick with possibilities.

They had coffee at the table, and when they had drunk it Shirley pushed back her chair and stood up. Her bag had slipped from her lap. She stooped to pick it up. It was an old-fashioned bag with a cut steel handle, inherited from Miss Emily Dale. The black velvet of which it was made was probably as old as the frame, and appeared to be as indestructible. It had such a good hasp that it surprised Shirley very much to find that it had opened with the fall.

Anthony came round the table and said, with the teasing note back in his voice,

"Do you always drop your bag?"

She said, "Nearly always," and put her hand on the clasp to fasten it.

And then an odd thing happened. It was just as if something ran tingling up her arm from the fingers which were touching the clasp. She moved a step nearer Anthony, and felt her shoulder brushed by the white fur wrap of the queer-looking woman at the next table. The tables were really too close together. A funny breathless feeling came up in her throat, and all at once her fingers moved with a jerk and the bag was open again. She didn't know why she had opened it, but as soon as it was open she saw a bright twist of silver cord sticking up against the black satin lining.

She said, "What's that?" in a quick uneven voice. Then she jerked at the silver cord, and up came the little shiny *diamanté* bag which had hung from the wrist of Miss Ettie Miller until half way through dinner. Shirley held it out to Anthony Leigh. "That's not mine," she said. "How did it get into my bag?" And with that Ettie Miller jumped to her feet, pushing her chair aside and crowding into the narrow space between the tables.

"I'm sorry, but that belongs to me," she said. Her voice was loud enough to attract attention. Heads were turned. A couple of waiters stood by uneasily.

Shirley looked towards the voice. She was rather pale, her eyes were wide and puzzled. The little shiny purse dangled from her outstretched hand.

"Is it yours? How did it get into my bag?" she said.

And then Anthony was at her shoulder with his hand slipped just inside her arm. He said,

"Yes, it's hers." And then, to the woman in red, "Miss Dale's bag was on the floor. Perhaps you picked it up by mistake."

Ettie Miller made no movement to take her bag. She said, still in that unmodulated voice,

"Well, it's a funny sort of mistake that gets your purse with the best part of five shillings or so inside it into someone else's bag."

Shirley held out the silver cord. Her eyes never wavered from Miss Miller's face.

"Won't you take it if it's yours? I don't know how it got into my bag."

The whole thing had only lasted half a minute, but it was half a minute too long. Alfred Phillips came round the table with a decided "That's enough, Ettie!" Whereupon Miss Miller said, "Oh, I'll take it all right," and did so with a very pronounced shrug of her shoulders. After which the pressure of Anthony's hand became insistent, and Shirley, obeying it, turned and walked away.

She had half the length of the Gold Room to walk, and some curious glances followed her and Anthony. She kept her head high, but the cornets of the room were full of a mist that stung her eyes. What a horrible thing to happen. But she mustn't let herself think about it yet—not whilst all these people were looking at her. She felt a terrified longing for some dark place to hide in. The lights were very bright. The room was full of people. She and Anthony were walking, but they didn't seem to be getting to the door. *Anthony*—Don't think about Anthony. Don't think about anything.

They came to the door at last, and through an archway lined with mirrors to an empty corridor. Shirley looked straight ahead of her as they passed the arch, but she could just see herself and Anthony reflected endlessly from either side of it—a hundred Anthonys and a hundred Shirleys. No, far more than a hundred, only it made you giddy to think how many there were. And every one of the Shirleys feeling as if someone had struck her a blow in the dark. And every one of the Anthonys wishing that he had never set eyes on her, because he hated scenes worse than anything else in the world, and there certainly had been a scene—

And then Anthony said, "You all right, Shirley?" and his voice was kind.

She said, "Yes." The answer was only just audible.

Anthony did not find it at all a convincing sort of answer. He pushed open a door inscribed "Residents only", and took her into a smallish room with some very comfortable chairs in it.

"But we're not residents," said Shirley, still only just above a whisper.

Anthony put her into the most comfortable chair. Her knees were shaking so much that she stopped bothering about not being a resident. The chair wasn't big, but it was very soft and comforting. He sat down facing her and said in a cheerful matter of fact voice,

"And now what's all this about?"

Shirley felt so grateful that she could have kissed him then and there. He wasn't going to treat her with stony politeness as if nothing had happened, or believe the simply frightful things which that horrible woman had hinted. He was going to be just ordinary, and friendly, and kind. She said, "Oh, Anthony!" and he patted her knee and told her to pull herself together.

"It was that woman's bag all right, because she had it dangling on her wrist all the time she was fidgetting with that beastly white fur thing, and then about half way through dinner she settled down and I didn't see it any more. But how on earth did het bag get inside yours?"

Shirley's right hand held her left hand very tight. She sat up stiffly and looked him straight in the face.

"Anthony—do you think I put it there?"

"Of course you didn't."

Her eyes held his with a strained, insistent look.

"I don't want you to be polite."

"I'm not being polite."

She did not move her eyes, but she lifted her right hand and brought it down upon her knee with a sort of despairing effort.

"It's no good saying the sort of things you think I want you to say. I want what you really think, because you see, it's happened twice in a few days, and I don't know how that woman's bag got on to my arm when I was waiting for the bus, and I don't know how this woman's bag got inside mine." She repeated the gesture with her hand. "Anthony, I don't *know*."

"What do you think?" said Anthony Leigh.

She drew in her breath sharply before she answered him. There was a look in her face as if she were trying not to wince away from a blow.

"It's not what I think. It's what you think, or what anyone would think."

He said, "Well?"

She was still looking at him. She was very pale.

"Anthony—either someone put that bag on my wrist and put this one into my bag, or else I'm a thief and took them deliberately, or else I've got a screw loose and I took them without knowing what I was doing. You don't think I'm a thief—but do you think I'm a kleptomaniac? Because why should anyone try and plant bags on me like that? It's too utterly balmy."

Anthony leaned forward and took the hand which lay upon her knee. It felt cold and stiff as he covered it with his own.

"Shirley—one minute—has anything of this sort ever happened to you before?"

"No, it hasn't." She paused, and added with a little catch in her voice, "It hasn't—*really*."

"Those people at the next table—have you ever seen either of them before?"

"No, never."

"You're sure neither of them was in the bus the other day?"

"Quite sure."

The hand in his was warmer, and it had begun to shake a little. She closed her eyes for a moment, and then looked at him again, but without the same fixity.

"No, they weren't in the bus, either of them—I'm quite sure. But everybody didn't get on." She shut her eyes again, screwing them up tight. "There were people left behind—quite a lot. They might have been there—either of them. I don't know—I wasn't noticing. I was thinking about the bag and how it could possibly have got on to my arm, and trying not to catch the eye of the vinegary woman it belonged to—and of course every time I looked up I did." She gave him the faintest of fleeting smiles. "You know how it is. And she had the horridest sort of eye to catch—like a half-cooked gooseberry—" She pulled her hand away suddenly and sat back. "Anthony, I'm not a kleptomaniac!"

"I didn't think you were," said Anthony.

"I don't know why you didn't—I very nearly did myself. I suppose it was the shock or something, but I had the most horrible giddy feeling that I might have done it. And then when you were holding my hand I sort of knew you didn't think so, and then the giddy feeling went away and I didn't think so either. For one thing, if I was going to steal, I'd take something that was worth having, and not a nasty little jingly bag with the best part of five shillings in it."

Anthony was sitting there frowning. She had said there were three possible explanations, and they had just disposed of two of them. There remained the third and most improbable of the three. But why should anyone plant alien bags upon Shirley Dale? There didn't seem to be any answer to that.

"It's difficult—isn't it?" said Shirley.

Chapter Six

ALFRED PHILLIPS CAUGHT a waiter's eye and ordered coffee. He had resumed his chair, and sat with his shoulder turned to the length of the room down which Anthony Leigh and Shirley Dale had taken their way, but Ettie Miller watched them out of sight with a furious gleam in those fine dark eyes of hers. Seen like that, she had a heavy brooding face, and a mouth that fell easily into angry lines. When Alfred Phillips spoke her name with impatience she turned the anger on him.

"Well, you're a nice one, letting her go like that!"

"Come, come," he said—"it all went off very well. And you mustn't look that way—you'll be having people noticing you."

"And why shouldn't people notice me? Haven't I just had my bag stolen, or as near as makes no difference? I should have thought the more people noticed me, the better. And they wouldn't expect me to be looking as pleased as Punch either—would they? I should have thought the more fuss there was, the better it would have suited your book. I tell you, Al, I don't understand you—I don't know what you're getting at. Why didn't you go on and run her in? You'll never get a better chance. There she was, red-handed as you may say, and instead of calling in the police all you've got to say is, 'That's enough, Ettie.' And there's me taking my bag back, and meek as a mouse—and I'm sure I don't know why I did it—and Miss Shirley Dale going off without so much as a cross word from anyone, let alone a policeman's had on her shoulder, which is what I thought you meant or I wouldn't have taken the risks I did and get no thanks for them either!"

There was an empty table on either side of them now. The hum of the room and the sound of the gypsy music which the orchestra was playing enclosed them. They could talk as intimately and privately as if there had been walls about them and a locked door to shut them in.

Alfred Phillips let her talk. Ettie always had a lot to say, and it was no good trying to stop her. When she had got to the end of it she would listen to him, and not before. She grumbled until the coffee came. Then, as she helped herself to sugar, she rolled her eyes at him and said,

"Lost your tongue, Al?"

"Using my eyes instead. That dress suits you, Ettie."

"Think so?"

He put a little warmth into his cold look.

"Red's your colour."

"Oh well, I don't know. I got it a bargain."

He looked at her approvingly.

"You're clever. But you got that all wrong just now, you know. You listen a minute and I'll put you wise. That little bit of a game with Shirley Dale—there wasn't anything serious about that."

She stared at him, angry and surprised.

"There wasn't?"

"Of course there wasn't, any more than there was yesterday when she got on a bus with another lady's bag on her arm."

"What did you let me do it for then?" said Ettie Miller. A heavy flush came into her face. "If I thought you were making a fool of me, Al Phillips—"

Mr Phillips moved impatiently.

"Fool nothing! This is business. Now you listen to me, Ettie! There isn't any sort of business in the world that doesn't need publicity. I'm not ready for the real job yet. Advertisement—that's what comes first—advertisement, publicity. Then when everything's set, put your business across and it'll go big."

Ettie looked stubborn.

"That's just a way of talking. But what I say is, you'll never get a better chance than you've had to-night, and if you go throwing chances away, you've only got yourself to thank if you don't get them again."

Al Phillips smiled.

"I can make all the chances I want. Now you freeze right on to this—to-night was only publicity. You've got brains all right, if you'll use them. Well then, how was it going to look if *you* ran her in—when the whole story came out—well, I ask you, what was it going to look like? Conspiracy, my dear—and then it would be you that would be in the dock on a criminal charge, and not her."

"Dry up!" said Ettie Miller angrily. "What do you think you're saying? What was the good of doing the thing at all if it was all going to fizzle out?"

Mr Phillips went on smiling.

"When the real job comes off, Anthony Leigh's going to remember where that bag of yours was found," he said.

Chapter Seven

SHIRLEY CAME BACK to her lunch next day to find Mrs Camber hovering. The door was no sooner shut than she made an agitated descent from the half-landing.

"If I might have a word with you, Miss Dale—"

Shirley looked at her in surprise. She didn't in the least want to have words with Mrs Camber. She wanted her lunch. She had been promised a good hot helping of beefsteak pudding and a baked apple, and she had been thinking lovingly about them all the way home, and Mrs Camber ought at this moment to be taking the pudding out of its cloth and helping it in portions instead of lurking on the stairs and fussing down on her like a stout agitated hen.

"If you'd come into the dining-room, miss, if you please," said Mrs Camber, very flushed, very short of breath, and still shiny from the kitchen fire.

The dining-room belonged to Miss Pym, but since she was in Paris, it was at their disposal.

"What is it, Mrs Camber?" said Shirley when the door was shut. Whatever it was, she hoped it wasn't going to take long. The room was stuffy and quite horribly cold. Miss Pym ran to silver photograph frames, and they were all lying down flat, as if a wind had passed over them.

Mrs Camber stood just inside the door and fidgetted with her kitchen apron. She had a round, flushed face and deeply sunk eyes. Her dark hair was brushed back as tight as it would go and pinned into a heavy coil at the back of her head. She said in a choked, gulping way,

"I'm bound to bring it to your notice, miss. And what you've got to say about it you can say it to me down here, for when all's said and done it's my house, and no getting from it, and so I told her."

The cold stuffiness of the room seemed to thicken about Shirley. It was rather a horrid feeling. She had an involuntary picture of being plunged in cold dirty water that had begun to freeze. What a stupid thing to think about. She said,

"Mrs Camber, what *do* you mean?"

Mrs Camber's flush deepened.

"And I told her straight, unpleasantness is what I've never had in my house before—no more than it might be a gentleman that had had a glass too much and come home a bit noisy, and if so be that it happened more than what you might call once in a way, I'd give him his notice same as I did Mr Peters that had the room Mr Wrenn's got now—and a nicer gentleman never stepped, only when it come to his falling downstairs three nights running and getting on for four in the morning and a-setting on the landing singing *Rule Britannia*, only he couldn't get along with it for the hiccups, well, I took and told him, 'Mr Peters,' I said, 'this is my house,' I said, 'and it's a respectable house, and those as don't behave as such, they must take and go elsewhere,' I said." She paused for breath, drawing it in with a sound between a gasp and a snort.

Shirley spoke quickly. Once Mrs Camber got going again, she wouldn't have a chance, and she simply must find out what all the fuss was about.

"Mrs Camber *dear*—what's the matter? I didn't come home drunk last night, did I?"

Mrs Camber looked scandalized.

"I never said no such thing, miss—and a drunk woman's a disgrace neither more nor less, and nothing to make a joke about if that's your meaning!"

A spurt of anger flared in Shirley. It made her feel better. She stamped her foot hard on Miss Pym's Brussels square. A little dust came up, because when a lodger was away neither Mrs Camber nor Mabel wasted time on an empty room.

"What *do* you mean? I want my lunch, and you keep hinting and hinting, and don't tell me a thing. What's the matter?"

Mrs Camber's manner changed. She stopped fidgetting with her apron, crossed her arms at the place where her waist would have been some twenty-five years ago, and said darkly,

"Don't you know, miss?"

"No, I don't."

"Then it's Miss Maltby," said Mrs Camber.

"Miss Maltby?"

"Miss Maltby," said Mrs Camber in a tone of heavy I gloom.

Shirley felt as if the dirty water of her imagining had changed to dirty glue. She was entangled and bewildered, and she hadn't the slightest idea what Mrs Camber was driving at, except that it was something unpleasant. The water might have changed to glue, but the dirt was constant.

"What about Miss Maltby?" she said impatiently.

Mrs Camber burst into speech.

"Seeing you won't let on that you know, I'm bound to tell you, and if there's anything you've got to say you can say it to me like I told you first go off. And I told Miss Maltby the same. 'There'll be no police sent for in my house,' I said, 'not till I've seen her myself and put it to her straight and heard what she's got to say.' And, 'Oh, Mrs Camber,' she says, 'I don't want no police brought into it.' 'And if you did,' I said, 'you wouldn't get them, Miss Maltby—not in my house,' I said."

Shirley's hand came out and caught her by the arm. Shirley's voice rang in the cold, stuffy room.

"What are you talking about?"

Mrs Camber gulped and went on.

"Down into my kitchen she come, and me with my hands in the flour, and 'Oh, Mrs Camber, can I speak to you?' she says. And I says, 'Not if you was Queen Alexandra you can't, not till I've finished with my crust, which if I leave it to Mabel it's spoilt.' I've not got nothing against the Salvation Army, and so I told the Curate when he came. 'Mabel's religion's all right so far as I can see,' I said. 'She don't tell lies and she don't carry on with the boys, and hymn-singing don't worry me, not so long as it's cheerful, which most of the Army hymns are, to do them justice. No, her religion's all right, Mr Smithers,' I said, 'but she's got a shocking heavy hand for pastry and there's no getting from it.'"

Shirley shook the arm she was holding, but that was as far as she could get. To shake Mrs Camber herself was an impossibility.

"What did Miss Maltby want?"

Mrs Camber gulped again.

"I told her straight I'd got to get my pudding on, and what did she do but hang around and watch me till I could ha' screamed? 'But why do you do it that way?' she says. And, 'Wouldn't it be better someways else?' she says. And, 'Oh dear, what a long time it takes to make a pudding,' she says. And, 'Isn't it funny to call it a pudding when it's got meat inside it?' she says. And Mabel singing in the scullery fit to burst your ears: 'Is there anyone there at the beautiful gate a-watching and waiting for me?' And I took and told her, 'You go along upstairs, Miss Maltby, and set down, or I won't be answerable for the pudding *nor* yet for my temper,' I said, and she took and went."

Shirley let go of the hard, hot arm and stood back. Hopeless to try and hurry Mrs Camber. She had to tell you everything that happened or she couldn't tell you anything at all. She didn't do it on purpose; it was just the way her mind worked. If you burst in, she just went back to the beginning and started all over again.

"Well, you finished the pudding, and then you saw Miss Maltby. What did she want?"

Mrs Camber tossed her head.

"Unpleasantness of some kind it was bound to be—I knew that right along. But when she up and told me what it was you could have knocked me down with a turkey feather. 'And I want you to come upstairs with me and search her room,' she says, 'and if I've made a mistake I'll be ready and willing to apologize for troubling you,' she says, 'but it's a thing that ought to be cleared up, if it's only for the sake of your house,' she says. And I said 'Right you are,' and up we went."

Shirley went back one step, two steps, until she touched the table. It was an oval table with a rosewood top and a single massive leg. It was very solid and strong. Shirley leaned against it. She said,

"You went up? Where?"

"Into your room, Miss Dale."

Shirley felt herself turning white with anger. Her face felt white, and her lips felt stiff. She said in a very slow, cold voice,

"You went into my room with Miss Maltby? *Why?*"

"Because this is my house, and I've always kept it respectable—that's why," said Mrs Camber.

Shirley put her hands behind her and gripped on to the edge of the table—hard. It was like the worst sort of dream she had ever dreamt. It couldn't be true—it really couldn't be true. Perhaps she would wake up in a minute. Perhaps she wouldn't. She said more slowly than before,

"I don't know what you mean. Will you please tell me?"

"There's things you can tell at once, and there's things you can't," said Mrs Camber with an air of aloof gloom, "which when she come and told me, 'Miss Maltby,' I said, 'I don't believe it.' And she says, 'Believe it or not, it's true.'"

An awful patience had descended upon Shirley.

"What did Miss Maltby say?"

She thought Mrs Camber's little sunk eyes had a pitying look. That was all nonsense, because why on earth should she be pitying Shirley? And why on earth didn't she come to the point?

"Some people says a sight of things they'd better by half keep to themselves."

"Mrs Camber, you really must tell me what Miss Maltby said."

"Which it's nothing anyone would be in a hurry to hear—not if they knew what it was. And I said to her, 'Well, by all accounts and at the very least of it you've been a-prying and a-poking.'"

Shirley's patience broke suddenly. She stamped again, and very much harder than before. There was a pair of old-fashioned lustres on the mantelpiece. The voice in which she said *"Mrs Camber!"* made them ring.

"And all very well to shout at me, miss, but shouting's no answer."

"You haven't asked me anything," said Shirley.

"Well, then I'm going to," said Mrs Camber—"and if you don't like it, it's not my fault! Was you in Miss Maltby's room day before yesterday round about half-past one when she was over in the bathroom and says she saw you go in and saw you come out through the crack of the bathroom door?"

A bright high colour flamed in Shirley's cheeks. Her skin burned and tingled with it. The lustres rang again as she said,

"What an absolute lie!"

"That's what she says—and couldn't come out along of having nothing on but a towel. And what she wants to go having a bath at such a ridiculous hour is what I can't understand and never shall. But that's her way, and as she says, there's no one in the house that don't know it. 'And what's easier,' she says, 'than to come down one pair of stairs and slip in and slip out again? And no one wasn't to know,' she says, 'that I count all my money regular every time I come in or go out,' she says."

"Is Miss Maltby mad?" said Shirley.

There was a faint sympathetic gleam in Mrs Camber's eye. She repressed it as in duty bound.

"Not that you'd take notice of," she said.

"She must be if she says I was in her room."

"That's what you say, miss. And what she says is she saw you there—leastways she saw you go in, and she kept her eye to the crack till you come out again, not above a minute or two it wasn't, she says, and when she'd got some clothes on her, and come back into her room and went over her money, there was two sixpences short."

"She must be absolutely raving," said Shirley.

A fleeting look that resembled pity appeared again on Mrs Camber's face. It was gone in an instant. She said in a flat, heavy voice,

"So upstairs we went and into your room, miss, and she says to me, 'I won't put a finger on nothing, Mrs Camber,' she says, 'but those two sixpences have got my mark on them same as all my money has and if you won't look and see if Miss Shirley Dale hasn't got them hidden away somewhere, well then I'll have in the police,' she says. And the first thing I see when I took up the toilet-cover off of your chest-of-drawers, there was two sixpences pushed in under, just where the looking-glass would be standing over them."

"Nonsense!" said Shirley. "Mrs Camber—"

"There they were and you can't get from it. And Miss Maltby she ups and says, 'I won't touch them nor handle them, but if they're mine they've got a little nick down aside the King's neck right along where the hair stops,' she says. And sure enough there it was on both of them, as plain as a pikestaff."

Shirley laughed, but it didn't sound like laughter. Even to herself it had a perfectly horrid sound. She said in a voice that matched the laugh,

"It would be—she'd see to that!"

And then all at once the stiff nightmarish feeling went out of her. She caught Mrs Camber by the arm and squeezed it with both hands and said,

"She's the world's champion liar. It's either that or bats in the belfry—lots, and lots, and lots, and lots of them. Mrs Camber *dear*, you don't really think I'd go sneaking into that awful Maltby's room and pinch sixpences and hide them in a perfectly idiotic place all nice and ready for you to find instead of putting them in my purse and squandering them quickly on lipstick or whatever female criminals do squander stolen sixpences on? It's too idiotic—isn't it?"

Mrs Camber bridled.

"I couldn't say, I'm sure. I don't know nothing about criminals nor I don't want to, and so I told Miss Maltby. 'And you can mark your sixpences in someone else's house and not in mine,' I said—'an' the sooner the better, Miss Maltby. And if that's your money you'd better pick it up and get back to your room, and when Miss Dale comes in I shall tell her what's happened and give her her notice to go, same as I've given you yours, and that's enough about it,' I said."

Shirley's hand dropped from Mrs Camber's arm.

"You don't believe I took her sixpences, Mrs Camber! You *can't*!"

Mrs Camber sniffed and gulped.

"Can't?" she said, and sniffed again. "Well, least said soonest mended, but I've got my house to think about, and a week from to-day will suit me if you'll be looking for something else." She stood aside from the door and held it open for Shirley to pass.

"But, Mrs Camber—"

Mabel came through the hall with a tray.

"If you're going to have time for your lunch you'll have to hurry," said Mrs Camber.

Shirley walked past her with her head in the air. The interview was over.

Chapter Eight

SHIRLEY SAT on the edge of her bed and stared straight in front of her. A generous helping of beefsteak pudding was rapidly congealing on its tray. Mrs Camber wasn't mean—she always gave you good helpings. Tepid beefsteak pudding was revolting. You had to snatch it from Mabel and eat it like lightning, because it was a long way up from the kitchen anyway, and the house didn't run to plate-covers. It didn't matter, because she wasn't hungry any more. Funny, because just before she had been quite ravingly hungry. Now the idea of swallowing anything made her throat close up. If she could have gone on feeling angry, it would have been much better. She had been angry when she walked out of Miss Pym's room past Mrs Camber, and she had been angry all the way upstairs, but the minute the door was shut and she was alone in her room the anger went away and left her feeling cold, and stiff, and rather sick. If she tried to eat anything she *would* be sick.

She didn't try to eat anything. She sat on the bed and looked in front of her. But in the back of her mind she knew that was all wrong, and she despised herself. She ought to think—think hard. It would be easier to think if she didn't feel so sick.

She didn't think. She sat where she was for twenty minutes, and then went back to Revelston Crescent. There was time to walk, so she didn't take a bus, and as she walked, some of the sick feeling wore off. It was colder—a bright frosty sunlight, and a pale blue sky. Miss Maltby and her fantastic accusation receded. Mrs Camber couldn't really believe a thing like that—nobody could. It was just silly—silly—silly—silly. She said the word out loud, and Miss Maltby shrivelled up and became of no account. It was tiresome to have to look for another room—landladies were such a chance. Anyhow it was no good making a song and dance about it.

Shirley frowned as she walked. That beastly stiff feeling was all gone. But why had she had it? She oughtn't to have been knocked over like that. She ought to have laughed in Mrs Camber's face. She ought to have raised Cain. She ought, bath or no bath, to have insisted on seeing Miss Maltby and telling her just what kind of crazy liar she was. She *had* waited on the landing as she went up and heard the rhythmic splashing which announced Miss Maltby's presence in the bathroom. But she oughtn't to have just let it go at that. She could have banged on the door and insisted—

A funny choky laugh came up in her throat, because in a minute she could see the whole thing like a scene in a perfectly lunatic play—Miss Maltby splashing in her bath, and Shirley Dale screaming through the keyhole, "I didn't take your sixpences, and I wouldn't go into your room if you paid me!" And then Jasper's head poking out of his room, and Mabel with a crowded tray singing "Father, dear Father, come home with me now," while Mrs Camber looked round the turn of the stair and said "A week from to-day will suit me if you'll be looking for something else." It was funny, but it was perfectly mad, and it was rather horrible.

She walked on quickly. There *was* something horrible about the whole thing. It was silly, and it was trivial, but somewhere behind the silliness there was something else. It was the something else that was horrible, and it was the something else that had made her behave like a spineless worm instead of—metaphorically—knocking Miss Maltby's teeth through the back of her head.

Somebody else's bag on her arm—somebody else's purse in her bag—somebody else's sixpences under the toilet-cover on her chest-of-drawers. Seven and elevenpence halfpenny and a paper of peppermints in the bag—the best part of five shillings in the purse—two marked sixpences under the toilet-cover.... Theft on the lowest and most sordid level. Furtive, trivial, magpie theft. And behind it something darkly horrible and menacing—something that wanted to get her into trouble, to crowd, and edge, and squeeze her up to the very brink of some horrid drop and then push her over. But why—why—*why?*... She hadn't any answer to that.

She began to wish that she hadn't gone without her lunch. She wasn't exactly hungry now, but she had that kind of thin, hollow feeling which doesn't help you to think along common-sense lines. Idiotic to go without your lunch.

An afternoon with Mrs Huddleston drove this home, because Mrs Huddleston talked about nothing but food—the kind of food she adored yet dared not touch; the kind of food she disliked and yet felt obliged to eat because it was so good for her; the diet prescribed by her medical advisers, or found beneficial by her friends, with a great many ramifications, illustrations, and examples—"Mrs Mallaby swears, simply swears, by raw salad before every meal, and much as I have always disliked uncooked vegetables, I should try it—one has a duty to oneself—if it were not for the fact that she *insists* on a tepid sponge all over at eight o'clock in the morning followed by breathing exercises at an open window—both naturally quite impossible in my case—and unless the treatment is adopted in its entirety she says it is no good at all. It seems extraordinary that anyone who knows me should imagine for one moment that I could attempt anything so—so—" Mrs Huddleston hesitated for a word, and Shirley dutifully offered her "drastic", which was refused with a frown. "Inhuman," said Mrs Huddleston—"and so I told Mrs Mallaby. 'It is all very well,' I said, 'for robust people like yourself, but for someone who has been as delicate as I have always been it is quite out of the question.' And do you know, Miss Dale, she looked as if I had insulted her. I am sure if I were robust I shouldn't be insulted at being called robust. It must be very pleasant to be one of those strong strapping women—what I call the cart-horse type—not, I think, very attractive. My dear husband always said that fragility was the essence of a woman's charm. But still it must be very nice to be so healthy and never to have any ailments, and I believe she puts it down entirely to the raw salads and the tepid sponge." Mrs Huddleston shuddered in a fragile manner. "One of the plainest women I ever met, and entirely lacking in charm, but quite well-meaning."

"I think your brooch is undone," said Shirley. It sounded most awfully bald, and probably Mrs Huddleston would take offence, but when she shuddered in that silly affected way the big diamond in her brooch winked sharply and the brooch fell crooked.

Mrs Huddleston put her hand to her breast, pricked her finger on the unguarded pin, and pitied herself profusely.

"Oh—my finger! Such a deep prick! Miss Dale—my handkerchief! It's bleeding! Such a deep prick!... Yes, yes of course I want it tied up. No, not so tight. Really, Miss Dale, you're very stupid this afternoon! And take care of the brooch—don't let it fall on any account—it is extremely valuable. The pin has always been perfectly safe—I can't think how it came undone."

Shirley had the brooch in her hand. She turned it over.

"The catch is bent, Mrs Huddleston. Shall I see if I can straighten it?"

"No, certainly not—on no account—the brooch is much too valuable to be played with. Let me see—I can't think how it can have happened—I can't imagine. No, don't touch it, Miss Dale! It must go to a competent jeweller. It is the most valuable thing I have except my emeralds. Put it on the mantelpiece. Now I wonder how the catch can have become damaged like that."

She continued to wonder at considerable length, and then announced that she would like a rest.

"I am feeling completely exhausted. No sleep at all last night—hour after hour, just waiting for the dawn. If I could drop off for half an hour before tea, it would be something."

Shirley pulled down the blinds and withdrew to the Study. She wondered how long she would have to go on enduring Mrs Huddleston. Commonsense said, "Until you can get another job," but something else, something unruly and wild and young, said in a very loud, dear voice of defiance, "Well, some day I shall throw something at her, and I expect it will be some day soon."

She sat down on the hearth-rug and considered what she would throw. One of the Dresden figures on the mantelpiece would make the most row, and a flower-vase full of cold water the most satisfying mess. "And golly—how she would yell!" She made a really good Woggy Doodle face and relaxed.

The warmth of the fire soaked pleasantly into her back. With any luck Mrs Huddleston would sleep till tea-time. It would be nice if

Anthony were to walk in. He wouldn't, because he was week-ending at Emshot, but it would be nice. She could tell him about Miss Maltby. No, she couldn't. It—it was too beastly. It made her feel hot all over to think of telling Anthony that she had practically been accused of stealing two six-pences and hiding them up in her room. She was glad that Anthony was out of town, glad that there wasn't any chance of his coming here, because she didn't want to tell him, or even to see him until she had got the taste of this beastly thing out of her mouth.

She got up resolutely, found herself a book, and curled up in the easy chair under the light.

Chapter Nine

BESSIE WOOD CAME softly up the kitchen stairs. She came very softly indeed. The quickest ear in the world could not have caught the sound of her feet on the treads. She opened the door into the hall and stood there looking and listening. There was nothing to see but the solid Victorian furnishings—table, chairs, hat-and-coat rack, and umbrella stand, and the grandfather clock which was a survival from an earlier century. There was nothing to hear except the ticking of this same clock. The hands stood at half-past three.

Bessie stayed there for quite a long time. Then she took a note out of her pocket and went across the hall to the table. She picked up a salver and went on to the drawing-room door, where she stopped again to listen. No sound came from the room beyond. Mrs Huddleston was certainly asleep, because her tongue never stopped so long as she was awake. Bessie's thin bitten-in lips took on an ironic twist. Extraordinary what a lot of sleep some people managed to put in. Swore she never slept a wink all night, but Possett, the maid, said that was all my eye. Well, Possett was safely out of the way, gone down to see her mother in Ealing, and Cook was having forty winks in the kitchen, a thing she'd never admit to, so she could be reckoned on to declare that Bessie hadn't left the room. With Mrs Huddleston asleep in here, and Miss Shirley Dale in the study, she could go in and have a look around and no one a penny the wiser. And if Mrs Huddleston did wake up, she'd got a note on her salver and every right to bring it in, and no one but herself to know it had come before lunch and she'd kept it back on purpose.

She opened the door as silently as she had done everything else. The room was very dark. Those green blinds fitted better than any blinds she had ever seen—no cracks round the edges. She waited for a moment to get her eyes accustomed to the green dusk, and as she waited, the steady rhythmic snoring of the Blessed Damozel Struck pleasantly upon her ear. She came into the room with the salver in her hand. The old grampus—she'd be cross if she waked, and she'd never own up to having been asleep, any more than Cook would.

The head of the sofa was towards her. She came up to it and looked over. Mrs Huddleston was lying on her back with her mouth wide open. The embroidered coverlet only came up to her waist. The laces of the blue silk tea-gown gaped above it unfastened. Bessie caught her lip between her teeth in her excitement. The diamond brooch had been fastening those laces at lunch-time, and it wasn't fastening them now. That meant that the damaged catch had done what she meant it to do when she damaged it. "Good work—good work, Bessie, my girl!" She bit her lip again, harder this time. What did she want to go and say that for—reminding herself about Ted? Ted was in jug, and she'd got to do this job for him. She wanted all her nerve for it, because she hated working alone, so what was the sense of thinking about Ted like this?

She looked about her with quick, prying eyes. She hadn't really expected to get a chance to-day, and so she'd told Al Phillips. It might be a day or two, she'd told him—"But with the catch damaged, the brooch'll lie about a bit before she sends it off to be mended. Never does nothing on the nail, so Possett says, and when things lie about there's always chances—only of course we've got to fit it in with Miss Dale being there." That's what she'd said, and now it looked like getting a chance right away. If she could only put her hand on the brooch—

She came round the couch, still holding the salver. The fire was burning brightly, and her eyes had got accustomed to the light. She looked along the mantelpiece and saw the brooch. It lay tilted forward against the spreading skirt of the Dresden shepherdess with the powdered hair and the silly fly-away hat with roses all round the crown. The skirt was a very pale blue. The diamonds leaned against it and winked in the firelight.

Bessie took two steps forward, picked up the brooch, and went straight on past the head of the couch and out of the room. She shut the door behind her carefully. Mrs Huddleston had never moved except to snore, and she had never stopped snoring. Nothing could have been easier.

She crossed over to the coat-stand. Only one coat hung there—Miss Shirley Dale's dark grey coat with the black astrakhan collar. As she passed the hall table, she got rid of the salver, and dived into her apron pocket for a pair of nail scissors. It doesn't take a moment to rip a hole in a pocket lining. She chose the left-hand pocket because Miss Dale wasn't so likely to slip her hand into it. She probably wouldn't notice the hole if she did, but there was no sense in taking risks. It was a good coat, and the lining was the very best quality silk. The fur was good too—none of your cheap imitations. Miss Dale couldn't have afforded to buy a coat like that. She must have had it given to her.

Bessie's mind was like that. It went sniffing round like a terrier after rats even in the midst of a job. It would mean jug if she was caught, and a hundred pounds from Al if she pulled it off, but she couldn't keep herself from wondering about Shirley's coat.

She pushed the brooch through the slit in the pocket, and then worked it along the hem until she got it right sound at the back where the coat was slit up and lapped over. It wouldn't show there at all. "A very neat job, Bessie, my girl." Stupid, stupid, stupid to go thinking of Ted again.

She turned round quickly and ran upstairs. So far, so good. But that was only half the job. It was she who had suggested piling up the evidence against Shirley Dale by taking the emeralds too. Al Phillips hadn't been so sure about the emeralds. He thought the diamond brooch would be enough. But then all he wanted was to get the girl into trouble, whereas Bessie had views of her own. It wasn't her first inside job, not by a long chalk. She had worked with Ted for five years, and if she'd started with forged references, she'd got genuine ones now, and never been so much as suspected. Al Phillips wouldn't have known anything about her if it hadn't been for Ted's sister that was married to a cousin of his. Funny how you came across people.

She came into Mrs Huddleston's bedroom and went straight to the built-in cupboard by the fireplace. It hadn't taken her long to find out from Possett that Mrs Huddleston didn't believe in safes or locking things up. She hid her jewellery, and put it in a different place every week. This week the emeralds were rolled up with her stockings. Possett had let that out when they were making the bed yesterday morning. She couldn't keep anything to herself, Possett couldn't. Bessie despised her a good deal.

There were drawers inside the cupboard door. There was a whole drawerful of stockings. Bessie ran her fingers over them, and found the emeralds easily enough. They were beautiful and valuable stones, and they were beautifully set. She looked at them with professional admiration. There was a headband of green leaves set so that they would lie flat against the hair, and there were long earrings, and two brooches, one smaller than the other. It seemed a most awful waste to plant them all on Miss Dale. The headband would be enough to make it look as if she had planned the theft, not just been tempted by the brooch lying, as you might say, to her hand on the drawing-room mantelpiece. She'd got to be in the thing up to her neck, had Miss Dale, but the headband would be enough for that.

Bessie slipped all the things into her apron pocket under her handkerchief and ran down the stairs again. Would Al Phillips find out if she kept some of the emeralds? She didn't see why he should. She could keep the earrings and one of the brooches, and no one would be any the wiser. If they weren't found in the hem of the grey coat, it would only look as if Shirley Dale had hidden them somewhere else—that's all it would look like. Bessie would be safe enough, and Ted's old fence would give her a price for the brooch and earrings. She made up her mind to keep them.

Then she hid the headband and the larger brooch as she had hidden the diamonds, pushing them down through the slit in the lining of Shirley's coat. The headband lay flat along the hem, and she worked the brooch round to the back on the opposite side to the diamonds, taking care to keep the two brooches sis inches apart so that they couldn't possibly knock against each other and give the show away.

Bessie stepped back from the coat-stand with triumph in her heart. There was rather a mouldy-looking fern in a pot on the hall table. Her eye lighted upon it approvingly. The earthenware pot was concealed by a majolica jar. She took it out, dropped the remaining emeralds into the jar, and when the fern had been replaced there was nothing of an incriminating nature anywhere except a dirty mark on Bessie's thumb. One minute later she was washing it off under the scullery tap with Primrose soap, and half a minute after that she was sitting close up to the kitchen window to catch the light, with her eyes bent on page 101 of a novelette entitled *The Perils of Pansy*, whilst her ears noted gratefully the fact that Cook was still snoring. Not much to choose between her and the old grampus upstairs, but Cook perhaps a bit louder and rather more on the bass side.

She became engrossed with Pansy, who was being subjected to the perfidious advances of an unscrupulous duke who had nothing except his wealth and his title to recommend him, while her heart remained perseveringly true to a virtuous commercial traveller who had been unjustly dismissed by his firm. Bessie more than suspected the duke of having a hand in this dismissal, and she had also begun to have a dawning suspicion that the persecuted Everard was going to turn out to be the real duke. She would have time for at least two chapters before she had to think about getting tea.

Chapter Ten

SHIRLEY CAUGHT the six o'clock bus. She had to run for it, because at the last minute Mrs Huddleston called her back to look up a number in the telephone directory. As she ran, the hem of her coat flapped against her legs. She was in too much of a hurry to bother about it. Something hard kept hitting her on the calf. She thought vaguely that there must be leaden weights in the hem to keep it down—tailors often put them there. But she had had this coat two years, and it was funny that it should suddenly have started banging into her when it had never done it before.

She caught the bus by the skin of her teeth, and was flung into the only vacant place by the violent lurch with which it started off again. She came down with a bump between a pale young man with an evening paper and a red-faced woman in a fur cap and a disintegrating plush coat trimmed with rabbit, and had great difficulty in reducing a scream to a gasp, because something very sharp indeed ran about half an inch into the calf of her left leg. She hoped no one noticed the gasp. It really had only just missed being a shriek, because the jab was so sudden. The young man continued to read his paper. The red-faced woman said darkly, "Don't care 'oo they knock down, do they? Talk about accidents on the road—seems to me, you don't 'ave to go out on the road to 'ave them."

Shirley bent down and felt her calf. It was still hurting abominably, but since it wasn't streaming with gore she supposed that the pin which had run into her hadn't really gone in as much as half an inch. It had felt like being stabbed to the bone. ("Draw it mild, my good Shirley—it's about two inches to the bone if you start that side"). She controlled a giggle and sat back. Well anyhow, whether it was half an inch or two inches, the main point was that her leg wasn't streaming with blood. It didn't in fact seem to be bleeding at all, which she thought showed great self-control considering the provocation it had had. And then she began to think about the provocation. What could possibly have pricked her like that? If her coat had been new, it would have been quite easy. You pin up a hem, and then you forget to take the pin away. But why should a pin lurk peacefully and secretly for years and then turn and rend you? She wondered if her stocking had laddered. That really would be a curse.

And while she was thinking about that, in a funny underground way she began to connect the pin which had jabbed her with the odd hard something that had kept on banging against her leg as she ran to catch the bus. She had taken it to be a weight, but it had puzzled her—and weights don't have sharp pins attached to them. Something clouded in Shirley's mind, faintly at first, and then with a gathering darkness. If you pour ink into water, it goes in black, and then spreads out and thins away until the black is all gone and there is only the water, with a tinge in it that wasn't there before. What happened in Shirley's mind was the opposite to this. It was as if all her thoughts were suddenly, lightly, tinged with fear and then the fear began to draw itself away and gather itself together until it wasn't part of her own thoughts any more, but just a dense blackness which had been dropped into her mind. On a terrified impulse she bent down again and felt the hem of her coat.

The young man was reading his paper. The red-faced woman had shut her eyes. The two people immediately opposite were getting to their feet. There was nobody to notice Shirley's sudden pallor. Her heart gave a frightful jump. The bus stopped at the corner of Emsworth Road, and she rose blindly and followed the people who were getting out there. A lot of people always got out at Emsworth Road. It wasn't her stop, but nobody was to know that.

She began to walk back along the way that the bus had come.

It wasn't true....

It was true....

It couldn't be true....

What's the good of saying 'couldn't' when a thing has happened? This thing was true because it had happened. The pin that had run into her was the pin of Mrs Huddleston's diamond brooch. The catch had come undone, and she had told Mrs Huddleston that it was undone, and Mrs Huddleston had told her to put the brooch on the mantelpiece, and she had put it there leaning up against the Dresden china shepherdess.

Well, it wasn't there now. It ought to be there, but it wasn't. It was in the hem of Shirley Dale's coat. She had felt the shape of it quite clearly through the stuff of the hem—the shape, and the big diamond which stuck up like a boss in the middle. She was cold, and hollow, and her legs shook. "The prisoner when arrested had the stolen goods in her possession." That's the sort of thing you see in the papers. It doesn't happen to real people. It can't happen to me—oh, it can't! Oh please, please, *please*!

With a sort of mental jerk Shirley pulled herself together. Something had made her get off the bus. She didn't quite know what, but it was good sound commonsense. What she'd got to do was to go straight back to Revelston Crescent, tell Mrs Huddleston what had happened, and insist, absolutely *insist*, on an inquiry. Because somebody must have put that brooch into the hem of her coat, and for her own sake as well as Shirley Dale's Mrs Huddleston was bound to find out who that someone was.

The minute she decided to do something she began to feel better. She must get back to Revelston Crescent as quickly as possible. It wasn't worth waiting about for a bus. She could do it in ten minutes if she hurried.

She began to hurry, taking three or four running steps and then a couple of walking ones. She must get there before Possett got back from seeing her mother at Ealing, but it was no good arriving out of breath. She was going to need it all to cope calmly with Mrs Huddleston. You could do this running and walking stunt indefinitely without getting out of breath.

Possett wasn't due back till half-past six, so there ought to be plenty of time, "*Loads* of time," Shirley said to herself as she ran. Sometimes Possett came in early. "Don't think of that'—don't, don't, *don't*! Why should she be early to-day? She *won't* be early." And until she came in at half-past six nobody would know that the brooch was gone. Mrs Huddleston wouldn't dream of telling anyone except Possett to put her jewellery away. No, she would wait for Possett to come in, and then she would tell her all about the catch being damaged, and how tiresome it was, and a lot of stuff like that. And when she'd said everything you *could* possibly say about a brooch that wanted mending, and said it twice over at least, then she would tell Possett to take the brooch off the mantelpiece—"carefully, because it is so valuable." With even the least little bit of luck she would get in long before it came to that.

Shirley didn't have any luck at all. Possett came home at five minutes past six. Her sister Mrs Hodgson had also been out to Ealing, and she had to get back not one minute later than six because Aggie, her eldest, was bringing a young man in to tea sharp at the half hour and she'd got scones to make and everything to see to. So the sisters took the same bus, Mrs Hodgson getting off back at the High Street, and Possett, who was Mabel in the family circle, reaching Revelston Crescent at exactly five minutes past six. She took off her outdoor things and went down to the drawing-room as she always did the minute she got in, and the next thing was Mrs Huddleston in hysterics, and Bessie being rung for, and Possett and Bessie applying restoratives. And the next thing after that was Possett at the telephone, trembling in every limb and ringing up the police station.

The loss of the emeralds was discovered a little later, after Possett had rung up the station, but before the policeman arrived.

Shirley Dale saw him arrive. She had turned into Revelston Crescent and had slackened her pace so as to appear with all the calmness and poise which the situation demanded, and there, advancing from the other end of the Crescent with majestic tread and all the calm and poise in the world, was a large and towering policeman. The same something which had snatched Shirley from the bus once more impelled her. She turned, ran up the steps of No 12, and stood there screened by the portico as if she were waiting for someone to come and let her in. She hadn't the slightest doubt that the policeman was on his way to No 15. She had never seen a policeman in Revelston Crescent before. The fact that one was there now most undoubtedly meant that Mrs Huddleston had discovered her loss and sent for the police.

Revelston Crescent was not at all well lighted. Shirley stood in the dark under the portico of No 12 and looked sideways between the pillars. The lamp which had enabled her to see the policeman was opposite No 20. She watched the massive form approach, at first silhouetted against the lamp-light, then growing larger and dimmer. The heavy tread sounded on the quiet pavement. It ascended the steps of No 15. And then, before there was time for the bell to be rung, the door was jerked open and for a moment the agitated twitterings of Possett actually reached Shirley's ears. The policeman went in and the door was shut. Shirley heard that too. And then without stopping to think or plan she ran down the steps of No 12 and went on running.

Chapter Eleven

SHIRLEY SAT in a third-class carriage, and was appalled at her cowardice. Behind being appalled there was a faint fresh tang of triumph. It felt rather like having a scolding from old Aunt Emily Dale in a stuffy room with a hot fire and all the windows shut, and hearing the wind blow in off the sea all cold, and salt, and gusty.

Her hands and feet were cold and her cheeks burned. She sat up stiff and straight with the damp air buffeting her as the train gathered speed, and called herself a puling, puking, pusillanimous pip-squeak, but away at the back of her mind something danced and shouted, "I've done it—I've got away!"

Shirley turned savagely on the shouting, dancing rebel. "Yes, you've got away—and shall I tell you where you've got to? Out of the frying-pan into the fire. You just panicked and ran, and in about half no time the police will be running after you. What you ought to have done was to run after that policeman and burst into the house with him, arm-in-arm so to speak, and tell him all about it." She stopped short. You can't scold anyone, not even yourself, when a sort of cramp of terror has taken hold of you. She waited for it to let go again. Presently it went. She was glad the window was open and the wind blowing in on her face. She was very glad indeed that she was alone in the carriage. She didn't bother about any more scolding, because what was the good? She *hadn't* followed the policeman into the house, and that was that. The milk was spilt, and she couldn't conjure it unspilt again however hard she scolded. When you haven't done a thing, it's just sheer waste of time saying "Why didn't I do it?"

Well, what had she done? Run away. And in the middle of running she had thought about Anthony. Just Anthony to start with, because she was horribly frightened, and he was someone to hold on to. And then, still running, she had thought about Anthony week-ending at Emshot, and Jane Rigg, her sister Jane whom she had never seen, living in Emshot in a ridiculously named Acacia Cottage. "I don't suppose there's an acacia within a mile of it," said Shirley as she ran.

And then and there the panic went out of her and she made a plan. She thought it was a very good plan. She Stopped running and elaborated it. She would whisk back to Mrs Camber's, pick up a toothbrush and pyjamas, and go down to Emshot. Jane Rigg would simply have to take her in. However snuffy and stuffy, and spare-bedroomless you are, you can't turn your own half-sister away from your doorstep in the dark— not in a village. It is just one of the things that can't possibly be done. Shirley had lived long enough in a village with old Aunt Emily to feel comfortably sure about this. Then, having planted the pyjamas and the toothbrush in Jane's alleged non-existent spare room—"which *may* mean that I've got to sleep on the sitting-room sofa, but was probably only meant to choke me off coming to stay"—well, then she must get hold of Anthony, press that horrible diamond brooch into his hand, and leave him to cope with the police and Mrs Huddleston. After all, what was the good of being a barrister if you couldn't cope with a policeman?

This was Shirley's plan, but some of it never got carried out. She had to begin, as it were, in the middle of it. It was the bit about going back to Mrs Camber's and fetching her things which didn't come off. Shirley really did feel ashamed about this, because now that it was over, she felt quite sure she had taken fright about nothing. But when she turned the corner into Findon Road and saw a policeman walking down the pavement about half-way between her and Mrs Camber's whitewashed steps, she didn't stop to think or argue with herself. She ran away all over again.

And caught the train to Emshot by the skin of her teeth. And sat in it between fright and triumph, with no toothbrush and no pyjamas but a sort of dogged conviction that she had done the right thing and that everything was going to be all right, and that if she hadn't done it she would have been completely, absolutely, and finally in the Soup.

She became conscious of feeling cold, and pulled up half the window. Then she leaned back in the corner and put her feet up. The one blessed bit of luck was its being Saturday. If it hadn't been Saturday, Mrs Huddleston wouldn't have just paid her, and she wouldn't have had anything to run away on. If the village shop hadn't shut, she would be able to get a toothbrush at Emshot. Village shops often stay open quite late, especially on Saturday nights. It was a pity about her luggage. Since she was falling on Jane out of the clouds, it would have been much, much better to have had at least pyjamas and a toothbrush to break the fall. And then with horrifying clearness it came over Shirley that by running away without so much as a change of pocket-handkerchiefs she was practically admitting her guilt. If she had gone home for her luggage it would have been all right, because why shouldn't she take a week-end in the country as well as Anthony Leigh or anyone else? But to run without luggage just gave the whole show away. Who was going to believe she was innocent after that? Would Anthony believe it?

She had a horrid picture of an unbelieving Anthony. His face came up in her mind with the astonishing clarity of an image seen on the dark screen of a camera. It was more Anthony than the real Anthony, it was more vivid than life, and it looked at her with cold and unbelieving eyes. In that moment Shirley felt her inmost self dissolve. Something wept in her and would not be comforted. There was no comfort for her anywhere in all the world if Anthony didn't believe.

Chapter Twelve

THE TRAIN REACHED Emshot at half-past eight. That is to say, it reached the station commonly known as Emshot, but whose proper name is Emshot and Twing. It is actually two and a half miles from Twing and a mile and a half from Emshot church, though the village straggles towards it, and Mr Pumphrey the postman can reach the platform in six minutes from his house, which is the last in Emshot.

Shirley set off along a pitch-black lane, encouraged by the assurance of the porter who took her ticket that she couldn't possibly miss her way. And just about the time that she got out of the train Mrs Ward, who was Mr Pumphrey's widowed sister, was shutting the door of Acacia Cottage behind her and putting the key under the mat.

"For if she does come by the eight-thirty—and there's no saying she will—I don't see staying any longer, and that's a fact."

Her daughter, Lucy Hill, agreed in her slow, determined voice.

"No call to go at all that I could see. And just like her sending a telegram like that on a Saturday afternoon! 'Get everything ready. Coming down to-night or to-morrow morning.' Slave-driving, I call it, and you'd no call to do it for her! And come eight o'clock when you weren't back, Bert said to me real angry, 'You go and fetch your mother home, Lu, and tell her the old cat can do her own clearing up.'"

Mrs Ward straightened herself up with a hastily repressed groan. "Well, I'm coming, aren't I? Of course by rights I ought to wait for the train—"

Lucy took her by the arm and propelled her towards the gate.

"Well, you'll do nothing of the sort, Mother! You'll take and come along home and have your supper and go to your bed! Bert's real angry at your going at all."

Mrs Ward sighed and acquiesced.

"Well, the water's hot, and I've left a bit of a fire, and the kettle on the side, and there's tea and butter and eggs, and a half pint of milk in the larder same as she always has, and I've boiled a bit of bacon along of to-morrow being Sunday and no meat in the house, so whether she comes to-night or don't come till to-morrow, there'll be something for her to eat. And the key's under the mat, same as usual."

"You come along home, Mother!" said Lucy Ward.

Shirley walked along the lane until she came to Mr Pumphrey's house. It had red curtains in the sitting-room window, and the light shone through them. After that there were houses all the way, which was rather tantalizing, because you kept hoping you had got there and finding you hadn't. The houses were a long way apart at first, but by the time she had been walking for twenty minutes they were getting more sociable.

The young man at the station had told Shirley that she couldn't miss Acacia Cottage. She didn't feel as sure about this as he did, but she hoped for the best. The reason she couldn't miss it was that it was right opposite the Green Man. Having lived in a village herself, Shirley appreciated this. In the country you steer by churches and pubs. At half-past eight on a Saturday evening the church would certainly be dark and deserted, but the Green Man would be going all out with lights, and drinks, and a full flow of village talk.

The young man at the station proved to be quite right. You come round a bend, and the Green Man more or less hits you in the eye. Well, then the house lurking in the darkness across the road must be Acacia Cottage.

Shirley lifted the latch of the gate. It swung in, creaking a little, and she found herself in the dense shadow of an over-arching yew. At the time she did not know where the shadow came from, only that it was there, and very black. She stood in the blackness and looked towards the house, but she could see nothing except shadow melting into shadow, all dark, and vague, and formless. Suppose there wasn't a house here at all.... Nonsense! She had seen it quite clearly from the other side of the road. Suppose she hadn't really seen it—Suppose she were to walk into the shadow and find there wasn't anything there.... Her spine crept all the way down. Nothing to eat since breakfast is apt to induce spine-creeping in the dark. The slice of toast and the cup of tea of which she had partaken twelve hours before seemed to belong to some remote previous existence.

"Stop it!" said she to herself with as much scorn as she could contrive. It was just enough to take her reluctant feet up what felt like a flagged path and land them on a most undoubted door-mat. At the same time her hand, feeling before her, touched the smooth painted wood of the door.

Well, here she was. But where was Jane Rigg? The house hadn't a blink of light in it anywhere on this side. Perhaps there was a room at the back. Perhaps Jane was a thrifty soul and wouldn't have a light in the hall. Shirley felt along the painted door until she found the knocker, and when she had found it knocked with a vigour calculated to reach every corner of the house. But when she stopped to listen, there was no sound nor any that answered. That was out of the Bible, when the prophets called upon Baal and he didn't hear them.... What a perfectly *horrid* thing to think about on a black doorstep when you haven't had anything to eat all day. But in spite of herself Elijah's mocking words came into her mind: "Cry aloud ... either he is pursuing, or he is in a journey, or peradventure he sleepeth and must be awaked."

She banged with the knocker again. If Jane was asleep, this ought to wake her, but if she was on a journey—She stopped to listen. The house positively oozed silence. Suppose Jane really *was* away....

Shirley stamped on the mat in sheer rage, and heard something tinkle under her foot. The sound touched off a bright firework of joy inside her. A tinkle under the mat meant a hidden key, and you don't hide your key under the mat when you go on a journey—you hide it there when there's only one key and two people use it, and it means you are coming in quite soon. In fact Jane had gone out to supper, and she probably had a maid who had gone out too, and whichever of them came home first would take the key from under the mat and lift up the latch and walk in, just as Miss Shirley Dale was doing now. Wait on the doorstep for Jane to return from riotous supping with some other old hen? Not for nuppence! Anyhow not for Shirley Dale. They might riot till midnight playing bridge for all she knew of Emshot society.

She shut the front door, felt her way forward round a bend, and saw a very faint rosy glow behind a door that stood ajar. She pushed open the door and went in. The room was the kitchen. The rosy glow came from between the bars of an old-fashioned range. There was a faint mingled smell of blacklead, and bacon, and floor polish, with a sort of general over-tone of paraffin. Helped partly by her nose and partly by the glow, Shirley located a lamp. It stood on the dresser breathing out oil—warm oil. Before she put her hand on it Shirley knew that

that lamp hadn't been out very long. It needs heat to draw out the full flavour of paraffin oil. There were matches lying beside it. She struck one and lighted the lamp. The yellow flame ran along the double wick and steadied down as she replaced the chimney. A tin reflector threw the light out into the room.

The kitchen sprang into view. There were red tiles on the floor, and Mrs Ward had polished them till they shone. The dresser and the table had been scrubbed white, and the range was as glossy as a newly blacked boot. Curtains of red Turkey twill were drawn across a long casement window.

Shirley looked about her with a sense of deep relief and comfort. If she liked Jane as much as she liked her kitchen, everything was going to be all right. There were old willow-pattern plates on the dresser, and dishcovers with little crouching lions on them. There was a row of Toby jugs on the ledge above the range. The smell of bacon meant that there was food in the larder. She loved Jane's kitchen.

The first thing to do was to make up the fire, and the next to put the kettle over it. It began to sing at once in the most encouraging way. It was the singing of the kettle that made her feel how very cold, and hungry, and frightened she had been, and how very, very glad she was to be here.

There were two other doors besides the one through which she had come. The farther one stood open into the scullery. The nearer one let in a draught of cold air as she opened it. It led into the larder—a very superior larder with a stone floor and wide shelves. On the bottom shelf there was a loaf of brown bread, half a pound of butter, a canister of tea, a little jug of milk, two eggs, two bananas, a sugar-basin half full of lump sugar, and a piece of bacon cooling down in the liquor in which it had been boiled.

A passionate affection for all this food welled gratefully up in Shirley. The only question was, how much of it could she decently eat? She considered this whilst she found a knife and fork and a teapot, tipped the bacon on to a plate, and set everything out on the table. Two eggs and two bananas looked like Jane and a maid each having an egg and a banana for Sunday breakfast, or if there wasn't a maid who lived in, it looked like two breakfasts for Jane. Just enough and nothing wasted seemed to be Jane's motto. And just where did an unfortunate starving half-sister who was running away from the police come in?

The contents of the larder rather confirmed all her worst fears about Jane. There was, to be sure, the piece of bacon. It looked terribly good, but there wasn't very much of it. Supper for one to-night, lunch for three tomorrow, and supper for three to-morrow evening—no, it just couldn't be done.

The kettle changed its singing tone to a boiling one. She made the tea, and then firmly boiled one of the eggs. If she didn't have something to eat—and not a snack but lots *and* lots and lots—she couldn't possibly confront Jane at midnight. Any village shop will sell you food out of its back door on a Sunday. She would leave one egg for Jane's breakfast, and a banana, and just not bother about anything else.

She had never enjoyed a supper so much in her life. The half cold bacon, the brown bread, the butter, and the egg all tasted too marvellous for words. She ate a great deal of the bacon, and she drank three cups of tea, allowancing herself rather strictly with the milk so as to leave some for breakfast. It was a lovely lingering meal and the kitchen was as hot as a toast, and the police, and Mrs Huddleston, and London were all as comfortably remote as something read in a book a long time ago. Her grey coat hung across the back of one of the kitchen chairs. Presently she would have to think about it again and get that blighted diamond brooch out of the hem, but not just now.

When she had finished her supper she put everything tidily away and washed up. It was now about a quarter to ten. If Jane kept early hours, she might come in any time after ten. Shirley thought suddenly about the telephone. Was there one in the house or not? If there was, she could ring Anthony now, at once, before Jane got in. Perhaps he would come down and see her—perhaps he wouldn't. Anyhow she must let him know she was here.

She took the lamp and went over the house. There was a dining-room, and a drawing-room, and some crooked stairs, two bedrooms in front and a tiny one at the back, and quite a big room over the kitchen which had been turned into a bathroom. Only one bed was made up, the one in the room over the drawing-room. The sheets and pillow-cases were clean, and there were two hot-water bottles keeping it warm. This meant that Jane hadn't a maid who slept in. There must be a daily woman, and perhaps she didn't come on Sundays, which would account for the food shortage. The clean sheets puzzled her a little, because it was Saturday, and no one changes their sheets on a Saturday. But of course that might be to save trouble if the daily woman didn't come on Sundays.

Shirley looked round Jane's room, and didn't like it very much. There were heavy dark brown curtains across the window, and an ugly brown linoleum on the floor, with a faded strip of carpet by the bed. The furniture was heavy, gloomy mahogany of the mid-Victorian period, so much too large for the house that she wondered how it had ever been persuaded into it. The wardrobe, which covered one whole wall and towered to the ceiling, gave her the feeling that its doors might open at any moment. It was rather a horrid feeling.

She went downstairs again. There wasn't any telephone upstairs, and there wasn't any telephone downstairs. In fact there wasn't any telephone. What was she going to do about Anthony?

She put the lamp down on the top of the upright piano in the drawing-room and considered. The piano had brass candle-holders and a front of pleated green silk with rosewood scroll-work over it. The room was quite astonishingly like Aunt Emily's drawing-room— the same sort of carpet with faded wreaths on a ground the colour of dried fog; the same odd-shaped chairs; the same table with a leg in the middle; the same silver photograph frames; the same determination to cover as much of the wall-space as possible with every conceivable kind of picture. There were oil paintings, and water colours, engravings, mezzo-tints, and a sampler or two bearing witness in tiny stitches to the industry of little bygone Riggs—Augusta aged seven, and Marianne aged five. Just behind the lamp there was a forbidding photographic enlargement of a man with whiskers. A momentary unpleasant sense of something familiar came over Shirley. She had certainly never seen the whiskers before, but there was something—some likeness—some—

She turned away quickly, and saw over the mantelpiece her mother's face smiling down from an oval frame. She knew it at once. She had a photograph in her room at Mrs Camber's, but this must be the original, an oil painting commissioned by Augustus Rigg at the time of his marriage. The bride of seventeen had been painted in her wedding dress of white moiré, high at the back, and cut to a modest square in front, with a ruched trimming and ruched elbow sleeves. Her dark brown hair was taken plainly back and caught in a demure knot at the nape of the neck. The hair was demure, and the dress was demure, but the lips had a mischievous smile and the eyes a teasing brilliance.

The queerest feeling came over Shirley as she looked up at Jane's mother and hers—regret—something missed—something that couldn't ever be made up to her. This teasing beauty that she couldn't remember—there was something all wrong about it. Jane couldn't remember her either. She had left Jane as a baby to marry Pierre Levaux, and she had left the baby Perrine to marry Humphrey Dale and go away over the seas with him. And she had lost their two grown sons in the war, and then she had left the little after-thought Shirley because she had died. And here she was, still seventeen, still with that secret mutinous smile.

Chapter Thirteen

THE 8.30, BY WHICH Shirley had come, is the last train scheduled to stop at Emshot station, but the 9.30 will stop long enough to drop a passenger if the guard is notified. Emshot people who like their money's worth when they go to town for the day very often return by the 9.30. They rather like the feeling that they can get the train stopped especially for them. Of course it very often doesn't stop at all, but goes roaring away past Emshot and past Twing with the red light in its tail getting fainter and fainter until the darkness swallows it up. On this particular Saturday night it stopped. A woman got out, and the train went on. The woman was carrying a suit-case. She left the station, entered the dark lane, and began to walk towards the village.

Shirley stopped looking at her mother's picture and looked at the clock below it instead. It was a gimcrack affair in a Dresden china case. The gilt hands stood at ten o'clock. On the other hand the clock in the kitchen had made it twenty minutes to ten only a few minutes ago. Both clocks were fully wound up and going. She went to have another look at the one in the kitchen. It said five minutes to ten, so she had been longer going over the house than she had thought.

She wondered how long it was going to be before Jane Rigg came home. That bed and those hot-water bottles were beginning to be the most frightful temptation. Not that she wanted to sleep in Jane's room or in Jane's bed, but she wanted—most frightfully she wanted—a room and a bed of her own. And a hot-water bottle. And to snuggle down and pull the eiderdown right up round her and go to sleep for hours, and hours, and hours. She gave herself a sort of mental shake. She couldn't possibly have any bed at all till Jane came home, but she could sit down in the kitchen armchair, and if she went to sleep she went to sleep, and that was all about it.

She left the lamp in the hall. There was a book-case there, and the lamp sat comfortably on the top shelf. It would be nice for Jane to find a light in the hall when she came in. Firelight would do very well to go to sleep by.

Shirley sat down in the kitchen chair and went to sleep. She seemed to pass at once into a dream in which old Aunt Emily Dale was scolding her. "You shouldn't have done it, Shirley," she kept saying—"you shouldn't have done it. Everyone knows that diamonds must never be cooked with butter." And there was Shirley in her nightgown, with a frying-pan in one hand and a little *diamanté* bag in the other trying hard to explain to Aunt Emily that there wasn't any butter in the house. And then the dream changed, and she and Anthony were dancing together at the Luxe, and all of a sudden he pushed her away and put on a judge's wig and a black square on the top of it, and she knew that he was going to sentence her to death. She tried to speak, and to cry out, and to say his name, but she couldn't. And then sharp across her dream there came the sound of a key being fitted into a lock, and in an instant she was awake. The key was being tiresome—not fitting, not turning.

Shirley jumped up and ran into the passage, because of course this was Jane come home and she must be ready to explain herself. The passage twisted to avoid the crooked stair. As Shirley came to the bend and looked round it, the key turned with a click, the door opened, and Miss Maltby stepped into the lighted hall with a battered brown suit-case in her hand. The shock made Shirley tingle all over. One bit of her mind told her that Miss Maltby was there, and another bit told her that it simply wasn't possible, and that Miss Maltby was a bit of the dream in which Aunt Emily had been accusing her of trying to cook diamonds in butter.

If Miss Maltby had been looking in her direction she would have seen the shuddering movement with which Shirley drew back behind the bend, but she had eyes only for the lamp which was wastefully burning in the hall. She made a clicking sound of disapproval, put down her suit-case at the foot of the stair, and turned to withdraw her key and shut and bolt the door.

The sound reached Shirley in the kitchen. It woke her completely. Miss Maltby wasn't something in a nightmare. She was real, and she was here. If she was also Jane Rigg, then Shirley had indeed jumped out of the frying-pan into the fire, and she hadn't a single moment to lose if she didn't want to be burnt to a cinder. She snatched her coat and ran into the scullery as Miss Maltby's footsteps sounded in the twisted passage. She tore at the bolt of the back door and got it open as the kitchen floor swung in and the light came brightly round it. Miss Maltby's voice sounded behind her querulously: "Mrs Ward—Mrs Ward—is that you?" The air blew cold in her face, and she was over the threshold and away.

It was very dark. She had run blindly to the corner of the house, one hand before her, the other clutching her coat. Some kind of thorny branch caught at her, tearing her sleeve and scratching her shoulder. She got off the path and felt under foot the soft damp earth of a garden bed. Then she was brought up short by a thrusting mass of evergreens. They were wet against let face, her neck, her hand. Her heart nearly choked her. She stood still, with the aromatic scent of bruised cypress in her throat and nose, and listened with terror for the sound of Miss Maltby's feet. She heard instead the unmistakeable slam of the back door and the sound of a bolt going home. She turned, shuddering, and saw the lamplight shining comfortably through the red Turkey curtains of the kitchen window. Miss Maltby was in the kitchen. Miss Maltby wasn't following her. It was even possible that Miss Maltby thought she was a burglar and had made haste to lock herself in.

The thought of Miss Maltby trembling in the lamp-lit kitchen had a very heartening effect upon Shirley. The glow from the kitchen window gave her her direction. She stopped shuddering, disengaged herself from the evergreens, and made her way quite easily round the house and out of the yew-shadowed gate.

As soon as she was outside she stopped and put on her coat, and it was when she was buttoning it up that it came to her with a crashing sense of disaster that she had left her cap and her bag behind her in Acacia Cottage. The cap didn't matter. Lots of people go about without hats in the country even in the middle of the winter. But the bag—that was the really frightful loss, because it had all her money in it—every single penny of it. And how was she to go on running away without so much as a single halfpenny to run with?

She stood against the hedge which bordered the garden and stamped her foot in desperate anger. "Oh, Shirley—you *blasted* food!" she said. It really was a most horrible situation. If she hadn't been wanted by the police, she could, of course, have walked up to the front door, knocked firmly and loudly, and explained with calm that she had left her bag in the kitchen. But if she hadn't been wanted by the police she wouldn't have been here at all. And of course the really awful thing was that Miss Maltby must know perfectly well by now that Shirley Dale was wanted by the police. They would have been to Mrs Camber's, and Miss Maltby would have told them her horrible lying story about the marked sixpences. It certainly was a very nasty mess.

The odd thing was that it wasn't until this moment that it occurred to Shirley to regard Miss Maltby's sudden appearance as anything except a breath-taking catastrophe, but now quite suddenly it seemed to require explanation. Acacia Cottage was Jane Rigg's cottage. Then why Miss Maltby? Had she followed her, Shirley, down from town? She couldn't have—not an hour later, and by a different train. And she had walked into the house as if it belonged to her.... Something in Shirley's mind said in a loud penetrating whisper, *"Suppose it does belong to her. Suppose Miss Maltby is Jane."*

Shirley's flesh crept all over from the top of her scalp to the tips of her fingers and the soles of her feet. Miss Maltby her sister! She said desperately, "Oh, no, no—she's too old!" and then remembered that Jane must be fifty-one. The bit in the family Bible—"John and Jane, b. 1884"—And how old was Miss Maltby?—Some people didn't look a bit old when they were fifty, and other people did—Miss Maltby might be any age—She might be sixty-five, or sixty, or fifty. *She might be Jane.*

The idea was so frightful that Shirley started to run away from it. She didn't know where she was going or what she was going to do. All she knew was that she must get away from Acacia Cottage and the revolting possibility that Miss Maltby might be Jane.

She might have run quite a long way if she hadn't bumped into William Giles. William was on his way to fetch the village nurse to his wife, and, it being a first baby, William was in a hurry, and in a very flustered and unnoticing state of mind, otherwise he would probably have avoided the collision. As it was, it was a head-on affair, and Shirley certainly saw stars. All William wanted was to get Mrs Gaunt as quickly as possible. He apologized—all the Giles have very nice manners—and then hurried upon his way. But before he had gone a dozen yards, there was the girl he had nearly knocked down coming up behind him and saying in a soft panting voice,

"Oh, please, *please* can you tell me how to find Emshot Place?"

William could and did, and as shortly as possible, because anything that came between him and getting Mrs Gaunt for Rosie had to be got out of the way as sharp as it could be done.

"Straight on the way you were going till you come to the churchyard, and there's the gate right along next to it—you can't miss it." He ran on into the darkness.

Shirley turned round and walked in the opposite direction. Whenever you asked anyone the way in Emshot they always told you you couldn't miss it. Well, she hadn't missed Acacia Cottage. She shivered, squared her shoulders, and marched along briskly. It was funny that knocking her head and seeing stars should have made her remember Anthony, but the moment the first bang was over that was just what had happened. She had been running blindly without an idea in her head except to get away from Miss Maltby who might be Jane, and then after an interval of stars her panic was gone and she was remembering that Anthony was at Emshot Place, and that she had better hurry up and get into touch with him.

She hurried.

William Giles was perfectly right—you couldn't miss the churchyard. Even on a dark night like this the whiter tombstones showed up. A polished marble angel gleamed wraith-like above a polished marble tomb, and just where the churchyard wall began there was a pair of open gates and a shadowy drive that went on, and on, and on, and out of sight. Shirley couldn't see if there was a lodge or not. Anyhow the gates were open. She turned between them and began to walk along the drive.

She had no idea what time it was, because she had no idea how long she had slept in the kitchen of Acacia Cottage. Everything had happened too quickly after she woke up for her even to have thought of looking at the clock. Suppose it was the middle of the night. Suppose it was the small hours of the morning. Suppose everyone in Emshot Place had gone to bed ... "Suppose fiddlestick ends! That man was out, wasn't he? And Miss Maltby had arrived from somewhere—she wouldn't be walking about in the middle of the night. Besides it hasn't got that after-midnight kind of feeling."

It was, as a matter of fact, a little short of half-past ten.

Shirley thought the drive was never going to come to an end. And then all of a sudden it came out of a particularly dark belt of shrubbery and she saw the lighted house right in front of her, a big square block with a glow coming from it as if it was full of people and all the rooms in use. She had been thinking about reaching the house, but she hadn't thought about what she was going to do when she got there. Ring the bell and ask for Anthony Leigh? Oh no, she couldn't possibly do that. Her hair was wild, her face probably coal-black after blundering in amongst those wet evergreens, and her shoes plastered with mud from the soft garden bed. She must look like a tramp. And even if she didn't, she couldn't go up to that door and ask for Anthony.

Well, what *was* she going to do? She didn't know.

The drive came out on a newly gravelled sweep before the house. New gravel makes the most ghastly noise when you walk on it. Shirley felt very modest indeed about making a noise. She wondered if there was a dog loose. It was horrid to feel that she would mind if there were. But when you are in someone else's grounds in the middle of the night and the police are after you it has a very undermining effect on your courage, and on the ordinary affectionate feelings you would have towards the Alsatian, or mastiff, or bull terrier who might be going the rounds of his master's property.

As she stood there hesitating, the veering wind brought her a faint snatch of music. It had the hoarse, tinny sound of gramophone or wireless heard in the distance. Synthetic music does not travel well. Shirley's feet moved at once and instinctively in the direction of the sound. Where there is a gramophone or wireless in full swing, there are people gathered together. Where there were people gathered together in this house, there would be Anthony Leigh. And if the music was making enough noise to reach her as far away as this, they wouldn't be likely to heat her feet on the gravel.

Nevertheless she skirted the edge of it until she came to the place where she could see past the end of the shrubbery and along the side of the house. A big lighted conservatory ran the whole length of it. She could see palms rising to the roof and spreading out there, black against the glow behind them.

When she had passed the front line of the house the gravel wasn't new any more. She crossed it without making any noise and stood by the glass wall of the conservatory looking in. The music was quite loud now that she was so near. A crooner with a voice dripping with sentiment was wailing out something about the "melancholy—folly—of loving you." There was a group of palms which prevented her from seeing in. They touched the glass, and their stems, which looked as if they had been wrapped up in matting and only partially unpacked, made a thick screen. She moved a little to the left and looked round them. The place was more like a palm room at an hotel than a real conservatory. There was matting on the floor, and green wicker furniture. There were bright banks of azaleas, and a lot more palms. Amongst the palms and the azaleas three bridge tables had been set out. At the nearest one Anthony was playing bridge.

Shirley felt a little tingling triumph. He was really here, and she had really reached him.

And then the triumph died, because the three or four yards between her and Anthony might just as well have been miles. There he was, all nice and clean and tidy, with the celebrated profile in full view. He had probably had a most frightfully good dinner, and he was playing bridge with a jolly red-faced old man, and a white-haired woman who drooped and frowned and fidgeted with her cards, and a girl. The girl had her back to Shirley. She looked exactly as if she had never been out of a glass Case in her life—rows of little shining curls coming down on to her neck, and the most wonderful waves. Her hair was exactly the colour of honey after the frost has thickened it. Her dress had a silver bib in front and nothing at all behind. At any other time it would have interested Shirley very much, because there didn't seem to be any reason at all why the bib should stay put. Unless it was *stuck* on—and then suppose it melted. She could hear their voices. Someone had just dealt, and the bidding was going on.

Shirley stood there and listened, and was hot with humiliation and anger. She felt like a beggar, standing here all muddy and grimed and untidy, looking in at that glass-case girl with her white flesh and her silver bib, and at Anthony, who wouldn't care if he never saw her again, and who was sitting comfortably in a warm, lighted place whilst she was out in the dark and the cold. And presently he would have an absolutely super bed to sleep in and as many eiderdowns as he wanted, and she, Shirley, would probably be sleeping in a ditch. No, she wouldn't—not without putting up a fight about it anyhow.

The bidding had finished. Anthony kid down his cards and got up. He stood there for a moment lighting a cigarette, and then moved away. Before Shirley knew what she was going to do she had stooped, picked up a pebble, and thrown it tinkling against the glass. The fidgeting, frowning woman started nervously, and the girl with the pale shining hair looked over her shoulder in a languid, unhurried way. Shirley saw that she had an odd heart-shaped face with pale blue eyes and artificially darkened eyebrows and lashes. There was no colour at all in her face except in the lips, which were painted a smooth, deep strawberry red. Her look was vague and uninterested. The fidgety woman played a card from dummy's hand, and the girl turned back to the game.

Anthony Leigh strolled over to the glass wall and stood there with his cigarette in his hand looking out. It was a dark night—dark and windy. The B.B.C. dance orchestra was playing *"Wein Weib und Gesang."* He loathed playing bridge to the wireless. He would rather have heard the wind in those black trees out there. He wondered who had thrown a pebble against the glass. You couldn't see a yard with all these lights behind you.

And then he saw Shirley looking at him through the hard, clear pane which divided them. He was startled to the point of immobility. Her face had swum out of the darkness like a face rising through water—a dead face coming up out of dark water—

The moment of shock passed. Her lips moved, and her eyes implored him. Then she was gone again, without sound and without visible movement.

Anthony walked round the palms, opened a glass door, and descended four steps. The wind caught the smouldering end of his cigarette and blew it into a bright point of fire. He said just under his breath,

"Shirley, where are you?"

Chapter Fourteen

SHIRLEY CAME UP like a shadow, caught him by the wrist, and ran with him across the old gravel. At the black edge of the shrubbery she stopped. Her hand was cold on his. She dropped it. She said in a whispering, panting voice,

"I had to see you—I haven't got any money—I'm running away—"

He took her by the arm.

"There's a path just here—we'd better get down it a little way. There—this will be all right, and I can keep my eye on the table. I shall have to go back as soon as the hand is over."

Shirley boiled with rage. She said in a furious whisper,

"I'm running away. I left my bag at Jane's blighted cottage—it's got all my money in it. I can't go back because Miss Maltby's there." And then it came over her that Anthony didn't know about Miss Maltby, and her horrible sixpences, and the lies she had told Mrs Camber. And he didn't know about Mrs Huddleston's brooch and the police. And all he wanted was to go back to the girl with the strawberry lips and go on playing bridge. She hated him with a fiery hatred, and it was the last humiliation on earth to have to ask him to lend her a pound.

"You're awfully cold," he said. "Why are you running away?" He was partly amused and partly annoyed. It was the first time he had stayed with the Parrys. Shirley turning up like this looked as queer as the devil.

She stamped her foot on the garden path.

"Lend me a pound and I'll manage! I don't want to keep you—you can go in! I'll pay you back!"

The quivering rage in her voice got home.

"Shirley—is anything really the matter?"

Shirley caught her breath.

"Oh no! I'm running away for fun—and the police are after me for fun—and you haven't got time to hear about it, so please go in!"

They were standing quite close in the narrow path with the dense blackness of holly, and laurel, and yew shutting them in. Anthony's hands came down hard upon her shoulders. He spoke with an angry tang in his voice.

"Cut that out! Tell me what's happened—tell me at once!"

Shirley began to tell him. His hands gripped her so tightly that they hurt. They held her squarely in front of him so that she couldn't move. Under all her anger was the dreadfully weak feeling that it would be nice to cry on his shoulder. Her voice went tripping and stumbling amongst a lot of difficult words.

"It began with Miss Maltby—she told Mrs Camber that—two sixpences were gone—from her room—*sixpences*, Anthony! She said she had marked them—and she said she had seen me come out of her room—and she made Mrs Camber look in *my* room—and they found the sixpences—under the toilet-cover—on my chest-of-drawers. That's only the beginning."

"Then you'd better go on," said Anthony.

He felt her quiver under his hands, and that surface annoyance of his was gone. The Parrys were gone too—off the map and out of the world. The world just now was this black shrubbery which enclosed himself and Shirley. In this world something was happening between them—an onset of anger shaking them both, and then, in himself, a vehement uprush of some feeling which he did not recognize. It was strange to him. It seemed to be blended of fear and a new sort of anger, and over and above the fear and the anger there was a warmth and a kind of aching sweetness.

Shirley stumbled on.

"Mrs Huddleston's brooch came off—her big diamond *brooch*. She said to put it on the mantelpiece—the catch was broken—I leaned it up against the shepherdess. Then she had her rest. Afterwards I didn't notice it. I got away at six—I had to run for my bus—and something kept banging against my leg. When I was in the bus I felt the hem of my coat to find out what it was—and it was Mrs Huddleston's brooch—"

"*What?*"

"It was. I could feel it—in the hem. I didn't know what to do—the bus had gone quite a long way. Then it stopped, and I got out and ran back. I thought if I went straight back and told her, we could find out who had put the brooch in my coat—because someone *must* have put it there."

"Yes, that was right. Go on."

Shirley gave a bitter little sob.

"No, it wasn't right—it all went wrong. She must have missed the brooch the minute I'd gone—they'd seat for the police, and there was a policeman going into the house when I got there, and—and I ran away. And I thought about Jane Rigg at Emshot—and I thought if I came down here she'd have to take me in, and then I could give you the brooch and that would be the next best thing to giving it to Mrs Huddleston."

"Yes," said Anthony—"yes." He took his hands off her shoulders. He picked her up suddenly and held her tight for a moment, "Shirley—don't! It'll be all right. You've got to do just what I tell you—you've got to. Do you hear?"

Shirley gave another sob.

"Darling, listen! Can you find your way down the drive? All right. Then go and wait by the gate—I'll be as quick as ever I can. I can't stop now, or they'll come and look for me. The rubber's just finishing, and then I'll cut out. You'll wait?"

Shirley said "Yes," and then he let go of her and was gone.

She stood at the end of the path and watched him go up the steps and cross behind the palms and come out into the lighted space where the bridge table was. It gave her the strangest feeling to see him there in the light, and to remember how he had held her a moment ago. He hadn't kissed her, only held her up against him hard and then let her go. She had felt the beating of his heart. She wasn't angry any more. She was shaken, and yet comforted.

She went on watching the conservatory for a little. The rubber must have finished, because they were all standing up. She saw Anthony stand and talk for a little and then go away through a door that led into the house. Then she turned, skirted the shrubbery as she had done before, and so found her way to the drive, and down to the gate.

Anthony had to find Mrs Parry. She came to meet him across the drawing-room, a pleasant, comfortable woman who couldn't be bothered with keeping slim and was in a state of perpetual distress because none of the girls who came to the house would eat the good food she provided for them. If Anthony had qualms about the plausibility of his story, Mrs Parry was the least critical audience for such a story. She observed Anthony's charming smile, liked his manner, and thought it showed very nice feeling for him to wish to ring up and ask news of a sick friend. There was a telephone-box in the hall, and she told him that he must be sure to let her know what his news was. Anthony liked her very much indeed, and wished that he could have told her the truth.

He came back presently with a grave face. Would Mrs Parry think it very rude of him if he did not stay the night? She had been so very kind, and he was in fact urgently needed. He felt he had really no choice in the matter.

It was all quite easy. She was kindness itself, and so was old Parry. They wouldn't tell anyone else till he was gone. He could just slip away. And he must be sure to come another time, or they would feel cheated, because you really couldn't count this as a visit at all.

His suit-cases were packed, his car was brought round, and in an astonishingly short time he was moving slowly down the drive and keeping a sharp look-out for Shirley.

She was by the gate, just where he had told her to be. The time which had passed so quickly for him had seemed long and slow for her. There was a dead darkness broken only by the glimmer of the white tombstones in the churchyard just across the wall—a dead darkness and a dead silence. Anthony's arms round her began to feel like a dream. Perhaps he wouldn't come. Perhaps the girl in the silver dress would ask him to stay and he wouldn't come. She was very tired and very cold, and she didn't like midnight churchyards very much. It was more and more difficult to believe that Anthony would really come. And then she heard the car, and saw the headlights make a straight, bright path from him to her.

When she was in the car, he turned out of the gates and drove through the village and along the station road until they were clear of the houses. Then he drew up, shut off the engine, slipped an arm round her, and said,

"Now—what's all this nonsense?"

Shirley made herself stiff. She had only a tiny little scrap of pride left—because it is very difficult to be proud when you are feeling very tired, and very cold, and most dreadfully lost dog—but she did just manage to gather up enough to keep herself stiff in the circle of Anthony's arm.

He didn't seem to notice that she was being proud. He said,

"Go on telling me what you did. I want to know exactly what happened when you got to Emshot."

Shirley shivered a little. It was the thought of Miss Maltby that made her shiver, because it was so really horrid to think about her being Jane, and a relation.

Anthony said at once, "Are you cold?" He said it in a new voice, as if he would hate her to be cold—or unhappy—or frightened.

She said, "No." It wasn't true, but she wasn't thinking what she said. She was only thinking about the new sound in Anthony's voice. And then because she felt suddenly frightened she began to tell him very quickly about coming to the cottage and finding nobody there.

"But the key was under the mat. So I went in—I thought Jane would be coming back—I thought she had just gone out to supper—so I went in and had something to eat. I hadn't had anything since breakfast, and I didn't think she would mind. And then I looked to see if there was a telephone because of ringing you up, and there wasn't one, so I sat down in the kitchen to wait for Jane, and I went to sleep. And the next thing was someone opening the front door, and of course I thought it was Jane. And oh, Anthony, it *wasn't*—at least I don't know if it was or not. That's the really frightful part, because she came in as if the whole place belonged to her, but it was Miss Maltby from Mrs Camber's—the one who said I'd taken her horrible sixpences. And I don't see how I can bear it if she's Jane—but I suppose she is."

Anthony put his other arm round her too. He found her almost unbearably funny and dear, sitting there frightened and shaky, but remembering to be proud. He said in a tender laughing voice,

"Oh, Shirley!" And then, "You won't have to bear it. The place does belong to her, but she isn't Jane."

Shirley tried to push him away. Perhaps she didn't try very hard. Anyhow he didn't go. She went on making herself stiff. She said,

"What do you mean?"

"Jane's dead," said Anthony. "She died six months ago, and she left everything to the friend who'd been living with her for years. The friend's name is Maltby."

"How do you know?" said Shirley with a gasp.

"Because I asked. As soon as I got down here I asked about Jane Rigg, and that's what Mrs Parry told me. She didn't seem to like Miss Maltby very much."

"Why did you ask?" said Shirley in a small angry voice.

"Why do you think?" said Anthony.

"I don't know."

"She was your sister—I wanted to go and see her. *Shirley—*"

"What?"

"Must you sit up all stiff like that? What's the matter?"

She said very low, "I don't want you to hold me."

"Why not?"

"You mustn't."

"Why mustn't I?"

Her hands caught one another in the dark. She said in a quick, breathless whisper,

"I don't know what's happening—but you mustn't get mixed up in it. Something's happening, but I don't know what it is. I think I'd better go away and hide. It's nothing to do with you—you mustn't get mixed up in it."

He kept his arms round her, but without trying to draw her any nearer. He said,

"But I am mixed up in it—over head and ears. I can't get out, and I don't want to. Shirley—don't you know why?"

"No—no, I don't! You can't—you mustn't!"

"I can—I do," said Anthony. He was half laughing, but his voice shook. "And how can I propose to you properly when you keep on being as stiff as a poker?"

Shirley put up her hands and covered her face for a minute. It couldn't possibly be true that Anthony was asking her to marry him, but it was a nice dream. It was a pity to wake up, but you couldn't stay in a dream. She said in a little melting voice,

"Will you please let go of me."

"Why?"

"Because I ask you. *Please*, Anthony."

He let go.

She took her hands away from her face and said,

"You don't really *love* me."

That wasn't what she meant to say at all. It was one of those undermining things that she most particularly oughtn't to have said. And the dreadful thing was that Anthony laughed and said coolly,

"You do know a lot—don't you?"

That hurt beyond all reason, because he might at least have *said* that he loved her. It would have been nice to hear him say it—once. She sat silent and forlorn, and had nothing more to say.

Anthony reached out and took her two hands in his.

"How am I going to make you believe that I love you?" he said, and all at once she did believe it. Whether it was the warm clasp of his hands, or something in his voice, or whether it was just because it was true, she didn't know, but she did believe it.

She said, "Why?" in a surprised, wondering voice, and Anthony caught her close and began to tell her why.

The car stood by the side of the road, and nobody passed it going to Emshot or going to Twing. Nobody does go to either of these places in the middle of the night.

Shirley sat up at last with a sigh.

"What are we going to do?" she said.

Everything was going to be all right now, but even in world of fantastic happiness you had to make plans.

"You'd better give me that blighted brooch," said Anthony.

Shirley had actually forgotten about the brooch. It seemed a pity to have to remember it again. She said,

"I'd forgotten all about it."

"Well, we can't do that, worse luck. You'd better hand it over."

"I don't know how it got in," said Shirley in a puzzled voice. "There isn't any hole." She was feeling in the hem of her coat, just as she had felt it in the bus.

The coat was split up the back and lapped over. The brooch with its heavy boss was in the corner of the hem where the slit began. It was about two and a half inches across and heavy for its size. No wonder she had felt it banging against her leg as she ran. But it puzzled her to think how it could have got down into the corner of the hem like that.

Anthony said, "Try the pocket."

And there sure enough was a slit in the lining. She had to work the brooch up between the lining and the tweed until she could get at it through the slit. She put it into Anthony's hand, and saw the big diamond in the boss catch up the faint light from the dashboard and give it back with a sparkle.

"And I'd like very much to know who handled it last," said Anthony.

Chapter Fifteen

THEY SAT AND MADE their plans in the dark. When Shirley had had to make a plan for escaping from the police all by herself it had been so sordid and frightening that she had felt as if she wasn't ever going to be clean again—like falling into dirty water and not being able to get out, and not having any clean clothes to put on if you did get out. Making plans with Anthony was quite different. The whole thing had turned into a gay adventure, with all sorts of nice things waiting for them at the end of it. So they made their plans very cheerfully.

Anthony was going to drive her to Ledlington and leave her at the station hotel with one of his suit-cases for luggage, and she was to stay there until he came for her. Meanwhile he would go up to town, and first thing in the morning he would go round to Revelston Crescent all dutiful nephew, and of course Mrs Huddleston would pour out the whole story of the lost brooch. Then Anthony would tell her that they hadn't looked for it properly, and would proceed to find it in the fireplace, or the coalscuttle, or slipped down between the back and seat of the sofa, or in any other place that seemed suitable. After which he could fetch Shirley from Ledlington. They would have the whole afternoon and evening together, and when she turned up at Revelston Crescent on Monday morning she would have been week-ending with friends in the country and it wasn't anybody's business but her own.

The same story would do for Mrs Camber. It was a beautiful plan, and it appeared to be quite watertight.

"But of course," Anthony said, "what we've got to do is to get to the bottom of all these things that have been happening."

Shirley made one of those murmuring sounds which may mean anything. This one meant that she was sure everything was going to be all tight, because everything *was* all right—now. It also meant that she was too happy, and too dazed, and too sleepy to bother. Her head was on Anthony's shoulder and his arm about her. But Anthony was frowning into the darkness.

"The things are all so unrelated," he said. "That's the bother. First you find somebody's bag on your wrist when you're getting into the bus at the corner of Acland Road, and then there's somebody's purse in your bag when we're dining at the Luxe, and then Miss Maltby says she has lost two marked sixpences and they are found in your room, and then the Blessed Damozel's brooch turns up in the hem of your coat. You see, there doesn't seem to be the slightest relation between these four happenings. But they must be related. I can't believe in four totally unconnected people all trying to fix a theft on you—that's the sort of coincidence that can't happen. Darling, you're not to go to sleep—you've got to talk."

Shirley started and blinked.

"I'm not!" she said.

"You were. You've got to keep awake. You see, there must be a connecting link, and I want you to go over every detail in your mind and try and get hold of something which does connect these things. There must be some one person behind these attempts to get you into trouble. It might be Miss Maltby. Are you sure she wasn't in the bus, or in the crowd that was waiting for it at the corner of Acland Road?"

Even on the edges of sleep Shirley was quite sure about this. She said so.

"Oh no—there wasn't anyone in the least like her."

"And she certainly wasn't at the Luxe, and I don't see how she could have got hold of Aunt Agnes' brooch. Still I think we'll have Miss Maltby watched. Then I'll try and find out if those people who had the next table to ours are known at the Luxe. I'm not a bit hopeful—they didn't look like habitués—but we've got to try everything. The bus affair seems hopeless, but you may remember something. Now these three things, which happened first, are all concerned with some very trifling sum. They look to me like an attempt to raise an atmosphere of suspicion about you. I don't think any of them were meant to be pushed home. But the brooch—that's different—it's very valuable. I can't help thinking that the other things were only meant to lead up to the brooch, so we'd better concentrate on that. Just tell me the whole thing all over again exactly as it happened."

Shirley lifted her head with a sigh. Her pleasant drowsiness had slipped away from her, and she was sorry to let it go. If Anthony hadn't been there, she would have been frightened. She tried to remember exactly what had happened—was it only that afternoon?

"Mrs Huddleston was going to have her rest," she said, "and when she moved for me to take the cushions I saw the brooch hanging crooked—"

"She was wearing it?"

"Oh yes—she always wears it. So I told her it was crooked, and we found that the pin was undone. It had come undone because the catch was damaged."

"How *damaged*?"

"It was bent. The pin wouldn't stay in it."

"Did it look as if someone had bent it on purpose?"

"I don't know—it was bent. You can look for yourself."

Anthony nodded.

"Yes. I just wanted to know how it had struck you. All right, go on—what happened next?"

"She told me to put it on the mantelpiece, and I leaned it up against the right-hand Dresden figure—the shepherdess."

"How did you lean it? Were the diamonds towards her—could she see it from the sofa?"

Shirley stopped to think.

"No, I don't think she could. The shepherdess stands back, and there was a vase with some violets in it—no, she couldn't see it from the sofa. I've been wondering why she didn't miss it till I was gone. I'd forgotten the violets."

"Go on," said Anthony.

"Well, I tucked her up for a rest and went into the study. At half-past four we had tea, and then I wrote some letters for her, and after that I was reading to her. And in the end I nearly lost the six o'clock bus, because she wanted me to look up a telephone number at the last minute, so I had to run, and the brooch kept banging against my leg, and I thought it was one of those weights they put in the hem."

"And it wasn't," said Anthony with half a laugh. "Now let's get back to the afternoon. Who was in the house besides you and Aunt Agnes?"

Shirley hesitated.

"I don't really know.... Oh yes—Possett was out—she'd gone to see her mother at Ealing."

"I'd go bail for Possett," said Anthony. "But we'll check up on her all the same. Was she back before you left?"

"No, I'm sure she wasn't. She always comes straight through to Mrs Huddleston. She doesn't generally get back till half-past six, but she must have been early, because I saw her when the policeman went in." A shiver went over her. It was dreadful to remember that she had run away from a policeman. She went on quickly. "I think she must have got back early—just after I left. And the first thing Mrs Huddleston would do would be to tell her about the brooch. And when they found it wasn't there they just *rushed* and sent for the police. And I've been thinking what a coward I was to run away, but if I *hadn't*, they'd have arrested me and I'd be in a prison cell at this very minute instead of here."

"Rather be here?" said Anthony softly.

"Much rather," said Shirley with a shaky little laugh.

There was an interlude, from which Shirley emerged in a state of hardened impenitence about having run away. She hadn't been cowardly—she had been clever. She had run away to Anthony, and here she was. It was much, much the best thing she could have done. Anthony said so, and he ought to know.

The cross-examination was resumed. It is not usual for counsel to have his arm round the witness's waist, or for the witness to have her head upon counsel's shoulder, but it may be quite an agreeable arrangement.

"Who brought in the tea?" said Anthony.

"That new girl, Bessie."

"I didn't cotton to her very much. What's her other name?"

"Wood. She had splendid references. I saw the last woman she'd been with—she said she was a treasure."

"How long was she there, and why did she leave?"

"Six months. She didn't get on with the cook."

"Give me the name and address. I'm going to check everything. Old Downie the cook has been with Aunt Agnes ever since I can remember. If anyone's been playing tricks, it's simply bound to be this Bessie. Would you have heard her if she had gone into the drawing-room?"

"I don't suppose I should."

"Would Aunt Agnes?"

"Not if she was asleep," said Shirley.

"But was she asleep? That's the point."

Shirley lifted her head and moved round to face him.

"Anthony—that's where we're *had*," she said. "She always does go to sleep in the afternoon, and when she's off, a pack of burglars wouldn't wake her—I've never seen anyone sleep so sound. But if you think wild horses would make her admit having slept a single wink—"

"Damn!" said Anthony with simple fervour.

Chapter Sixteen

THEY DROVE ALONG the black lanes, and never met a soul until they came out on the Ledlington road. They had repacked one of Anthony's suit-cases, and every time Shirley thought about unpacking a large male hairbrush, and yards and yards of jazz dressing-gown, and Anthony's enormous pyjamas she began to have an inward giggle. She hoped it would go on being inward, because the only thing that could be more compromising than her luggage would be to giggle about it under the eye of a reception-clerk or a chambermaid. She dwelt on this horrid possibility, and then, to get away from it, she said,

"Why should Miss Maltby want to get me into trouble?"

"I don't know why anyone should want to get you into trouble," said Anthony, "but it's a sure thing that somebody does."

Shirley considered that for a little. The Ledlington road ran wide and straight. The black hedges rushed by. The hands of the clock on the dashboard stood at five minutes to twelve. It didn't seem possible that so much could have happened since they had stood there last. Last time it had been twelve o'clock she had been reading the Stock Exchange news aloud to Mrs Huddleston. Shirley found it very dull, but Mrs Huddleston loved it. Shirley considered it a morbid taste.

Well, that was only twelve hours ago. It really didn't seem possible.

She said suddenly, "Anthony—didn't you ever think I had taken those things? You really don't know very much about me. Suppose I turn out to be a thief, or a kleptomaniac or something."

"I hope you won't," said Anthony. "I mean, it would be a bit embarrassing."

Shirley laughed breathlessly.

"The embarrassed barrister! It would—wouldn't it? That's why we oughtn't to be engaged—not till we've found out who's been doing all this."

"We *are* engaged," said Anthony. "You can't not be engaged once you are."

"I can break it off."

"Then I'd run you in for breach of promise."

"You couldn't!"

"Oh, couldn't I? You just wait and see! I should conduct my own case, and have the jury sobbing into their pocket-handkerchiefs at my description of how you lured me on, and promised to marry me, and then turned me down."

"Have I promised to marry you?" said Shirley.

Anthony's left hand shot out and caught her by the wrist.

"If you haven't, you'll do it now! *Swear!*"

Shirley began to laugh.

"Anthony, do let go—it isn't safe!"

He set the car on a zig-zag course, and said *"Swear!"* with a floe rolling "r" and the voice in which the villain of a melodrama presents the virtuous heroine with his well known ultimatum.

Shirley gave a little shriek as they skimmed the edge of the ditch on one side of the road and then headed for the bank on the other.

"Anthony—*don't!* I'm going to scream!"

The grip on her wrist tightened. The villain's voice became more villainous.

"It is useless to shriek—there is none to hear you. Swear that you will marry me—by all that you hold sacred *swear it!*"

They shaved the bank and took a long diagonal towards the ditch again.

"I swear," said Shirley with a terrified giggle. She screamed as they escaped the ditch and came back into the middle of the road again. "Oh, Anthony, what a fool you are!"

Without stopping the car he pulled her close, kissed her lightly, and let her go.

"Don't forget you've sworn," he said.

Shirley thought about that. Her head was whirling, and it wasn't easy to think at all. She couldn't marry him if they sent her to prison. He wouldn't want her to. Or would he? It came dimly into her mind that there might be something behind his fooling. There had been something in his voice when he said, "Don't forget you've sworn." But he hadn't answered her question. She said that aloud.

"You didn't answer my question."

"What question?"

It had been so hard to say it at all. She didn't want to say it again. She said piteously,

"I don't want to say it again."

His left hand came out once more. This time it rested on her knee with a heavy, comforting pressure. He said,

"Don't be silly, my dear."

There was an everyday matter-of-fact sound in his voice that was more convincing than many protestations. She knew that he had never thought, and could never think, anything about her that wasn't true. Something in him knew what was true about her, and what wasn't true. If two strings are close enough together, one vibrates when the other is touched. It is the same with people. If they are very close to each other, not with their bodies but with their selves, there is something which sees, and knows, and is sure without any words.

Shirley gave a deep satisfied sigh and said in a sleepy voice,

"Then that's all right."

Then she went to sleep in her corner, and woke with a start when they stopped at the Station Hotel. She got out blinking and a little bewildered.

Anthony was very high-handed with the hotel. He was going straight on to London, but his sister wanted a room for the night. He registered Shirley as Miss Alice Lester to correspond with the A.L. on his suit-case, and adjured her in a last private moment not to forget and relapse into Shirley Dale, and to sit tight till he came for her.

"And I'll try and get down for lunch, but if the Blessed Damozel's having hysterics I may have to stop and see her through them." And with that and a grip of her arm he was back in the driver's seat.

Shirley stood clear and watched the red tail-light draw away and then go out suddenly like a dead spark as the car turned out of the station yard.

She went up to her room. Her face was even dirtier than she expected, but the night-porter who had brought up her suit-case—no, Anthony's suit-case—didn't appear to notice anything. The bathroom was just opposite, and he seemed quite sure that the water would be hot. It was boiling. As Shirley wallowed in it, she blessed the name of Ledlington, and its station, and its Station Hotel.

When she was most beautifully clean and warm, she arrayed herself in Anthony's blue and white pyjamas. The legs trailed on the floor and the sleeves flapped down over her hands, but she got back to her room somehow by clutching at the knees and taking up handfuls of stuff. Then she locked the door—Aunt Emily had been very particular indeed about locking your door in a hotel—and got into bed.

She had wondered what the bed would be like. Beds in country hotels are chancy, but she went to sleep so quickly that she had no time to find out. One minute she was climbing into bed and switching out the light, and the next, sleep rushed down upon her with the darkness and swept her away. At first she didn't dream at all. She lay on her left side with her hands doubled up under her chin and slept like a baby. The very ugly yellow wall-clock on the hall landing struck two, and three, and four, and five, and six. Then Shirley began to dream. It wasn't light yet, it wouldn't be light for a long time, but the night was passing. People were beginning to wake and turn over, and go to sleep again because it was Sunday morning. Without waking, Shirley came up out of the deep waters of sleep into its shallows and began to dream.

She dreamed she was in a cave. It was quite dark there, and she knew—because in a dream you do know that sort of thing—that the cave ran deep into a cliff, and that the mouth of it was blocked by the sea. So that she could never get out. She was in prison, and she couldn't ever get out. Then the sea came roaring in with a noise like thunder, and she ran away from it, deeper, and deeper, and deeper into the cave.

The dream broke. She was in a swing, and Anthony was in a swing. The two swings crossed one another, so that for one flying instant she and Anthony were close together, and then swooped apart again, and up with a rush to the top of the arc, and down with a rush again. Every time they passed Anthony called to her, but she couldn't heat what he said, and he put out his hands and caught her as she flew, and the swing broke and they went crashing down into another dream.

It was a very odd dream. At first she didn't know where she was. Then she saw old Aunt Emily in her night-gown, and her cap, and the woolly shawl with the blue crochet border which Shirley had knitted for her the Christmas before she died. She had her bedroom candle-stick in her hand, an old-fashioned white one with little bunches of flowers on it. The candle was lighted. Shirley was very glad not to be in the dark any more. And then she saw her mother's picture, just as she had seen it hanging above the drawing-room mantelpiece in Acacia Cottage, and all of a sudden that was where they were, she and Aunt Emily, and Aunt Emily gave her the candle and said "Be a good girl, Shirley," just as she had said it a little before she died. And then she wasn't there any more, but Miss Maltby was letting herself in with a key as long as her arm. Shirley wanted to run away, but her feet wouldn't move. Her heart thumped with terror, her feet stuck to the carpet, and Miss Maltby stood in the doorway and said in a horrible hating voice, "It isn't fair. Why should you have it all?" And then Anthony came running like the wind and caught her hand, and she ran too, and the candle turned into a star, and the wind carried them away.

She woke up then and thought it was a pity, and turned over and went to sleep again....

When she waked, the wall-clock in its hideous case of yellow maple had just finished striking ten o'clock, Shirley got up. She was hungry. She dressed, had breakfast, and wondered how soon Anthony would come. She packed away the pyjamas, and the dressing-gown, and the compromising hairbrush before she left the room, but as the suit-case had no key and she couldn't very well take it down to breakfast, she would have to hope for the best. If the chambermaid was inquisitive, it was all up—the breath of scandal would certainly blow. No one brought up by old Aunt Emily in a village could be quite indifferent to the breath of scandal, but with prison so to speak looming, it didn't seem to matter as much as it would have done before she started running away from the police. Anyhow she had done her best for Mrs Grundy, and if she didn't like it she would have to lump it.

After breakfast she went upstairs again. The suit-case didn't seem to have been moved. She extracted her coat from the vast emptiness of an old-fashioned wall cupboard and looked it over for possible damage. She had rushed out of Acacia Cottage with it bundled up anyhow over her arm and then gone blundering into Jane's shrubbery. There might be stains, or even a tear. Stains would sponge, but a tear would be a calamity.

She laid the coat out on the bed and looked it over breadth by breadth, beginning with the right front and working round to the slit in the back. There was a little bulge where the heavy brooch had been, but otherwise this side was all right. The coat was slit up the middle of the back and overlapped by about four inches. Shirley turned her attention to the left-hand back breadth. There was no stain or tear, but there was something funny about the hem. It had a cockled, lumpy look. She put out her hand to touch it and snatched it back again. She had been stooping over the bed. She straightened up and stood looking down at the cockled hem. After a minute she took hold of the rail at the bed foot. She went on looking at the hem, but she didn't touch it. She was afraid to touch it.

At last she said, "Coward!" Then she stamped her foot and went over to the door and locked it. And then she came back to the bed and felt the hem of the coat. There was something there. The brooch wasn't the only thing that had been planted on her. She had known it the moment she saw the lumpy, cockled hem. There was probably a slit in the left-hand pocket too.

There was.

She doubled the hem up to meet it, and pulled out Mrs Huddleston's emerald hairband and her large emerald brooch. There wasn't anything else. She made quite sure of that. Then she sat down on the bed and stared at the emeralds.

Chapter Seventeen

Somebody tried the handle of the door. Shirley gave a most frightful start. There was a murmur of apology and a scurry of retreating footsteps—a chambermaid's footsteps, not a policeman's.

Shirley put out the tip of her finger and touched the emerald hairband. It was real. She had been staring at it for so long that it had swum away from her in a green dazzle, but when she touched it it came into focus again. It was real, and it was there, and what was she going to do about it? She tried to think.

The thing was dreadfully valuable. It was a band to go right round the head, and it was made like a laurel wreath, the leaves set with emeralds, and at every fourth pair of leaves there was a large single diamond which might be meant for a dew-drop or a berry. The brooch was two laurel branches crossed, with a diamond between them, and both wreath and brooch had an N engraved on the pale gold setting at the back of the laurel leaves. They were part of a set which Napoleon had given to Josephine after his Italian victories. There should be another brooch, and a pair of long earrings. There might once have been a necklace too, but if so, it had become separated from the rest of the set.

Shirley knew all about the set. That was what made the whole thing so damning. Mrs Huddleston had told her a hundred times about her grandfather buying it when he was in Paris in '48, and how he got it cheap because everything was in the melting-pot, with kings coming off their thrones all over Europe and court jewellery at a discount. And Mrs Huddleston's grandmother had worn Josephine's emeralds when she made her curtsey to Queen Victoria as a bride, and again at the marriage of the Princess Royal. And Mrs Huddleston was most inordinately proud of them. It wasn't the slightest bit of good for Anthony to smuggle back the diamond brooch and pretend to find it in the drawing-room. The emeralds were about fifty times more important than the diamond brooch, and quite fifty times as damning to Shirley. She knew all about them. She knew just how valuable they were, and she could easily, so easily, have gone upstairs and taken them whilst Mrs Huddleston was resting. Because she knew where they were kept.

She had helped Possett to take them out, and she had helped her to put them away. Mrs Huddleston didn't wear them, but she was very fond of looking at them and talking about them. It was utterly damnable and utterly damning.

Shirley jumped to her feet. If she sat and stared at the wretched things till her eyes popped out of her head, it wouldn't do the slightest bit of good. What she had got to do was to get on to Anthony at once, before he saw Mrs Huddleston or did anything about the diamond brooch. But meanwhile what was she going to do with the emeralds? She thought about putting them back in the hem of her coat, and she thought about rolling them up in a handkerchief and pinning them inside the pocket of her jumper suit. But it was no good, she just couldn't. The thought of having them on her or near her induced a feeling of absolute panic. The best she could do was to put them in the pocket of Anthony's pyjamas, and, oddly enough, that made her feel better. The emeralds were Mrs Huddleston's, and Anthony was Mrs Huddleston's nephew. It was the best she could do.

As she shut the suit-case, the wall-clock on the landing struck eleven. Shirley unlocked the door and rang the bell. There wasn't a moment to lose. She had lost far too many moments already. She must get on to Anthony, and she was most dreadfully afraid that she wouldn't catch him at his chambers.

The chambermaid told her that there was a telephone-box at the end of the passage. She took the suit-case along, and had a moment's agitated wonder as to whether she could remember Anthony's telephone number. She had called him up often enough for Mrs Huddleston, but could she, did she, remember the number now? She could, and she did.

She lifted the receiver, and then remembered that she had no pennies ready. Anthony had left her with five pounds and a handful of change. The notes were pinned to the elastic of her knickers, and the change was in the left-hand pocket of her jumper. She started all over again, and as she put the pennies in, she remembered that she would have to be most horribly careful what she said, because this was only an extension, and if the hotel clerk liked to listen in she could hear every word.

Ten minutes later she realized that she hadn't got to worry about that. She had missed Anthony. There was no reply. He shared rooms with a friend, and a man came and did for them. Anthony had expected to be away for the week-end, and his friend was probably away too, in which case the man-servant would have a day off and it was no use asking the exchange to ring again, because there just wasn't anyone there.

She hung up the receiver, and felt desperate. She simply must get hold of Anthony before he did anything about the diamond brooch. It was no good his pretending to find it now—it would only make things worse. Really the only thing they could do was to go to Mrs Huddleston and tell her the truth. Shirley really did feel that it would be an enormous relief just to stick to the truth and make a clean breast of everything. One of the first things she remembered was Aunt Emily making her learn:

> *"Oh, what a tangled web we weave*
> *When first we practise to deceive."*

And another even more drastic verse which ran:

> *"Behold the man of lies,*
> *A bandage on his eyes.*
> *He falls into the Pit,*
> *And cannot rise from it."*

There was a picture of the man of lies, very black and repulsive with the bandage tied in a neat bow at the back of his head and one foot overhanging the Pit, from which issued long pointed flames and a quantity of very black smoke.

These early impressions are very hard to shake off. Shirley hadn't actually told any lies, but she had a feeling that Anthony might be telling them for her, and that was really worse, because it was adding meanness to deceit, and she had always despised mean people.

The only thing she could do now was to take her courage in both hands and ring up Revelston Crescent. She could disguise her voice—at least she hoped she could—and if Anthony was there, she would just say, "Don't do anything at all until you have seen me again." Perhaps she might say, "Something else has turned up." She didn't see how it could do any harm to say that. Anthony was as quick as lightning—he would know what she meant.

She got through very quickly to Revelston Crescent, and it was Bessie Wood who answered the telephone. Shirley knew her quiet, toneless voice at once—quite different from Possett's agitated bleat. She tried to make her own voice sound elderly and fat as she asked for Mr Leigh.

Bessie Wood held the receiver a little away from her and bit her lip. The telephone was in the hall. At certain hours of the day it was her duty to answer it, and if necessary to switch the caller through to the extension in Mrs Huddleston's bedroom or the drawing-room. After eleven o'clock the telephone usually stayed switched through to the drawing-room until it was time for Mrs Huddleston's rest. She had been a bit later than usual this morning, and Mr Leigh was in there with her now. And here was this voice asking for him. Well, that was a bit of an odd start, wasn't it? Mr Leigh was supposed to be out of town for the week-end. He had given her the surprise of her life when he walked in not five minutes ago. Her eyes went to the fern in its ornamental pot on the hall table. It was a good hiding-place, and there was nothing to connect her with it whatever happened. The emeralds she had hidden under the fern were perfectly safe, and so was she.

She felt a thrumming in the receiver as she held it away from her. A faint ghostly thread of a voice said "Mr Leigh," and all at once she knew whose voice it was. She hadn't anything to go by, but she was quite sure it was Miss Dale who was ringing up. She put the mouth-piece to her lips and said in her toneless voice,

"I beg your pardon?"

In the telephone-box at the Station Hotel Shirley mumbled,

"Is that 15 Revelston Crescent? Is Mr Leigh there? I want to speak to him."

Bessie's voice came back to her without hesitation.

"Oh no, ma'am, Mr Leigh isn't here. Can I take a message?"

A giggle caught in Shirley's throat. What sort of message could she leave for Anthony? Suppose she said, "Shirley Dale speaking. Please tell Mr Leigh that I've got Mrs Huddleston's emeralds, and will he please come and fetch them at once." It would be so nice and simple if she only could. What would Bessie do—scream and tell the police, or just say politely "Very well, miss—is that all?" What was the good of thinking about it? She couldn't possibly leave a message for Anthony.

She said, "No, there's no message," and rang off.

As Bessie hung up the receiver, Anthony Leigh opened the drawing-room door and looked out.

"Mrs Huddleston wanted to know who was ringing up," he said. She turned, quite cool and glib.

"Just a wrong number, sir—someone wanting a Mrs Bartholomew."

Shirley felt quite distracted. What on earth was Anthony doing? If he wasn't at his chambers, or at Revelston Crescent, where was he? Somewhere between the two, she supposed—and how on earth was she going to get hold of him? If she hadn't been hiding from the police, she could have left a message and the telephone number of the hotel and asked him to ring her up as soon as he arrived. But if she did that, Bessie would tell Mrs Huddleston, and Mrs Huddleston would tell the police, and the next thing that happened would be a Ledlington policeman coming to arrest her. And how was anyone going to believe that she hadn't stolen the emeralds if they were found in her suit-case—no, Anthony's suit-case? They would probably think that she had stolen his pyjamas as well. No, the only thing she could do now was to wait in this blighted hotel until Anthony came. After all, he had promised to try and get down to lunch. It was eleven o'clock—no, it must be about ten past by now. Suppose he didn't reach Revelston Crescent till half past.... That was nonsense—he *must* get there before that. Well, suppose he didn't. How long would it take him to soothe Mrs Huddleston?... She dismissed several gloomy estimates, and decided that he wouldn't let it take more than an hour because of coming down to fetch her. If he got away at half-past twelve, he would be here by two, and if he really trod on the gas, it might be any time after half-past one.

She pushed open the door of the telephone-box and bent to pick up the suit-case. Voices reached her from a half open bedroom door. There were two girls on the other side of it. She heard the sound of a bed being moved. One of the girls said with a giggle and a strong local drawl,

"What would you do if the police was after you, Vi'let?"

Another, shriller voice said,

"Go on! What are you talking about?"

The first girl giggled again.

"They'll get her all right—the police have got a clue. You know—that girl that's in all the headlines. She had a nerve, I don't think. Walked off as bold as brass with the stuff in a suit-case, and not her suit-case neither. They say there's a man mixed up with it. The Sunday papers are full of it. I got a chance at the *News of the World* while 17 was having his bath."

"You'll be getting us into a row talking like that with the door open," said the second girl.

The door banged.

Shirley clutched the brass handle of the door of the telephone-box with one hand and Anthony's suit-case with the other. Her feet and hands were cold, and her forehead was wet.

It was a frightful thing to have a guilty conscience. She hadn't seen the Sunday papers, and therefore knew nothing about the mysterious affair of the Disappearing Typist and the Missing Bearer Bonds. She tiptoed out of the telephone-box and past the bedroom door. At the top of the stairs she made herself stand still. She had got to get away. She hadn't left anything in her room, but Anthony's treasury notes were pinned to the elastic of her knickers. She couldn't unpin them here or in the office, and she had got to unpin them before she could pay her bill— and to run away without paying her bill would be asking for trouble.

She went back to her room, detached two pound notes, and then descended the stairs feeling horribly cold and sick. Suppose they wouldn't let her go. Suppose they pretended to let her go and sent a policeman after her. Suppose they searched the suit-case …

None of these things happened. She paid her bill, put the change in her jumper pocket, and walked out of the hotel.

The Station Hotel has two entrances, one upon the station yard and the other upon Albert Road. Shirley came out into Albert Road. Facing her across the way was one of those small crowded shops which sell sweets, tobacco, and newspapers. In the middle of a Sunday morning, when all other shops were closed, this one had an open door. It also had a row of posters with starting headlines. Shirley only saw one of them. If seemed to leap at her as she came down the steps. It said in big black letters:

DISAPPEARING GIRL. IMPORTANT CLUE.

Chapter Eighteen

BESSIE WOOD might have felt surprised when she opened the door and admitted Mr Anthony Leigh, who was supposed to be away in the country for the week-end, but her face remained as passive and uninterested as usual. That was one of the things that had made her so useful to Ted—no matter what happened, she could keep a straight face and not let on that she so much as noticed there was anything to get upset about. She hung up Anthony's hat and coat, and saw him go through to the drawing-room with an indifferent eye, yet behind this appearance of calm she was both angry and frightened. Mr Leigh must have been sent for, and that Possett must have known that he had been sent for. Mrs Huddleston would never have put through a trunk call herself—a deal too much trouble for *her*. Possett must have done it for her, and Possett must have known he was coming back, and she'd kept a close mug about it, damn her!

Bessie wondered whether Mrs Huddleston suspected her. If she didn't suspect Shirley Dale, she was bound to suspect Bessie Wood. Well, if there wasn't any risk about the job, Al Phillips wouldn't be paying her a hundred pounds for doing it. It was a bit awkward Mr Anthony turning up like this. It was as plain as the nose on your face that he was in love with Miss Dale. Meant her no good most likely, but he wouldn't want her to go to prison till he was finished with her.

She stood there frowning at the drawing-room door. Things weren't going just the way they'd planned them. Mr Leigh was to have been out of the way until the girl was safe in stir. Once the police had their hands on her, it'd be too late for Mr Anthony to get his aunt to call the show off. But it wasn't going right. The girl had gone off into the blue, and here was Mr Anthony shoving his oar in. She made a small clicking sound with her tongue against the roof of her mouth. And then the telephone bell rang and Shirley's call came through.

All the time the call was going on she was getting more and more sure that it was Miss Dale on the line, and if it was, she had got to find out where she was speaking from. But here again things went wrong. First Mrs Huddleston wanting to know who was calling, and sending Mr Anthony to find out. And then Cook coming half way up the back stair to ask if she'd taken in a parcel of groceries last night, because if she had, where had she put them, and if she hadn't, they were clean out of coffee, and Mr Anthony staying to lunch as like as not.

By the time she got back to the telephone and on to Trunks nobody seemed to have the least idea where the call had come from. She put the receiver gently back on its hook and went downstairs with rage in her heart and an expression of dull indifference on her face.

In the drawing-room Anthony was receiving a series of shocks. Mrs Huddleston's diamond brooch was no longer in his pocket, because at the moment of stooping over the sofa to kiss her, he had pushed it down as far as it would go between the padded back and the equally padded seat. There was a space quite six inches deep into which the loose cover was tucked, and it seemed to him an admirable way of disposing of Aunt Agnes' diamonds. Pleased and exhilarated, he drew up a chair and sat down.

Mrs Huddleston instantly prepared for the first blow by sniffing at a new and very powerful bottle of smelling salts and then dabbing at the resulting tears with one of those handkerchiefs edged with Honiton lace which used to be showered upon Victorian brides.

"Oh, my dear boy—such a shock!"

"Has anything happened, Aunt Agnes?"

"Such a terrible shock!"

"What's the matter?"

"That wicked, *wicked* girl!" said Mrs Huddleston with sudden energy.

So far the conversation reminded Anthony of one of those duets in which each of the singers has different words and a different tune and just goes on perseveringly with his own part. He had to wait for a lead, because officially he was completely in the dark.

"What wicked girl, Aunt Agnes?" he inquired with no more than a fleeting frown.

Mrs Huddleston sniffed against the handkerchief.

"It only shows that you can't trust anyone. I couldn't, couldn't have believed it."

"What couldn't you believe?"

"I'm *forced* to," said Mrs Huddleston with a fine gloomy stare.

"My dear, if I had the slightest idea what you were talking about—"

"I've always been far too foolishly trusting—your poor uncle always said so. And I never really liked the girl. I remember saying so to Possett right at the very beginning when she first came to me—"

"When Possett first came to you?"

Mrs Huddleston waved that away with a sweep of the hand. Three diamond rings flashed in the firelight.

"No, no, not *Possett*—Miss Dale. And I wish you would go and ask Bessie who that is ringing up. If it's the police and they've arrested her—"

Anthony went out into the hall, glad of an excuse to hide his face. He thought his Aunt Agnes the silliest woman in England, but generally speaking he had an affection for her. Just at this moment it would have given him the greatest possible pleasure to shake her till her teeth rattled in her head.

It wouldn't help Shirley if his feelings showed in his face. He came back and sat down again.

"It was only a wrong number. What's all this about Miss Dale? You haven't told me what's happened yet."

She began to tell him in detail. Nothing so exciting had happened to her for years—a thief in her own household, her jewellery stolen, the police called in. She meant to extract the ultimate thrill from all these things. The smelling-salts were kept in action. Tears of sensibility flowed. The Honiton lace handkerchief was pressed against long dark lashes.

Anthony let her run on until she stopped for breath. Then he said firmly,

"But it couldn't possibly be Miss Dale, Aunt Agnes."

"She put the brooch on the mantelpiece," moaned Mrs Huddleston. "She told me it was hanging crooked, and when I gave it to her to look at she said the catch was damaged. I expect it was all part of the *plot* really. And I told her to put it on the mantelpiece, and when Possett came in it was gone."

"It must be somewhere in the room. It's impossible that Miss Dale can have taken it. Have you looked for it? Anyone may have moved it, or it may have fallen down. Where have you looked?"

"Everywhere," said Mrs Huddleston with a despairing gesture. "It was the first thing I said. And Possett is so thorough. She and Bessie have had the carpet up and all the covers off, and there wasn't a sign of anything at all."

Anthony felt himself blenching.

He said, "What covers?"—just like that, quite baldly, and Mrs Huddleston explained with her usual wealth of detail.

"The sofa cover, and all the chairs. Such pretty stuff, don't you think? Possett saw it last year at Barker's sale, and she came home quite excited about it and said if I would buy the stuff she would try her hand at making the covers. And they turned out so well—quite professional."

Anthony gazed in horror at the faint die-away pattern of the chintz which covered the sofa. He was not concerned with its æsthetic aspect. He was realizing that he had made a most horrible bloomer. If Possett had really had that cover off this morning, he wasn't going to be able to persuade Aunt Agnes that the diamond brooch had been lurking there all the time. Unfortunately it was lurking there at this moment, and he couldn't see any way of getting hold of it again. To be sure, its presence there would exonerate Shirley, but he didn't want to get Possett into trouble. He said, in a tone that he hoped was firm,

"It must be somewhere."

"Not in this house," said Mrs Huddleston with as much dramatic intensity as if she had been playing Lady-Macbeth. "That wicked, wicked girl took it away in her pocket, and as likely as not everything's been melted down, or broken up, or whatever it is they do with jewellery when they steal it and don't want it to be traced."

Anthony leaned forward.

"Aunt Agnes—why are you connecting Miss Dale with all this? It's quite impossible that she can have anything to do with it."

She stared at him with the angry tears running down her face.

"Then where is she? Can you tell me that? The police went round to her rooms at once, and they didn't know anything about her there. She hadn't come in—and she didn't come in, for I rang up the police this morning on purpose to find out. She never came in at all. And what do you think of that?"

Anthony smiled his most ingratiating smile.

"Why, that she had gone out of town for the weekend. Thousands of people do it, you know, and they haven't all been stealing diamond brooches. I do it myself."

"But you don't go away without any luggage," said Mrs Huddleston with an indignant sob.

"How do you know she went away without any luggage?"

"Oh, my dear boy! Of course it was the very first thing the police asked the landlady—I should have thought, being a barrister, you would have known that—and she hasn't taken so much as her toothbrush."

"It's always possible to buy a toothbrush if you have a sudden invitation and want to catch a train. I've done that too. You know, Aunt Agnes, you've got to be careful about this—you don't want to be run in for defamation of character. Miss Dale is perfectly free to go away for the week-end when she's finished with her job here. When did she leave, by the way?"

"Six o'clock," said Mrs Huddleston, dabbing her eyes. "I remember the clock struck while she was looking up Mildred Hathaway's number, and she seemed quite impatient to get off. I thought it *very* inconsiderate of her at the time, because she *knows* how anything like a hurry upsets me. I remember it was the thing Dr Pocklington always impressed on me—'Don't hurry—never hurry—take things quietly.'"

Anthony forgot to be tactful. This Saturday afternoon business had riled him for a long time.

"Well, most girls expect to get off at one o'clock on Saturdays," he said crisply.

"So terribly selfish," sighed Mrs Huddleston.

He let that pass.

"Well, if she didn't leave here till six or a little bit after, and she had any sort of date in the country, she probably had to leg it for her train and hadn't any time to go home first."

"Date?" said Mrs Huddleston faintly, but with a gleam of curiosity.

"Appointment," emended Anthony—"engagement—anything you like."

Mrs Huddleston repeated the original word.

"Date," she said—"date? Oh no, my dear boy—if she had any, what do you call it, date at all, it was with a *receiver* who was going to get rid of the jewellery for her."

Twice during this conversation she had used a phrase which had puzzled Anthony. The word jewellery puzzled him now. Is one diamond brooch jewellery? He did not find himself anxious to investigate the puzzle. He took a mental shy at it and went on.

"Then why didn't she go home after the assignation?"

She cast her eyes to the ceiling.

"Don't ask me why that sort of girl does *anything*. She probably knew the game was up and thought she would get away whilst she could. She must have got a lot of money for the emeralds."

The word hit Anthony right between the eyes and made him blink. Then he said, *"What?"* and his voice was a great deal louder than he meant it to be. He said it again, and this time he had hardly enough breath to finish the word.

"My dear boy—didn't you know?" said Mrs Huddleston.

"The emeralds?" said Anthony.

She dissolved into a fresh flood of tears.

"My lovely emeralds—the entire set—so historical! Napoleon gave them to Josephine after his campaign in Italy, and my grandfather gave them to my grandmother when they were on their wedding tour in 1848—and of course he wasn't as famous as Napoleon, but he was thought a great deal of in the County, and they made him Vice-Lieutenant at the time of the Chartist Riots. Napoleon had the set made for Josephine in Italy—a wreath, and earrings, and two brooches—and some people think there was a necklace as well, but your uncle always said no, because if you look at the pictures of the people then— Josephine, and Hortense, and Madame Récamier—they all have things round their heads, but not necklaces, so he always said he didn't believe there had ever been a necklace, and of course I'd much rather think so, because it makes the set complete as it is, and so very interesting. Josephine very nearly didn't get it after all—I expect you remember she had been flirting with somebody else, and when Napoleon came back they had a most dreadful quarrel and there was very nearly a divorce, but she got round him and they made it up, and that is when he gave her the emeralds. And now, I suppose, I shall never see them again."

Anthony sat stunned amid the flow of tearful words. The emeralds! Oh lord! What a debacle! No question of their value. No question of their having slipped down somewhere, or being mislaid. Possett would have gone between warp and woof of everything under her charge before giving in to the shattering idea that the emeralds had been stolen. He asked a question or two for form's sake, but he already knew what the answers would be—Yes the emeralds had been hidden. She always hid her things, because burglars went straight for a jewel-case. And she changed the hiding-place every week. Last week the emeralds were in a sponge-bag in her wash-stand drawer. This week they were rolled up with her stockings. And how could anyone know where to find them if they didn't know the ways of the house? Only the stockings had been moved—Possett could sweat to that. Every other drawer was just as she had left it. The person who had taken the emeralds had known just where to put her hand on them, and if it wasn't that wicked girl Shirley Dale, perhaps Anthony would tell her who else had helped Possett put them away in that very drawer no farther back than Wednesday afternoon, when she had had them down to show to Mildred Hathaway.

Anthony couldn't tell her anything. He had only three ideas in his head. To get away. To think. To tell Shirley about the emeralds.

He sat where he was for five minutes, because he had to make up his mind whether to try and retrieve the diamond brooch or leave it pushed down between the seat and the back of the sofa. He found it difficult to decide, but in the end he left it where it was. As he walked away from the house, he felt sure that this was the best thing to do. The brooch was quite safe. If he had tried to get it out, he might have bungled, and then the fat would have been in the fire. It was no good having an explanation about the diamond brooch when the far more valuable emeralds were still missing and he had no idea of their whereabouts. He must get to Shirley without delay and talk things over. This idea swallowed up all others.

It was still dominant when he drew up in the station yard at Ledlington and ran up the steps into the hotel. And then, as the porter moved to meet him, it came upon him with all the force of a sudden and unexpected shock that he had registered Shirley last night under a made-up name, and he no longer had the slightest recollection of what that name might be. The initials must have been A.L. to correspond with his suit-case, and the Christian name—yes, the Christian name was Alice—unless it was Agnes. But when he tried to recover the surname, half a dozen names like Leslie, and Lawlor, and Lester, and Lyons slipped into his mind as easily and inconclusively as they slipped out again.

Meanwhile the hall porter stood attentive. Anthony was rather pleased afterwards with the way he got out of the mess. There was no perceptible hesitation before he said,

"I think a friend of mine is staying in this hotel. May I see the register?"

The man came back of course with the expected, "What name would it be, sir?" but a tip and a repetition of the word register did the trick.

Anthony gazed at the words in his own writing which described Shirley as Miss Alice Lester, British, and the nest minute he was asking for her with a pleasant confidence which did him credit.

"Yes—Miss Lester. Will you please tell her her brother is here."

The pleased confidence was disastrously shattered by the hall porter's reply. He said in the casual tone in which he would have said the most casual, humdrum thing,

"Miss Lester's gone."

Anthony said, *"What?"*

The man repeated the blow.

"Miss Lester paid her bill and left round about eleven o'clock, sir."

Chapter Nineteen

SHIRLEY SAT in the slow Sunday train which was making its way station by station to town and Anthony. That was the only clear idea in her mind—she had simply got to get to London before Anthony left for Ledlington. She couldn't risk waiting for him at the Station Hotel. The horrible placard she had seen said, *"Disappearing Girl. Important Clue,"* and she had instantly jumped to the conclusion that the hunt was up, her hiding-place discovered, and that she might at any moment be arrested with the emeralds in her possession. They were as little in her possession as she could help, but the fact that they were in the pocket of Anthony's pyjamas inside Anthony's suit-case wouldn't really help her very much with the police, since she and the suit-case were quite obviously running away together.

The train stopped at Snedholm. A cold, horrible trickle ran down Shirley's spine. She didn't feel safe when the train was going, but she felt like a microbe under a microscope the moment it stopped. All her bones turned to jelly, and the platform and the booking-office were like something in a bad dream. They were empty, but at any moment they might sprout police—dozens of them, each with a warrant for the arrest of Shirley Dale.

Nobody got out at Snedholm, and nobody got in. The guard had a short conversation with a lounging porter on the subject of Ledlington United's chance of getting into the Second Division. Both appeared to belong to the gloomy type of football fan whose home team never has a dog's chance owing to the perversity of the club officials.

"Now if they was to play Lanky Stevenson—" said the porter as the train began to move.

"Not much they won't," said the guard, after which Snedholm receded and Shirley's bones became bones again.

The worst time of all had been when she was screwing herself up to take her ticket and get into the London train. It wouldn't have been so bad if there had been a crowd, as there would have been on a week-day, but at eleven-ten on a Sunday morning there was only one other passenger, a young man who looked as if he had been up all night. He yawned as he took his ticket, yawned as he waited for the train, and vanished, yawning, into a third-class compartment next the engine. Shirley got in as far away as possible, and from first to last she had the carriage to herself.

After Snedholm there was Rainwell, and after Rainwell, Melbury, and after Melbury, Chington St. Mary, and Repford. There seemed no end to the sleepy country stations, each with its single porter. All the potters looked as if they had just waked up and would go to sleep again as soon as the train had passed. But no matter how innocently bare, at every station Shirley dissolved in terror and expected the worst.

The country villages gave place to bungalows and semi-detached houses in every stage of construction, merging gradually into rows of yellow brick houses. The next stop was a junction, and the next after that the terminus. Shirley had to nerve herself to get out, walk along the platform carrying Anthony's suit-case, and give up her ticket at the barrier. When she found herself on the other side, she was conscious not so much of relief as of a kind of flat bewilderment. She had made such a tremendous effort, and now that it was spent, she had a come-to-the-end kind of feeling.

She walked about twenty yards, and then put the suit-case down and stood there. She didn't know what she was going to do next. She lifted her eyes and saw on the station wall immediately opposite the large round face of a clock. The hands stood at five minutes past one. Shirley stared at them. Five minutes past one ... Then she had missed Anthony.... Why, he had said that he would be down in time to lunch with her in Ledlington. He would arrive, and she wouldn't be there. He might be arriving at this very minute, and she wouldn't be there....

Her mind began to wake up, and the waking hurt.

What a fool she had been to think that she could possibly catch him in London. No—not a fool to think that she could catch him, but a fool who just simply hadn't thought at all—had seen that placard, panicked, and rushed blindly along the first way of escape—had landed herself thirty-five miles from Anthony, who was probably calling down the most hideous curses on her head. Shirley had never been so ashamed of herself in her life. She had run like a rabbit, and she had always despised rabbits. The most dreadful part of it was that she couldn't feel in the least sure that she wouldn't do it again.

She stared forlornly at the clock and wondered what she was going to do next. In the dim and faraway time before she had slipped out of the ordinary world into a nightmare one o'clock was lunch-time. This was Sunday in a bad dream, but on an ordinary week-day Mrs Huddleston's lunch would be coming in on a tray and Shirley Dale would be saying "Cheers!", scrambling into her coat and cap, and bursting into Revelston Crescent with the joyous feeling that she wouldn't have to listen to any more symptoms for an hour and a half. She would be ragingly hungry, and she would be wondering what Mrs Camber was going to give her for lunch.

She woke up still more. The word hungry seemed to be wandering round in her mind. It occurred to her that perhaps she *was* hungry. Perhaps some of this cold, sick, empty feeling was plain everyday wanting something to eat, and not sheer shameful cowardice. Perhaps if she had something to eat, her knees would feel stronger and her head less like a balloon which might at any moment float away. Anyhow it was worth trying.

The refreshment-room was empty. She tried to remember whether refreshment-room tea was nastier than refreshment-room coffee, or whether Bovril and milk would be worse than either. She made it coffee and a ham sandwich, and retired with them to one of the depressing little tables against the wall.

The coffee wasn't too bad. It was hot and sweet, and it helped the sandwich down. It wanted a lot of helping, but when it *was* down her head had stopped feeling like a balloon. She got another cup of coffee, and the least repulsive bun on view. If she went on sitting still and eating and drinking in a perfectly ordinary way, perhaps her mind would begin to work again and she would be able to think what she had better do next.

Someone else had been drinking coffee at her table. The cup had left a sticky brown ring, and there were cake crumbs. A blasé winter fly crawled languidly on the outskirts of the ring. A crumpled newspaper lay sprawled across the chair on the opposite side of the table. Shirley put out her hand to take the paper and drew it back again. *"Disappearing Girl. Important Clue"*—the headlines which had been on the placard would be inside the paper. She ought to pick it up and find out what had happened. If she hadn't the nerve to do it she was a triple rabbit and had better go down the drain and have done with it. She certainly didn't deserve ever to see Anthony again.

She picked up the paper, unfolded it, clenched her teeth to prevent them chattering—and had her reward. For the very first thing she saw was the heading, *"Disappearing Typist In Bearer Bonds Mystery. Police Clue"*; and, a little way down the page, a portrait of a damsel with a great deal of smile and permanent wave labelled *"Gladys Filentz. The Disappearing Girl. Have You Seen Her?"*

Gladys and her permanent wave swam away from Shirley into a quivering mist. She shut her eyes, drank some more coffee, and waited for the mist to clear, after which she read all about Miss Filentz and the bearer bonds she had carried away in a suit-case. She even felt a little sorry for her, because it didn't seem at all likely that she would get away with them, and, thief or no thief, Shirley was sorry for anyone who was just going to be arrested. Only what a joyful, joyful, *joyful* relief that it wasn't Shirley Dale.

She went rapidly through the rest of the paper just to make sure that there were not any lurking references to emeralds, or a missing diamond brooch, or Mrs Huddleston, or Revelston Crescent, or Shirley

Dale. There was a headline about an American millionaire's will, but she passed it without a glance, because of course it couldn't have anything to do with her. If she had been less sure of this, she might have discovered that the millionaire was William Ambrose Merewether, and if she had gone on reading to the end of the paragraph, she might have come upon her mother's maiden name. It was there for her to read: "My cousin Jane Lorimer." But she didn't read it. She was looking for her own name, or Mrs Huddleston's, or *"Robbery In Revelston Crescent,"* or, *"Historic Emeralds Stolen."*

When she didn't find any of these things, she put the paper down on the opposite chair and sat back with a thankful sigh. What a mugwump she had been. If she hadn't panicked and run away, she might have been having lunch with Anthony at this minute. She wondered where he was and what he was doing. And then suddenly her mind got to work and she realized that she had been sitting here for the best part of half an hour drinking coffee and wallowing in refreshment-room sandwiches and buns when of course she ought to have been telephoning to let Anthony know where she was. She picked up the suit-case, looked at the clock on the dingy wall, and ran. It was thirty-five minutes since she had got out of the train. It was five-and-twenty minutes to two, and if Anthony had got down early to Ledlington and found her gone, she might very well have missed him. She called herself all the worst names she could think of as she stood in the telephone-box and waited For "Enquiries" to find out the number of the Station Hotel.

It seemed a terribly long time before she got through. The hall porter's "Hullo!" sounded faint and far away:

"Ullo, 'ullo, 'ullo!"

And Shirley in the telephone-box:

"Is that the Station Hotel, Ledlington?"

"Hall porter speaking."

She tried hard to keep her voice from sounding frightened. She said,

"Is there a Mr Leigh in the hotel? He was coming down for lunch. Has he arrived?"

And then on the last word she remembered all in a devastating flash that Anthony hadn't been Mr Leigh last night but Mr Somebody Else, and she had been his sister, but what their name was supposed to have been she hadn't the very faintest idea, and unlike Anthony she couldn't fall back on the register. The receiver chattered at her ear, the hall porter receded. She racked her brain for the name, and found nothing but a blank. Things had gone on happening yesterday with such unremitting speed and intensity, what with being accused of stealing sixpences from Miss Maltby, and finding Mrs Huddleston's diamond brooch in the hem of her coat, and running away to Emshot, and finding Miss Maltby there, and running away to Anthony, and getting engaged to him, that by the time it came to being Anthony's sister at the Station Hotel in Ledlington her mind had reached saturation point and absolutely refused to take in another thing. It was no use searching for the name, because it wasn't there. Her mind had simply never taken it in. Besides, she had already asked for Mr Leigh. What would the hall porter think if she suddenly said, "I don't mean Mr Leigh—I mean somebody else"?

Here a very helpful squib went off with a bang in the middle of her frightened thoughts. "What on earth does it matter *what* the hall porter thinks? Damn the hall porter!" And right on the top of that, here he was on the line again.

"No one of the name of Leigh in the hotel, madam."

Shirley braced herself. After all he couldn't even see her, and she might be speaking from anywhere in the world. She toyed with the thought of Japan. How very, very comforting to be talking to the Station Hotel at Ledlington from Osaka or Tokyo. It was a lovely, lovely thought. But even if she wasn't in Japan, she was an anonymous and disembodied voice as far as the hall porter was concerned. She said,

"Did any gentleman arrive for lunch and ask for a lady who had been staying the night?"

It sounded very odd, but of course it didn't matter about a disembodied voice being odd.

The porter went away again. He said he would inquire, and faded out. A much nearer and more business-like voice asked Shirley whether she would like another three minutes, and invited her to drop more coins into the slot on her right. She dropped them, and there was the hall porter again.

"Are you there, madam?"

Shirley said that she was there. She began to feel as if she had been there for weeks.

"There was a gentleman that was asking for Miss Lester about one o'clock."

"Yes?" said Shirley, "Yes, yes—can I speak to him?"

"He asked for Miss Lester, and when he found she was gone he had some lunch and went off again."

"He's gone?"

Shirley's voice was so despairing that the hall porter was moved out of his official telephone manner.

"Not above a quarter of an hour ago. Asked about the trains both ways, and had his lunch and a fill-up of petrol at the garridge at the corner, and off he went."

"Do you know which way he went?"

"Turned to the right by the garridge—but he'd be bound to do that unless he was going to Trayle or Little-cote Green, which wouldn't be very likely."

It sounded very unlikely indeed. Shirley said "Thank you," and hung up the receiver. If she hadn't behaved like a complete nit-wit and a blithering, brainless chump, she would have caught Anthony easily at the Station Hotel. At this very moment he would be on his way to her, or she would be on her way to him and she would be within measurable distance of handing over Mrs Huddleston's emeralds to Mrs Huddleston's nephew. As it was, she hadn't the slightest chance of getting rid of them of the slightest idea what to do next. Anthony was probably blinding into the blue, and getting farther and farther away from her every moment.

Of course he might come to London, or he might go back to Emshot. He might reason that having rushed away from London in a panic, she wasn't likely to return there, or he might guess that something had frightened her and sent her flying into the first train that came along. She didn't find this last theory very convincing, because Anthony wouldn't know about the disappearing girl and that really terrifying placard. On the other hand, if he had no idea where she had gone, wouldn't he be quite likely to come back to his own chambers? Shirley hoped he would.

Odds and ends of plans began to shape themselves in her mind. The very first thing she must do was to get rid of the emeralds. Trail round with them any longer she simply wouldn't. The mere feeling that they were there inside the suit-case in the pocket of Anthony's pyjamas made her knees shake and her head swim. She went straight to the Left Luggage office, pushed the suit-case across the counter and received a check for it. She would have liked to post the check to Anthony, but she had neither paper, envelope, nor stamps. She was about to give up the idea, when she remembered that the railway hotel would provide her with all three if she had the nerve to walk in and behave as if she were staying there. She could order a cup of coffee at a pinch. But the nearer she came to the hotel entrance, the weaker she felt about it. She wasn't the disappearing girl of the placard, but she *was* Mrs Huddleston's companion, or secretary, or whatever you liked to call it, and she *had* run away with Mrs Huddleston's diamond brooch and Mrs Huddleston's Napoleonic emeralds. Mrs Huddleston's screams were probably still rending the roof of No 15 and Mrs Huddleston's moans were certainly penetrating by telephone to every police-station in the neighbourhood. It behoved Shirley Dale to be as inconspicuous as possible. It didn't behove her to get into the limelight by pinching hotel notepaper. She recoiled from the hotel entrance, picked up the loose end of a plan almost haphazard, and walked out of the station.

Chapter Twenty

ALFRED PHILLIPS paid for the lunch which he and Miss Ettie Miller had just eaten. He looked at her with one of his sharp, darting glances.

"We'll go out," he said.

Ettie's eyebrows went up.

"Out where?"

"The Park for choice. We've got to talk."

She didn't look at all pleased. The Park in the middle of winter, with a wind fit to cut you in two, when you might be sitting comfortable over a good hot fire! It wasn't her idea of a pleasant Sunday afternoon. She told Mr Phillips so with a good deal of vigour.

"And why can't we talk here?"

He frowned and shook his head.

"You never know who's listening in this sort of place."

"This sort of place," was one of those small hotels which exist shabbily in the cheaper parts of London. They are dirty, respectable, and extremely depressing, but they do not suffer from overcrowding.

Miss Miller said, "Rats!" And then, "You can say what you like Al, I'm not going out. That little tinpot writing-room half way up the stairs is dead certain to be empty, and nobody's going to listen to us there. We can have the gas fire and be comfortable. I'm not going to get pneumonia sitting about in the Park this weather, and that's flat."

Al Phillips gave way. The room was safe enough—nobody ever went there. He watched Ettie light the fire and then turn round with a satisfied smile.

"You haven't said whether you like my new rig-out," she said, preening herself.

Mr Phillips frowned.

"It's all right," he said shortly.

"Is that all you've got to say? I thought you liked me in red."

She was conscious that she was looking well, and she meant Al to be conscious of it too. She was very pleased with the dark wine-red three-piece suit and the smart little hat which matched it. The three-quarter length coat was becoming, and the colour set off eyes and hair. She had used a more discreet shade of lipstick. Al always said that scarlet was too bright, and the least he could do now was to tell her he had noticed the change. He might pay her a compliment or two whilst he was about it. Funny how quickly men went off telling you they liked your looks, and yet they expected you to go on telling them how clever they were, day in day out. She didn't mind that, but she did think Al might oblige a bit too.

It was borne in on Mr Phillips that there would be no serious conversation until he had obliged. That was the worst of having to do business with women—they always wanted it mixed up with love-making. He had no objection to making love to Ettie at the right time and when he felt like it, but it put his back up having to do it to order, and when he wanted to talk business. However—

He put an arm round her waist, tipped up her chin, and kissed her.

"You look fine."

"Think so? The fur collar suits me."

"The whole thing suits you. Now come along—we mustn't waste time."

"You didn't always think it was waste of time making love to me."

Gosh—what an insatiable appetite she had! A furious impatience sprang up in him, but he controlled it.

"I don't now. But look here, my dear, we've got to talk."

Ettie gave a regretful sigh.

"All right." She pulled up a dingy chair and settled herself. "What's the matter, Al? Anything wrong?"

Al Phillips went to the door and opened it. The dark stair ran empty down into the hall, and empty on to the landing above. A haunting odour of lunch came in to mingle with the gassy fumes of the long untended fire. He shut the door again, came back, pulled a chair close to Ettie, and sat down.

"The will's in the papers this morning."

"What—the whole thing?"

"The gist of it. It's darned awkward."

Ettie shrugged her shoulders. No Englishwoman born could have shrugged them just like that, yet nothing could have been more English than voice and accent. Both were of London and no other place—the London of shops, and offices, and the hundred ramifications of the business world.

"I don't see it matters," she said. "It was bound to come out anyway."

His long, sharp nose twitched with impatience.

"It wasn't bound to come out now! The girl ought to have been out of the way first! I didn't think they'd cable it. They wouldn't in the ordinary way. It's because the legatees are English, I suppose."

Ettie nodded.

"That's right—but I don't see it matters."

"Then you don't see very far! I've told you all along we've got to be careful or it'll look like a conspiracy."

Ettie Miller shrugged again.

"Rats!" she said.

"You wouldn't say 'Rats!' if you found yourself in the dock."

She laughed good-humouredly.

"Well, you'd be there too. And I don't see it matters a bit about the papers. If Shirley Dale's a thief, well then she is, and that's all there is about it. She's got the things on her, and if you've told me once you've told me a dozen times since yesterday that she has as much chance of getting away with them as she has of flying over the moon. I expect they've arrested her by now, and if they haven't they're bound to by to-morrow. She hasn't any money, and there isn't anyone who'd take her in. So there you are—why worry? They're bound to get her, and when they do, there's a perfectly straight case and an absolute cert of a conviction. Then out goes Shirley Dale, and we're on velvet for the rest of our lives."

Al Phillips did not reply. He leaned forward, frowning at the fire. When Ettie put out a hand and tweaked his ear he could have struck her. She attracted him—sometimes she attracted him very much—but she was too hearty, too demonstrative. There were times when she irritated him to such a point that he wondered whether it was worth it. He dealt sharply with himself on these occasions. When you had as much money as they were going to have, you didn't need to see enough of a woman to get her on your nerves—you had a big house where you didn't need to be right on top of each other all the time. Worth it? Of course it was worth it, Al Phillips!

"What's the matter, dearie?" There was a sugary, cooing tone in Ettie's voice which made him jerk away from her.

He moved his chair, swinging it round so as to face her.

"A bit of darned bad luck the will getting into the papers like that."

"Fidgety, aren't you?" Ettie's voice was still good-tempered. "I can't see what you're bothering about myself."

"It's not safe," said Al Phillips—"that's what I'm bothering about. And there are too many people mixed up in it—Bessie, and the Maltby woman, and you, and me."

She stared at him.

"Well, what's the matter with us?"

"Three too many of you—that's all."

Her shoulders went up again in that foreign shrug.

"Well, you couldn't have done without us—could you? And if you don't trust the others, I suppose you trust me. Nice sort of a husband I've got if you don't."

He said, "Shut your mouth!" in a tone of such cold fury that she sat back staring and without a word to say. Leaning forward and touching her on the knee, he dropped his voice to an edgy whisper and went on, "You say that word again, and you won't have one of any sort. Do you hear? You say 'wife', or 'husband', or 'married', and I'm through!"

Ettie's fine dark eyes opened to their fullest extent. When Al spoke like that it sent a shiver down her back. She admired him a good deal, the way he'd flare out at her, and the way his eyes seemed to go boring into her, and the way his voice gave her that shiver down the back. If he'd been a bit taller, and his hair had been black instead of that funny pale red, he'd have been the very one for a Sheikh.

"Well, I never!"

"Now you just listen!" He was tapping her knee again with a very hard bony finger. "If it gets out that we're married, we'll be in Queer Street. And if it gets out through you, you'll have done the worst bit of work you ever did in your life."

"That's all very well, but where do I come in? That's what I want to know. What's the good of being married when you don't even treat me as if we were engaged half the time? And I mustn't wear my wedding-ring—and I mustn't tell anyone—and not so much as a kiss or a kind word from one week-end to another—" She broke off with a sob.

"Come, come, Ettie—it's not so bad as all that." He pulled her forward and kissed her. "And it's only for a bit. Just so soon as this girl's out of the way and the will's proved, we can go and get married all over again, and nobody'll be a penny the wiser. Now, now—you don't want to spoil your eyes crying. There's a good time coming. You be a good girl and do as I say, and we'll be the happiest couple in the world. But we've got to be careful, my dear, we've got to be careful. Now just suppose she saw me in the crowd at the bus-stop when she got that bag which didn't belong to her on her arm. I mean just suppose she saw me to notice so that she'd know me again. And then suppose she connected that up with you and me dining at the next table to her and Mr Leigh at the Luxe, and you missing your purse and it being found in her bag. Well, that would be a bit awkward, wouldn't it—awkward and dangerous? Ought never to have given way to you over that purse business, and that's a fact. It wasn't safe."

"Oh, put it on me! It wasn't you that thought about it, and planned it, and was full of how Mr Leigh was going to remember about it afterwards when his aunt's things had gone missing! But there, I don't mind—put it on me if you want to. You know, Al, I've been thinking if more than a hundred people get killed on the roads every week—and I'm sure it's enough to give you the creeps the way they keep giving it out on the wireless—well, I was thinking if all those people are going to be killed, it does seem a pity one of them couldn't be Shirley Dale." She paused, looked at him with narrowed eyes, and added, "It *does* seem a pity—doesn't it?"

Al Phillips sent her one of his sharp, darting glances. "You quit that kind of talk! Do you hear? Do you know what, Ettie—if you could quit talking altogether for a month, we'd be a lot safer, and I'd be a lot happier in my mind."

"Why, I didn't say anything." Her tone was one of innocent surprise.

Al Phillips laughed. It was not a pleasant sound.

"And by the time you've said nothing, and Bessie's said nothing, and the Maltby woman's said nothing, we'll all be in the dock, I should-n't wonder!"

Ettie blinked and winced.

"I don't know how you can say a thing like that! I don't talk, I'm sure. And if you've told me once you've told me fifty times that Bessie Wood's as close as a clam. And as for that old Maltby, she's so loony crazy with rage because Jane Rigg didn't live long enough to come in for her share and leave it to her dear friend Estella Maltby along with what she did leave her, that it's not very likely she's going to talk, or if she does, what'll anyone think except that she's got a screw loose?"

"And that's why I'm afraid of her—she *has* got a screw loose."

"Well, she hates Shirley Dale," said Ettie in a lazy, comfort-able voice.

Chapter Twenty-One

SHIRLEY'S STRAY END of a plan had brought her into Redfield Terrace. Redfield Terrace led by way of a narrow paved alley at its farther end into the bottom of Findon Road, and No 14 Findon Road contained the room which she rented from Mrs Camber. The plan which had looked all right in the station now showed signs of wilting. It seemed insufficient, insubstantial, and well on the way to a complete fade-out,

Shirley stood in the alley-way and looked through it at the small section of Findon Road which appeared beyond the painted posts at its lower end. She could see a piece of pavement, and the width of the road, and another piece of pavement, and bits of two houses. There was nobody on either pavement, and nothing was passing in the road.

The plan had been to walk boldly into Mrs Camber's, pack a suit-case, and walk out again. It had seemed quite a good plan, but it was perishing so rapidly that she already regarded it as a has-been. It was a pity, because, having parked Anthony's suit-case and the emeralds in the left-luggage office, she now had no luggage, and without at least a suit-case nobody would take her in. Also she yearned for her toothbrush, and something to sleep in, and her dressing-gown, and a change of clothes, and her hot-water bottle. If it hadn't been Sunday, she might have bought a toothbrush and a suit-case, but it would have been a wicked extravagance. The balance of Anthony's five pounds wouldn't last for ever, and she had no idea how long she might have to go on running away.

She made an eleventh-hour effort to revive the plan. It was now somewhere between half-past two and a quarter to three. Mrs Camber would have had her Sunday dinner and would be just slipping into her Sunday afternoon nap. The Monks were always out on Sunday. Miss Pym was still in Paris. Miss Maltby was at Emshot. It was Mabel's afternoon out, and if she had finished washing up she would be putting on her navy-blue coat and her Army bonnet in the basement bedroom with the little barred window high up in the back wall. In fact the only person there was the slightest chance of meeting was Jasper Wrenn. She had her key, and what was there to prevent her slipping noiselessly into the house and creeping upstairs? As to meeting Jasper, he didn't matter. He could help her carry the suit-case to wherever she was going to carry it. The plan hadn't got as far as that, and now it never would, because even while she tried to revive it she knew that it was dead. She just couldn't walk out between those posts into Findon Road and up the steps of No 14. Even if there wasn't a single person in sight, she would feel as if the eyes of Scotland Yard were upon her—countless eyes of countless policemen, all watching for Shirley Dale who was *wanted*. No, she couldn't do it. She could walk almost down to the posts, but she couldn't pass them. It was no use—she simply couldn't.

She was just going to turn round and walk back to Redfield Terrace, when something happened, something that seemed too good to be true, and yet was true. Jasper Wrenn came into sight on the other side of the posts.

Shirley did what she had just decided she couldn't possibly do. She darted out into Findon Road and caught him by the arm. Then before he had time even to be astonished, she had dragged him back into the alleyway and was saying a great many incoherent things without quite enough breath to say them properly.

"Oh, Jas! *Angel!* We'd better walk. Darling—if you knew how glad! Angel—tell me—are there any policemen? I mean is the coast clear—I mean could I get into the house and get a suit-case, or would somebody arrest me? Because I haven't even got a toothbrush, and I don't see how anyone is going to take me in without one, Oh, Jas, you *are* an angel to turn up like this!"

She was hanging on his arm and impelling him away from Findon Road. No windows looked into the alley. Jasper lost his head a little. The whole thing had been so very sudden. Shirley was hugging his arm and burbling in his ear. Her lips were very near, and very red. He missed them, and landed an awkward kiss somewhere between her cheek and her chin. Shirley found it rather comforting. She felt none of the fury which had boiled up in her at Anthony's careless kiss—was it really only two days ago? But then she was in love with Anthony, and when you are in love with someone a careless kiss hurts worse than any blow. And she wasn't in love with Jas, she was only very fond of him, and he was an angel, and a Godsend, and what old Aunt Emily would have called a Providential Occurrence. She didn't mind his kissing her in the least, but she did have a sort of feeling that perhaps Anthony wouldn't like it, so she said, "No, Jas, *please*—there's no time," and got a little farther away from him.

Jasper experienced a feeling of relief. His heart was beating with great violence. His head swam with triumph. He had kissed her and they were both still, so to speak, here. He didn't quite know where he expected them to be, but he had the feeling that something might have blown up. She might have been horribly angry, she might have sent him away, she might not have let him help her—all horrible things to contemplate when your twentieth birthday is still three months ahead. Hence the relief. Perhaps next time he wouldn't miss her lips. Perhaps—

Shirley was shaking him by the arm.

"So you see, I simply *must* have a suit-case! Oh, Jas—you're not *listening*!"

For the moment Jasper had been quite incapable of listening, but it was borne in upon him that if he didn't pull himself together and listen now, Shirley would be annoyed. He said,

"I *am* listening."

"You weren't—but you've got to. Jas, do you think you could sleuth into the house, and pack a suit-case, and bring it here?"

He had no difficulty in listening now.

"Of course I could."

Shirley very nearly kissed him. It was so difficult not to kiss people when you were fond of them and they were being angel lambs. But perhaps better not. Jas had had a kind of yearning look just now, like a dog watching the cake at tea and hoping it is going to get some. Perhaps kinder not to raise false hopes, because of course the cake belonged to Anthony, so it wasn't any good encouraging Jas to yearn.

She said, "Angel!" and kept her arm stiff in case he tried to kiss her again. But he didn't—only said in a tone of melancholy devotion,

"What do you want?"

"Everything," said Shirley with an expansive gesture.

The realist in Jasper asserted himself.

"You can't get everything into a suit-case."

"I know, darling—isn't it a pity?"

"Well, what do you want most?"

The realist produced a blotted piece of paper and a fountain pen and prepared to make a list. Shirley began to tick things off on her fingers.

"*Must* have a toothbrush. Aunt Emily would have had a fit if she'd seen me cleaning my teeth with the corner of a station hotel face-towel."

"Toothbrush," said Jasper, and wrote it down.

"My blue dressing-gown—it's hanging behind the door. And a pair of pyjamas out of the left-hand corner of the first long drawer— not the blue ones, because they want mending, but there's a pink pair underneath. And the top pair of cami-knickers—they're in the same drawer—at least I hope the top pair's all right, but you'd better just have a look at the shoulder-straps."

"Why?"

"To make sure they're all right. If the top pair's wonky, take the next."

Jasper gloomed at the list.

"Anything else?"

"Brush and comb—right-hand top drawer. Powder-puff and powder-box. And there are some handkerchiefs in that drawer, and *stockings*. If you love me, don't take a pair with a hole."

Jasper gloomed at her instead of at the list.

"And what happens if the Maltby comes up whilst I'm rummaging in your drawers finding shoulder-straps and testing out stockings for holes?"

Shirley stamped her foot on a paving-stone.

"Don't be silly! How can she come up? She isn't there."

"Isn't she then?"

She stamped again, with a cold shiver going over her.

"Jas, she isn't, she *isn't*—she's at Emshot. I saw her there last night."

"Well, you've come back, and so has she."

"She's really here? You're not saying it to frighten me?"

He stuffed the fountain pen into his pocket and caught her by the arm.

"Shirley—what's up? Why should you be frightened of the Maltby? She's an old beast, but why should you be frightened of her? What's been happening—what's all this about? I can't just make lists and fetch suit-cases and not know what it's all about. You're driving me mad. I thought I'd go off my head when you didn't come home yesterday and the police came." He choked, staring at her with tortured intensity, and then suddenly let go of her and turned away. "I don't care what you've done. Don't tell me anything you don't want to. It doesn't make any difference, only if I *knew*, it wouldn't be so—so—" His voice broke off.

Shirley was in two minds as to whether she was going to cry or fly into a rage. Fortunately the rage had it. There was a good deal of bright colour in her cheeks as she jerked him by the sleeve.

"Will you look at me! What do you suppose I've done? I thought you were my friend. Are you going to stand there and dare to tell me you believe—you actually believe—I went into the Maltby's pig of a room and pinched her sixpences?"

"Shirley!"

"She says I did. And of course you believe what she says!"

"I don't know what you're talking about—I never heard of her blighted sixpences. *Shirley!*"

He was looking at her with such a desperate appeal that the anger went out of her. She said with a little gurgle of laughter,

"What an ass you are! Did you really think I'd been stealing? I wouldn't believe a hundred policemen about you."

"I nearly went mad when you didn't come back."

She slipped her hand inside his arm again.

"Well, you can't go mad now—there isn't time. Now tell me, what did that policeman say?"

"He searched your room. He said things were missing at Mrs Huddleston's—and when you didn't come home—"

She patted his shoulder.

"I know—you nearly went mad—you keep on saying so. Now look here—this is what really happened."

"I don't want you to tell me unless you really want to."

Shirley made a most hideous Woggy Doodle at him.

"Oh, Jas, do dry up! I want you to *help* me. Now listen—some one's trying to get me into a mess. I don't know who it is, and I don't know why they're doing it. All sorts of little things have been happening. The Maltby's sixpences was one of them. And then yesterday when I came away from Revelston Crescent something banged against my leg, and after I'd got into the bus I found out what it was—Mrs Huddleston's big diamond brooch. Someone had slit my pocket lining and pushed it right down into the hem of my coat."

Jasper stared at her.

"But why?"

"I don't *know* why—I keep telling you so. Well, I lost my head and ran away. I did start to go back and tell Mrs Huddleston, but when I got in sight of the house there was a policeman going in, and I funked it and bolted."

"Where did you bolt to?"

"To Anthony Leigh—Mrs Huddleston's nephew. I thought he'd be the best person to explain to her, and I knew where he was—he'd gone down to Emshot for the week-end. So I went after him and—Jas, the most awful thing, after he'd put me into an hotel and gone off with the diamond brooch—he had to park me somewhere, because it was getting on for one o'clock in the morning—"

The mention of Anthony Leigh had chilled Jasper to the bone. The realist came to the fore again, breaking in upon Shirley's disjointed narrative with a stern.

"You're getting all tied up. Where were you?"

"At the Station Hotel, Ledlington. I was telling you."

"No, you weren't!"

"Yes, I was!"

They glared at each other. Then Shirley broke down into a laugh.

"I was trying to, darling. You weren't being terribly helpful. And what I was trying to tell you was that after Anthony had been gone for hours and hours I found out that the diamond brooch wasn't the only thing that had been hidden in my coat. There were a lot of Mrs Huddleston's emeralds there as well in the hem on the other side."

"Mrs Huddleston's emeralds?"

Shirley nodded.

"Napoleon gave them to Josephine, and Mrs Huddleston's grandpapa gave them to Mrs. Huddleston's grandmamma." She gazed at him with an awful solemnity, and then began to giggle.

"Wasn't it *awful*?"

Jasper's frown was an attempt to conceal the fact that he was now completely bewildered. He said with an angry note in his voice,

"Are you making this up?"

Shirley went on giggling.

"No, darling—I'm not clever enough."

"Then what's Napoleon got to do with it?"

"N-nothing. He just gave them to Josephine—when he came back from Italy, you know. They've got N's all over them."

"What have?" Mr Wrenn was now scowling like a brigand.

Shirley patted him on the arm.

"The emeralds. I *knew* you weren't attending. There's a whole set of them—a headband, and earrings, and two brooches, but they only planted me with the headband and one of the brooches. Perhaps I shall find the earrings in my toothpaste when I get hold of it. Do you know, I had to wash my teeth with hotel soap on the corner of a towel this morning. It tasted revolting."

Jasper pulled himself away with a jerk.

"Is this true?"

"Absolutely. Darling, why should I deceive you? It was bright pink soap like a sugar sweet, but it tasted of tallow."

"I don't mean about your teeth—I mean about the emeralds. You're not making it up—you've really got them?"

"Not now," said Shirley with modest pride.

"How do you mean not now?"

"I've parked them." She was just going to say that they were in the pocket of Anthony's pyjamas, when it occurred to her that perhaps she had better not. Perhaps better be tactful about Anthony, not, so to speak, rub it in. And the pyjamas would need explaining. She decided not to explain them, and went on hastily, "You know, darling, I *had* to park them, because if a policeman had arrested me red-handed, I wouldn't have had an earthly—would I?"

"Where are they?" said Jasper very crossly indeed.

Shirley hesitated.

"Of course if you don't *trust* me!" The scowl was terrific.

"Jas, I do wish you'd stop being a fool! Of course I trust you!" She dived into her handbag. "They're in the left-luggage place. Here's the receipt. And when you've collected my toothbrush I want you to go and find Anthony Leigh."

"Why?" It was an angry and explosive monosyllable.

Shirley sighed with exaggerated patience.

"You said you wanted to help me—that's why."

He caught at her hand.

"I'll do anything in the world!"

"Well, find Anthony. I've been a complete mutt. I lost my head and ran away instead of waiting for him in Ledlington, and now he doesn't know where I am, and he doesn't know about the emeralds. I want you to find him, and tell him, and give him the receipt, and fix up somewhere for me to meet him. I think he's bound to come back to his chambers some time to-day. You could ring up to start with and then go round if he's there. I'll give you the address and the telephone number."

The angry colour came into Jasper's face. She knew the fellow's telephone number without having to look it up. She must have used it dozens of times. She must know him awfully well. He began to say something, and gulped it down.

"You will—*won't* you?" said Shirley in a coaxing voice. Then, on a note of anxious pleading, "*Angel* Jas."

"Oh, all right," said Mr Wrenn in a far from angelic tone.

Chapter Twenty-Two

WHEN JASPER HAD DEPARTED to fetch the toothbrush and a quite considerable number of other things of which he had made a careful list upon the back of a poem entitled "Cosmos", Shirley walked up and down the alley-way and sustained herself with the thought of a joyous reunion with, (a), her own clothes, and, (b), Anthony. Anthony should of course have been (a) both alphabetically and romantically, but in point of time the reunion with a probably bulging suit-case would come first—"And I only trust Jas won't *over*-bulge it, because the hasps are on the wonky side, and if they suddenly go pop and scatter my undies all over the stairs or on the front doorstep, what fun for the Maltby!"

The hasps were holding nobly when Jas came hurrying between the posts. He was running as he came up to her and without a word caught her by the arm and started her running too.

She looked back when they came to the posts at the other end of the alley. There was no one in sight. They turned right, and dropped into a fast walk.

"What happened? Did anyone see you?" She was a little breathless from the sudden run.

"I don't know," said Jas. His voice sounded startled.

"How do you mean you don't know? What happened?"

"A door banged. We'd better hurry."

"I'm not going to run—it attracts attention. How do you mean a door banged?"

"I don't know." His voice was rather sulky.

He wouldn't have minded dying for Shirley, the details of the decease being veiled in a mist heavily charged with romance, but he did bar being scolded by her. Here he had just been crawling up the stairs, and rummaging noiselessly for all the things she wanted—and nobody who hasn't tried to rummage noiselessly has any idea how difficult it is—and then creeping down those flights of stairs again thinking what a fool he'd look if anyone came out of a room and wanted to know what he was doing with Shirley's suit-case—well, after all this, instead of glowing with gratitude she kept saying things like "How do you mean you don't know?" And he didn't know. A door had banged when he was nearly down. A door had shut—shut with a sudden bang, as if the wind had caught it, as if someone had come out of a room to look down over the stairs and see what he was doing and a draught had caught the door and banged it to. That was what it had sounded like. He told Shirley so.

She pursed up her lips, emitting a faint whistle.

"Whose door was it?"

"I tell you I don't know."

Shirley laughed.

"Oh well, if there *was* a door, there's only one door it could be. If anyone was snooping and spying, it would be the Maltby. So we needn't hurry—I don't see her sprinting after us."

"She might take a taxi."

"She wouldn't—she's too mean. And you can't get a taxi like that all in a hurry on a Sunday afternoon, and she doesn't know where we're going."

"Where *are* we going?" said Jasper.

Shirley's eyes danced at him.

"I don't know either."

Jasper the realist was shocked and exasperated.

"You *must* know."

"Darling, I don't. I wish I did. It would be lovely to feel that there was a gas fire waiting for me somewhere, and crumpets for tea. It's been Sunday for weeks and weeks and weeks, and I've been running away all the time, and the last meal was about a week and a half ago in a railway refreshment-room—and I think it was a bun and a cup of tea, but it's so definitely a has-been that I can't be sure—it may have been coffee and a sandwich. I could do a plate of crumpets very nicely, and the sort of tea Aunt Emily never let me have, very hot and very strong with the sugar sticking out of the top of the cup."

"It sounds foul," said Jasper gloomily.

They turned out of Redfield Terrace and came into what on a week-day would have been a crowded thoroughfare. With the shops all blind and shuttered, it had a deserted look.

"But if you don't know where you're going, why are you going this way?"

"Must go some way, darling. Perhaps I shall meet a crumpet and follow it home."

He grabbed her by the arm and brought her to a standstill outside a hairdresser's shop. The lower part of the window was covered by a half blind of green shaded silk over the top of which there appeared the heads of three wax ladies.

"Look here, Shirley—talk sense! I've got to take you somewhere before I can go off and look for your Anthony Leigh, haven't I?"

He waited for her to say, "He isn't my Anthony Leigh," but she didn't say it. His throat went dry. He waited a little longer. She only said in a thoughtful tone,

"Well, there's something in that. But where can I go?"

"A friend—"

She shook her head.

"There's no one I can go to like this. But I've got some money—I could take a room if I knew where to go."

She gazed at the wax ladies as if for inspiration. The one in the middle had auburn hair slicked sideways in a series of flat waves, and a parting which bristled with diamond triangles. Shirley was wondering how on earth you would keep them on, when Jasper's voice broke in,

"We can't just stand here, you know."

She turned round regretfully. Running away by yourself was depressing and rather frightening, but running away with someone else whom you could tease and provoke, and who would carry your suit-case, was fun. She didn't want to go back to the lonely sort of running away a bit, but she supposed she'd got to. She said in a resigned voice,

"All right—you push off and find Anthony."

"I can't just leave you here."

"I know.... What shall I do? I suppose I could go and sit in a station. They don't turn you out till about one in the morning, do they?—and you're bound to have found Anthony by then."

"You can't do that," said Jasper crossly.

She contemplated saying "Why can't I?" but abandoned the idea. The prospect of spending nearly eleven hours in a railway waiting-room, and then perhaps having to stagger forth with a heavy suit-case and sleep on the Embankment, or wherever you did sleep when they turned you out, was not one which inspired her to battle. She gazed at Jasper with comparative meekness and said,

"All right, suggest something. It's your turn."

Jasper brightened a little.

"I've got a cousin—"

"Male or female?"

"Female—name of Helena Pocklington. She's only a sort of a cousin really."

"Well? What about her?"

"She lives in Pattenham Mews. She's by way of being an artist. She's got a studio and a bedroom."

"How's that going to help me?"

"She's away," said Jasper.

"Then how—"

With subdued triumph he said, "I've got her key."

Shirley said, "Oh—" Then her eyes began to sparkle. "You've got it with you?"

"In my trouser pocket."

"Lovely!" She went on sparkling. "Where is it? Will there be any food? I don't suppose there's anywhere we can buy anything, is there? If I can't have crumpets I must have muffins. I suppose there won't be any food."

"Only canary seed," said Jasper. "That's why I've got the key. She's got a canary, and she made me promise to go in every day and see to it."

"Darling, I can't live on canary seed! I should be a desiccated corpse! You'll have to burst into a pub and buy bread and cheese, or sandwiches or something. You can pretend you're a hiker. Hikers always want sandwiches. They used to pour into our village like locusts in summer, and Aunt Emily made me pull down the blinds because of the girls in shorts—only I'm not sure she didn't think flannel trousers worse—anyhow all very corrupting and—where did you say your cousin's Mew was?"

Jasper frowned at her levity. He was not very happy in his mind about using Helena Pocklington's key. She was one of those determined women to whom a relative originally known in the schoolroom remains there for the term of his natural life. She made Jasper feel an uncomfortable eight years old. When bidden to visit her flat and feed her canary, he had said, "Yes, Cousin Helena," and gone on saying "Yes" at respectful intervals while she told him just how much seed Chippy ate, and just how much water Chippy drank, and just how careful he must be not to make a mess when he cleaned out the cage. If Helena ever found out—

Shirley's voice cut in impatiently.

"Jas—wake up! Where is this Mew of yours?"

The consequences would be absolutely grim. He said in a tone of gloom,

"Just round at the back of Redfield Terrace."

"Then we'd better go there," said Shirley briskly.

He acquiesced. There was a snag in it—there were several snags. He said so aloud, and the light of controversy glinted in Shirley's eye.

"What do you mean by a snag?"

"Snags—plural," said Jasper. "And then some."

Her foot tapped the pavement, the glint brightened.

"Jas, you're enough to make a saint hit you over the head. What *are* the snags?"

"The Maltby's one of them."

Shirley's eyebrows went right up out of sight.

"The Maltby!!!"

He nodded with an air of sheepish gloom.

"How *can* she be a snag?" Her voice had an edge on it. "What can she possibly have to do with your Helena Pocklington?"

"They were at school together," said Jasper.

Shirley stamped so hard that her leg pringled all the way up.

"They *can't* have been!"

"Well, they were. That's why I'm at Mrs Camber's. The Maltby told Helena that it was a nice respectable place for me to live, so she made me go there. I stayed because of you."

"Nice of you," said Shirley in rather an absent manner. Then she made up for it with a brilliant smile. "Jas, I don't see that it's really a snag—not to matter. I shall only be there an hour or two—at least I hope so. And after all it's you who have got the key, not her."

"She's got one too," said Jasper.

"She *hasn't*!"

"She has."

Shirley stamped again.

"Why?"

He smiled an embittered smile.

"To make sure that I feed the canary."

Shirley said, "Help!" And then, with a rapid reversion to being practical, "Well, I haven't anywhere else to go. We'll have to chance it. Better get a move on."

They came into Pattenham Mews, and stopped at the third door on the left. It was painted a screaming shade of blue, and looked as odd in that row of shabby doors with blistered paint, and peeling paint, and very little paint at all, as a peacock would have done among the noisy sparrows which thronged the place.

Jasper produced the key and they went in. It was the oddest place inside. A stair which was little more than a ladder ran up from a yard inside the door to a square hole in the floor above. The ground floor had been partitioned—kitchenette in front, bedroom and bathroom behind. The kitchen contained a stove, a sink, a frying-pan and two saucepans. The bedroom contained a bed, a chair, and a chest of drawers. The bathroom contained a geyser and a bath. All the wood-work had been painted I the same bright peacock-blue as the front door.

They went up the ladder, through the hole in the floor, and arrived in the studio. More blue paint, and a great many windows—a row of them looking out in front, and a row of them looking out at the back, and a skylight looking up at the sky. All round the walls stood the products of Miss Helena Pocklington's brush. They stood because there was no room for them to hang—large canvases, and middle-sized canvases, plastered with paint so vivid that Shirley gasped.

"Golly!" she said in tone of awe.

"Enough to put the canary off his feed—aren't they?"

"What are they meant for? What's that one?" She pointed at the canvas which faced them. It appeared to present a design of a vaguely geometrical character. Lopsided circles of viridian green were intertwined with blood-red pyramids and yellow hexagons.

"She calls it the Potato Field."

"Why?"

"I don't know."

Shirley made a malignant Woggy Doodle at it, and behind her back the canary burst into song. She swung round and saw a large cage hanging from the rafters. On the perch a handsome yellow canary stretched his throat and trilled. In the angle between the back row of windows and the main wall stood an anthracite stove which gave out a very pleasant heat.

"Lovely and warm!" said Shirley.

Jasper scowled.

"I have to keep it up for him."

"For the canary—a whole stove?" She giggled appreciatively. "My poor Jas! The Canary's Friend, of Always Be Kind to Dumb Animals! Only he isn't dumb. Be quiet, you little wretch!"

Jasper produced a sudden schoolboy grin.

"He's nothing to Helena, and when they get going together—"

"Business," said Shirley firmly. She reached up and shook the cage, which had a temporarily discouraging effect on the canary. "Be quiet, you little wretch! All right, chirrup, if you like, but you're not to sing. Now, Jas—the first thing is food. Here's ten shillings. There must be places that are open on a Sunday, and I've got to have food in case of your having to follow Anthony to Timbuctoo or something like that. You wouldn't like to get a wireless message when you were half way there to say I'd been found starved to death—would you? It would make a lovely headline—wouldn't it? *Mystery Girl In Mews!* But I expect you'd rather not, and so would Anthony, so get me some eggs, or sandwiches, or something. And is the gas turned on? Because if it was, I could have a geyser bath."

Jasper looked panic-stricken.

"Oh, I say—you can't do that! She reads the meter. And it isn't on—at least—I mean—of course I could turn it on—but I don't think I'd better. She'd want to know why I had been using the gas."

"You can say you were giving the canary a bath, darling," said Shirley firmly. "Come and turn it on at once!"

Chapter Twenty-Three

ANTHONY LEIGH CAME BACK to town because it seemed the most sensible thing to do. Shirley had disappeared into the blue without leaving a message for him, and the only deduction he could make from that was that something had startled her and she had run away. No one seemed to have noticed her getting into any train, and he had therefore no clue to her probable whereabouts. He could have pushed his inquiries a little farther afield, but he did not want to attract attention, and if he disappeared into the blue after Shirley, *she* would then have no clue to *his* whereabouts. Whereas if he returned to town and sat within reach of a telephone, she could, and surely would, ring him up. He came back therefore, put the car away, and let himself into an empty flat. Manders wouldn't be back till ten o'clock. All the windows were shut. The place was cold and stuffy, and there wasn't a vestige of a fire.

He lit the gas fire in the dining-room, opened a window only to shut it again as the north-east wind came bounding in, threw himself into a comfortable shabby chair by the side of the hearth, and opened one of the Sunday papers which he had brought with him.

A headline about disarmament, a headline about road accidents, a headline about a film star, and—*"Millionaire's Amazing Will."*

Always something interesting about a will. Mortmain—the dead hand trying to pull strings, to go on pulling them, to go on having a finger in the pie. Extraordinary sidelights on human nature to be got out of wills.

He settled down to find out what William Ambrose Merewether had done about his millions.

Everything to his cousin Jane Lorimer if still alive....

Well, she'd be fairly old by now. William Ambrose wasn't any chicken....

Anthony looked away from the print to the photograph half way down the column. A good-looking old boy. Might have been a judge. Thick white hair standing up in a crest. More hair like that in America than over on this side—must have something to do with the climate. Keen features, bright malicious eyes. Looked as if he'd been a bad man to cross....

He went back to the print again.

"Jane Lorimer ... provided she has not, up to the time of this will being proved, been in prison on a criminal charge...."

Anthony laughed to himself. Something behind that. Interesting to know what. Pleasant for Jane Lorimer if still alive....

He read on to find out what happened to Mr Merewether's millions if his cousin Jane Lorimer were dead or had done time.

"Any children of the said Jane Lorimer ... equal shares ... same condition to apply ... survivor takes everything ... if no survivor, or condition not complied with, grandchild or grandchildren of said Jane Lorimer to inherit—still under the condition...."

Vindictive old boy. He must have had it in for Jane all right. Wonder what she did to him. How pleased the family must be. But I daresay the millions will sweeten the insult.

He had got as far as that, half interested, half trying to be interested—because what was the good of wondering all the time where Shirley was?—when suddenly the half interest became a whole interest and he was staring at the concluding paragraph with all his eyes. A name stood out, stared back—the name of Augustus Rigg.

Anthony's eyes looked at the name. He wondered why it should hold them like that. His brain made nothing of it yet—not consciously. He just looked at the name and couldn't let it go. Jane Lorimer had married Augustus Rigg, Esq. of Emerton House near Harrogate in the county of Yorkshire—Augustus Rigg, J.P. She had married him in 1883, and he died in 1884, leaving issue John and Jane, twins, born 1884.

John and Jane ... Augustus Rigg ... Jane Rigg ... Shirley giving her funny little gurgling laugh in the study at Revelston Crescent and saying, "I've got a half-sister called Jane Rigg. Sounds grim—doesn't it?"....

Light broke in violently upon his waiting brain. Mr William Ambrose Merewether's cousin Jane Lorimer was Shirley's mother. She had married Augustus Rigg and had twin children, John and Jane. And then she had married a French artist—what was his name?—Le-something or other—and he left her with a baby called Perrine ... The odd name stuck in his mind.... And then she married Dale and went off with him to New Zealand, and had two boys and, as an after-thought, Shirley....

Shirley—Shirley and William Ambrose Merewether's millions. Out of that mixed bag of Jane Lorimer's three marriages who was there left, and how did they all stand?

Jane Lorimer was dead, years and years ago as Jane Dale in New Zealand. That put her out of it. She and William Ambrose must settle their quarrel somewhere else—a little more than kin and less than kind.

The children came next—children of her three marriages—share and share alike unless any of them should have been in prison.

First the Rigg twins, John and Jane....

They were out of it too—both dead, John in the war (Shirley's voice again, very clear: "The John twin was killed in the war like my two real brothers") and Jane six months ago. The Riggs were off the map as far as the millions were concerned....

Next Perrine—the French child Perrine Levaux. (Shirley again, "Perrine's dead too, a long time ago.")

Cross off Perrine and come to the Dale family.... Three of them—two boys and Shirley. Two boys ... What were their names?—Hugh and Ambrose ... *Ambrose*.... There must have been something between Jane and old William Ambrose for her to have given his name to one of her boys so long afterwards—on the other side of the world....

Hugh, and Ambrose, and Shirley Dale....

But the Dale brothers had been killed in the war, both of them. He remembered Shirley saying, "Hugh was twenty-three and Ambrose was twenty-two"....

Cross out Hugh and Ambrose, and there was only Shirley left. Out of Jane Lorimer's six children there was only Shirley left. And Shirley came in for the Merewether millions unless—

Unless—

Unless—

Unless the very thing happened that was in imminent danger of happening....

He went back to William Ambrose Merewether's condition. If Shirley was arrested on a charge of theft, what would happen to the Merewether millions?... Something clicked in Anthony's brain. What *would* happen to the money if Shirley was disqualified?

He wanted to know that very badly.

Sharply on that the telephone bell rang.

He had crowded a writing-table in between fireplace and window. The telephone stood to his hand. He had only to lean sideways to reach it. A voice that was strange to him asked him if he was Mr Anthony Leigh—a male voice, young and not too pleased about it.

He said, "Anthony Leigh speaking. Who is it?" Whereupon the line did something odd and the voice from a very long way off said something which sounded like "Hens"—or it might have been pens—or one (singular) hen or pen. He raised his voice, said that he had neither a hen nor a pen, and what about it?

"Don't speak so loud," said the remote voice. And then all of a sudden there it was, blaring into his ear, "My name is Jasper Wrenn."

Anthony removed the receiver to a distance less jarring to the ear, and said,

"All right—what about it?"

And then in a flash he was remembering the exact tone of his own voice teasing Shirley—"You absolutely can't go about with a fellow called Jasper. It's asking to get into a melodrama." If Jasper was calling him up, it must mean—

He said quickly, "All right, Wrenn—there was something the matter with the line, but it's got going again. What is it?"

"Shirley asked me to ring you up."

Chapter Twenty-Four

SHIRLEY SURVEYED the provisions which Jasper had brought back from his foraging expedition. Two lumpy sandwiches, made without mustard, but the ham looked all right and the bread not too bad. Two currant scones, rather pale and undecided-looking, the sort that need lots of butter and are better toasted. Half a bag of biscuits, the frightfully dull kind that you don't take even with cheese *and* butter unless they're the only ones left in the box. Regarded as food, without so much as a cup of tea to wash them down, they were discouraging in the extreme. Jas had probably done his best, and that was all you could say about it.

Shirley had a bright thought. The word toast was, so to speak, the germ from which it sprang. Why not toast the scones? Lightly browned and crisp, they might be quite attractive. Even the biscuits would probably be edible if they were toasted. Also it would be amusing to play about with the gas stove, and it would help to pass the time till Anthony came.

She took everything down to the kitchenette, applauding her own cleverness in having made Jasper turn on the gas, and embarked on a fascinating game of make-believe in which she and Anthony were married, and this was *their* Mew, and she was expecting him to come home for tea—"Only it wouldn't run to ham sandwiches every day. Or would it? I haven't the slightest idea how much money he's got. But anyhow I should think he'd hate them—and so should I if I hadn't been running away all day."

She ate the sandwiches while she was toasting the scones. There was a toasting-fork, rather bent and rusty, but usable. She washed it well before she stuck it into the scones. It seemed to have been used for other than culinary purposes, because it was up in the studio amongst the canvases, and it smelt suspiciously of turpentine.

The scones toasted very well. Shirley felt a good deal better when she had eaten them. If she could have made herself a cup of tea she would have been quite happy. Cold water does not go at all well with scones. She left the biscuits alone. After the sandwiches and the scones, she wasn't hungry enough to embark on them.

She took the bag and wandered upstairs again with the idea that Chippy might like one. She would have to crumble it up of course. Chippy watched her with interest. She took a biscuit out of the bag, and he cocked his head, edged along the perch to the side of the cage and said "Tweet" on a piercingly hopeful note.

She was just going to break the biscuit in half, when a key clicked in the lock at the foot of the stair and the door was pushed open.

Shirley stood still with the biscuit in her hand. She doesn't know to this day why she didn't call out, or what stopped her. If it was one thing more than another, it was the slowness of that opening door—the key fumbling in the lock—a lot of little scratchy noises like a hen picking at something. And then the door opening with a slow push. And no one coming in—

With a biscuit in one hand and the paper bag in the other, she went to the top of the stair and looked down over it. She could see the blue edge of the open door, and the top of a dusty black felt hat with a little bunch of mauve flowers on one side of it, and a black coat, foreshortened because the stair was so steep that she was very nearly straight overhead, and a pair of hands in black kid gloves, the right hand holding an umbrella with an ebony crook, and the left hand holding a shabby black suède bag. Just for a moment she was so frozen with horror that she couldn't have moved to save her life. The hat, the umbrella, the handbag, and the gloves were as familiar as if they had been her own. But they weren't her own. She wouldn't have been seen dead in a ditch with them. They were Miss Maltby's.

It was frightful, it was unbelievable, but there didn't seem to be any way out of believing it. Miss Maltby had chosen this moment to inspect Miss Pocklington's premises and cast a fostering eye upon Chippy. *And that meant that she would be coming up into the studio.*

At her first movement in the direction of the stair Shirley became galvanised into terrified activity. Her brain raced. She was gone from the top of the stair in a flash. Her suit-case stood out in the middle of the floor. She snatched it up and sent it with a sliding push behind the neatest of those leaning canvases. The biscuit broke against the handle and fell in scattered crumbs and fragments. There was no time to pick them up. There was no time for anything at all except a dive behind the green circles, the blood-red pyramids, and the yellow hexagons of the Potato Field.

She reached the dusty space and crouched in it, still clutching the paper bag in her left hand. The rough stretched canvas tilted back against her hair, her cheek. A smell of paint, and fluff, and soot came up into her nose and throat. Miss Maltby's step sounded upon the studio floor.

Shirley was so frightened that all her natural reactions to dust, and soot, and paint, and a tickle at the back of the nose were at a standstill. They were not in fact reactions at all, because they had entirely stopped acting. The tickle was there, the smell of dust which had produced it was there, but the fear which was freezing her froze these things too.

If she stopped being frozen she would probably sneeze. She went on being frozen.

Miss Maltby's head and shoulders emerged through the square hole in the studio floor. She stood like that for quite a minute, sending her sharp glances darting to and fro. No one downstairs. No one up here. No one at all. She must have been mistaken. Something had said to her when she saw that young Wrenn go out of the house with what she was convinced was a suit-case belonging to Shirley Dale—something had said to her, quite loud and plain, "He has the key of Helena Pocklington's studio. Suppose he takes that girl *there*. *What* would Helena say?" Something had said this quite plainly. Intuition. Woman's intuition. Now it appeared, most annoyingly, that woman's intuition had let her down. She climbed the rest of the stairs and took another look round. There really was nobody there. Nobody, that is, except Helena's canary. She advanced a step or two into the room, looked up at the cage, and saw Chippy regarding her with a black unwinking eye. She made a little chirruping sound at him, to which he did not respond.

Miss Maltby turned from the cage and looked about her. Bits of biscuit lying about on the floor. Waste. Litter. The bird appeared to be well fed. That young Wrenn was evidently coming here regularly. The water-tin had been freshly filled, the cage was clean. She felt decidedly disappointed about this. If the canary had been neglected, it would have been her plain duty to write and acquaint Helena with the fact. It was always pleasant to do one's duty. It would have been pleasanter still if the bird had been dead of neglect. Helena was absurdly soft about that young Wrenn. She didn't show it, but you can't deceive a friend of fifty years standing. Helena was soft about him. Helena had probably made a will leaving him money. Taxed with this, she had not denied it, but merely shrugged her shoulders and said in a downright unpleasant manner, "Well, it's my own money, isn't it?" A queer cold gleam came into Miss Maltby's small grey eyes, a queer cold resentment rose in her. The thought of a will—anybody's will—brought her Grievance before her so strongly, so clearly, that she found it difficult to control herself. She began to walk up and down, clutching the black crook of her umbrella, and the black handle of her bag, whilst thoughts about the Grievance poured into her mind, bubbling, frothing, and boiling there, until they forced their way into speech.

Shirley crouched behind the Potato Field, and heard those uneven, pattering steps go to and fro. And then the words began to come—one here and there at first, disjointed, coming out like a plop of steam from a kettle which is boiling over, then running into crazy broken sentences. The terror which had sent her diving for shelter had been the terror of arrest—of Miss Maltby screaming out of the window for the police, of a heavy gloved hand on her shoulder, and of all the heads in the Mews popping out to see her being taken away to prison. It was enough to make anyone afraid, especially when they had been running away from that very fear for the last twenty-four hours. No, not twenty-four hours until six o'clock—about twenty-two hours, and quite long enough. It felt more like weeks. *"Time lengthened to an endless, timeless span."* Where had she read that? Somewhere—it didn't matter where. Anyhow that was what it felt like.

That was what she had been afraid of—not Miss Maltby herself, but the policeman behind Miss Maltby. But now the fear was changing, not all at once, but little by little, as those pattering steps went up and down and the voice went muttering by. Or rather, it was not so much a change as a withdrawal of one fear whilst another drew slowly on to take its place. The old fear was there in the background, but the new one stared her in the face with cold, light eyes. It was the fear of Miss Maltby herself. And after a few minutes of this new fear she yearned towards the solid comfort of a policeman. Because Miss Maltby was mad. She was certainly quite, quite mad.

Up and down she went, to and fro, pattering jerkily, and talking in a loud angry whisper to Jane Rigg—Shirley's half-sister Jane, who had been dead for six months.

"You shouldn't have done it. No—no—you shouldn't. You've let me down, Jane Rigg. There's never been anyone so badly let down before. You can't say there has. All that money. All those millions. Millions, Jane!" The voice went up into a sharp, thin sound like a bat's cry. "Just another six months. Six months. Only six months. If you'd taken care of yourself. But you wouldn't. I wanted you to. But you wouldn't. You didn't care about *me*—did you, Jane Rigg? You didn't care. You didn't care. If you'd lived another six months, there'd have been all that money between you and Shirley Dale. All that money! Millions! Millions! And once you'd got your share it would have come to me. Millions! To me!

You could have died then if you'd wanted to. It wouldn't have mattered then. Six months! Six months too soon! It's no good saying you left me what you had. It's no good, Jane! Two hundred a year and the cottage. Two hundred a year! And all those millions to Shirley Dale! Another six months and I'd have had half! It's no good, Jane Rigg! No good! You could have lived six months. If you'd tried. You didn't try. Said you were tired. I won't forgive you. You needn't think I'll forgive you. Because I won't. All that money to Shirley Dale!" The footsteps stopped in the middle of the floor. The voice dropped low, not muttering any longer, but bitter and hard. "*She shan't have it. She shan't have it. She shan't have it!* He said she shouldn't have it. They'll give me my share. Not half. No, not half. Not what I ought to have had. Why not? Why *not*?" The voice rambled off again, "They'd better take care. They'd better not upset me. They'd better treat me fair. Do you hear that, Mr Phillips? You'd better treat me fair. Because I know more than you think. I could put you in prison. Oh yes, I could. Ettie too. And then she won't get anything. None of us would. But I won't do it. As long as I get my share. And why shouldn't it be half? Why shouldn't it be my own proper half? That ought to have come to me from Jane."

Shirley crouched down behind the picture of the Potato Field. Her left arm had begun to feel as if it was broken. She was leaning on it with her hand on the bag of biscuits. A broken biscuit was running into the palm of her hand. The edge was like the edge of a knife. All her weight was on the hand and on her left knee. Something was boring into her kneecap. It felt like the head of a nail. The tickle in her nose, which seemed to have been going on for about a hundred years, had now reached the point at which a shattering sneeze might at any moment explode. The rest of her was still more or less frozen with terror, but the sneeze was rapidly unfreezing, and mad and absorbed as the Maltby was, she wouldn't be able to help noticing the sort of sneeze it was going to be. At the expense of driving the nail and the biscuit deeper into her she managed to get her right hand up to her nose. If savage maltreatment could deter it from sneezing, savage maltreatment it should have. She pinched and wrung until the tears ran down her cheeks. The sneeze hung in the balance and was checked.

Flinching and gasping, Shirley drew breath. Sounds from the studio had ceased to reach her, but that did not mean that there had not been any sounds. She released her nose, and wished urgently that she might solace it with a sniff. And then the paroxysm was upon her. There was no help in pinching and wringing now. She sneezed with a violence beyond belief, and went on sneezing until she had no breath left. After which there seemed to be nothing to do except to crawl ignominiously out from behind the Potato Field.

Chapter Twenty-Five

THE STUDIO was empty.

Shirley got to her feet and looked about her with incredulous relief. There was only the empty floor, the stacked canvases, and Chippy in his cage. There was no Miss Maltby. She could go on sneezing, she could sniff as loud as she liked—there was only the canary to hear her. Of course, now that it didn't matter, she no longer wanted either to sniff or to sneeze. She only wanted to know what had happened to Miss Maltby.

She ran to the window which looked out in front, and saw the whisk of a black skirt and a bit of a black umbrella just vanishing round the corner. A frightfully urgent question now arose. Was it the skirt and the umbrella of someone who was hurrying to fetch the police, or was it not? In other words, had Miss Maltby gone away before the sneeze or because of it? She might have gone whilst Shirley was still wringing and pinching her nose and therefore much too much taken up with the horrible disaster of that impending sneeze to notice anything that was going on in the studio, or she might have rushed away terrified after the sneeze had actually broken loose. She couldn't possibly have known that the sneeze belonged to Shirley Dale, but if she thought there was someone hiding in the studio she would probably go and fetch the police just the same.

Shirley stared at the corner and tried to remember exactly how the skirt and the umbrella had vanished. Were they in a frightful hurry as if they were rushing to the police-station, or were they just pattering along in the Maltby's usual undecided way? Shirley thought they had been pattering, but she wasn't sure enough to feel happy about it or to leave the window.

Chippy said "Tweet" behind her in a tentative sort of way, and then Anthony Leigh came into sight. Shirley's heart gave an ecstatic jump. She ran down the steep stair and unlatched the door. The moment, the very moment, Anthony touched the knocker she would open the door and let him in. He couldn't be much longer coming now. But supposing he didn't know which door to come to. Of course Jas would have told him. He wouldn't be coming at all if he hadn't seen Jas. And there was only one blue door—he couldn't possibly miss it.

The key moved in the lock. She flung the door wide open, and there was Anthony quite large and real on the doorstep. He didn't wait to take out the key. He flung an arm round her and kissed her, and she had to pull him in, and remind him about the key, and bang the door, all with a frightfully beating heart, because she wanted to kiss him quite as much as he wanted to kiss her.

"Oh, *Anthony*!"

Anthony kissed her and laughed, and kissed her again, and shook her, and said,

"Horrible child! Where have you been?"

"Running away," said Shirley with a deep sigh of content.

Anthony had both arms right round her. She could just reach his shoulder. She found it very comforting. They stood in the narrow place between the front door and the bottom of the stair and rocked to and fro. Sometimes he kissed her, and sometimes she kissed him.

She said, "I ran away," and sighed again.

"I know you did, you little fiend. What do you suppose I felt like when I got down to Ledlington and found you'd gone? Why did you do it?"

"A poster about a disappearing girl and the police having a clue, and I thought it was me. And I thought—no, I didn't think—I just hared for a train, and dithered all the way up to town. And then someone had left a paper in the railway refreshment-room, and the girl wasn't me at all, so I rushed to a telephone-box and tried to catch you, but by the time I'd got through to Ledlington you'd gone. And there I was with your suitcase and those awful emeralds. *Darling*, I forgot! You don't *know* the worst! I haven't *told* you about the emeralds! It's *too* awful!"

He said quickly, "Aunt Agnes told me they were gone. She let it off like a bomb just when I'd been really clever and slipped the diamond brooch down between the back and seat of her sofa. I did it while I was kissing her, and I was still patting myself on the back when she burst the bomb. As a matter of fact there were two bombs, because when I put out a suggestion that the brooch was probably only mislaid, she said they'd had the carpets up and all the covers off, and anyhow what about the emeralds, which were hidden in her stocking drawer and only you and Possett knew where they were."

Shirley raised an indignant head.

"I expect everyone in the house knew! I'm dead certain that girl Bessie did. She's the sort of girl who knows everything, but I suppose I oughtn't to say that, because she had a very good character. But, Anthony—it's definitely grim for me, because when Mrs Hathaway came to tea on Wednesday she was talking about the emeralds, how valuable they were, and Mrs Huddleston sent me up to fetch them. Possett took them out of the stocking drawer in front of me, and I helped her put them away again afterwards. It's *frightfully* grim."

"Yes—she told me that," said Anthony.

They moved a little apart and looked at each other. Shirley sat down on the bottom step but one because her knees were shaking. Anthony sat down beside her.

"I gather you've got the emeralds. Where did you find them?"

She put her head on his shoulder again.

"In the hem of my coat—same like the diamond brooch, only the other side. I suppose I was a perfect fool not to find them before, but I hardly ever stopped running away for ten seconds except just when you were proposing to me, and—"

"When did you find them?"

Shirley took a long breath and considered.

"It was only this morning really—it seems like weeks and weeks ago."

"Where are they now?"

"Didn't Jas tell you? They're in your suit-case—in the pocket of your pyjamas—the ones you lent me. Because I thought, supposing I was arrested—well, it was your suit-case, and your pyjamas, and your aunt, and I thought it might look a little better than if I had them. Besides I wanted to get rid of them. Suppose they'd been stolen—I mean suppose someone had stolen them from me—it would just about have put the lid on. But, darling, where's Jas? Because he was to find you, and give you the cloakroom ticket so that you could fetch away the suit-case—and if he didn't find you, and you haven't seen him, how did you know I was here?"

"He found me all right. He got me on the telephone. I told him he'd better go and collect the suit-case whilst I came straight here."

Shirley giggled against a masterful shoulder.

"Poor Jas!"

"Why?"

"Well, it isn't his suit-case."

"And you're not his girl!"

There was an interlude. Then Shirley said,

"What are we going to do next? I mean when Jas comes along with the emeralds. What are we going to do about them?"

"Ah!" said Anthony. "That's where we're up against it. Speaking roughly, we can either tell the truth or think up a really good lie."

"I'd rather tell the truth," said Shirley in a tone of modest virtue.

Anthony sat back against the banisters and surveyed her. There was a lot of dust on the side of her hair, and two or three fierce smears on her forehead and cheek. Her nose was still rather pink from being pinched. He had never seen her look so plain before, but as he loved her more than ever, the smudges and the pinkness were rather gratifying, because they made him feel quite sure that he wasn't just in love with Shirley, he loved her. He looked at her, all pale, and dishevelled, and dusty, and loved her dreadfully.

"I'd *rather* tell the truth," she said again, and this time her voice didn't sound priggish, but quite simple and a little frightened.

He took one of her hands and held it.

"All right, you take the emeralds, and walk in on Aunt Agnes and tell her where you found them."

Shirley blinked rather hard.

"I'd l-like to—but I d-don't think I can."

"Well, I wouldn't like to, and I'm quite sure I'm not going to try. Aunt Agnes doesn't know the truth when she sees it—she never has, she never will. You know what she's like as well as I do—she talks all the time, and she doesn't say what she thinks, she thinks what she has just heard herself say. I don't think she's got anything to think with.

She just talks, and when she hears herself talking she believes what she hears—every word of it. And you see, she has said several times that you must have taken the emeralds, so now she believes it firmly. If we told her the truth, she'd simply ring for Possett and tell her to call up the police-station."

It was all quite true—one of those depressing truths. Shirley said in a discouraged voice,

"Well, what *are* we going to do?"

"Get the things back into the house and persuade her they never left it."

"But you did that with the diamond brooch."

"I know, I know—you needn't rub it in. It was a perfectly sound scheme, and if it hadn't been for Possett being in such a devil of a hurry to turn the room out, and the emeralds being missing, and one thing and another—"

Shirley made a fleeting Woggy Doodle—not one of her best—a mere hurried sketch.

"I know—it went wrong on you. Plans do. But, darling, you can't put any more brooches and necklaces and things down the sides of the chairs and sofas, because even Possett would smell a rat if you did—especially if she's had all the covers off. And I expect she's turned out everything in Mrs Huddleston's bedroom. She's a sort of human ant, you know—*frightfully* thorough and persevering. So it's all very well to say get them back into the house, but what are you going to do with them when you've got them back? That's the question."

Anthony laughed.

"And the answer is I haven't the slightest idea, but something will probably turn up. And now I've got something really important to talk to you about."

Shirley clapped her hands together.

"Oh, but so have I! And she may be back at any minute *with* the police—only, I don't really think so, because I'm practically certain she must have gone before I began to sneeze or she wouldn't have been going round the corner by the time I got to the window, if you see what I mean."

"I don't in the least. How can I? I don't know what you're talking about."

Shirley caught him by the arm and pinched.

"The Maltby, darling. Where's the trained legal mind? Because it had better get going on the Maltby. She's got a key to this place, because she went to school with Jas's aunt, or cousin, or whatever she is. And she and Jas look after the canary when Miss Pocklington's away—at least Jas looks after it really, and the Maltby snoops round to make sure he's doing it properly. And this was one of her snooping days, only when she got here she didn't snoop—she just walked up and down and raved about Jane Rigg, and how she'd done her out of millions by dying six months too soon. You've no idea how she went on. She must be absolutely mad—"

Anthony put out a hand and stopped her.

"Wait a minute—this is important. I want you to try and remember exactly what she said."

Shirley stared at him.

"She was just raving. I've never been so frightened in my life. I quite *longed* for a policeman."

He said quickly, "Do you mean she saw you—she knows you're here?"

"No. I was behind one of the Pocklington woman's pictures—a most frightful thing—and I'm practically sure she had gone before I began to sneeze. You've no idea what a lot of dust there is in that studio. Jas isn't at all a good housemaid."

Anthony leaned forward and shot the bolt at the bottom of Miss Pocklington's bright blue door.

"Is there a back way out?"

She nodded.

"Because you mustn't be caught here in case she *has* gone to the police. Now listen! Was your mother's name Jane Lorimer?"

"Yes. Why? I told you."

"I remembered the name when I saw it in the paper to-day."

"In the paper?"

Anthony took both her hands and held them.

"Don't talk—listen. Listen, Shirley! Jane Lorimer had a cousin named William Ambrose Merewether. He went to America and made a lot of money there, and he's left that money first to Jane if she's alive, and secondly to Jane's children if any of them are alive, and thirdly to Jane's grandchildren—all *on condition—*"

"*What?*" said Shirley in a whisper. Her hands were shaking.

"*On condition* that none of them has ever been in prison on a criminal charge. No, I put that badly—any one that's been in prison is disqualified, and the others take the lot."

"*What?*"

"Yes," said Anthony. "So you mustn't go to prison."

"I mustn't?"

"You most particularly mustn't. You see, your mother Jane Lorimer is dead, and all her six children are dead except you, so all William Ambrose Merewether's money is due to come to you, provided— *provided* you can keep out of prison until after the will has been proved."

Shirley pulled away her hands and pressed them over her eyes. She wanted to be in the dark and think, but her hands didn't make a darkness, and she didn't seem to be able to do anything with her thoughts. She looked at Anthony and said,

"Say it again."

He said it again, and added,

"If your half-sister Jane Rigg had lived another six months she would have had half. That's why Miss Maltby raved—Jane left her everything, and the everything might have been half the Merewether millions."

Shirley said, "I see—" And then, "But she wouldn't get anything *now*—if I went to prison."

"That's just it," said Anthony. "Who would?"

She frowned in a puzzled way. He went on insistently.

"You're the last of the children. If you're disqualified, who comes next? The will says Jane Lorimer's grandchildren. But are there any? That's what I want to know. Did any of Jane Lorimer's children marry and leave a child or children?"

"Perrine did," said Shirley.

"Perrine—" Anthony searched his mind.... Of course—the French child of Jane Lorimer's second marriage.

They were facing each other on the narrow stair, Anthony on the outside, Shirley against the wall. He leaned forward a little.

"Yes—Perrine—you said she was dead."

"Ages ago." Her breath caught in her throat. "Ages, and ages, and ages ago. But she got married first, and she had a baby—Aunt Emily told me."

"Who did she marry?"

"He was French—or Swiss—I don't know which. He had a French name—Meunier. And she died when her baby was born."

"And the child—what happened to it? Was it a boy or a girl?"

"Girl," said Shirley. "Pierrette—Pierrette Meunier. I don't know what's become of her. Aunt Emily didn't know."

"We'll have to find out. It won't be difficult. If she's alive she'll come forward. She'll want to find out whether she's got a claim under this will."

But suppose she knew too much already—then she wouldn't come forward. She'd lie low for a bit and allow herself to be found. Only she had no claim unless Shirley was disqualified. It all came back to that. Someone was undoubtedly trying to land Shirley in prison. If Shirley went to prison, Shirley was disqualified. If Shirley was disqualified, Pierrette Meunier would get the Merewether millions. He wanted to know a lot more about Pierrette Meunier.

"You can't tell me anything more about her? Do you know how old she is?"

"Yes—I can tell you that. Perrine was born in '86, and she married when she was only seventeen. She died on her eighteenth birthday—Aunt Emily always remembered that. So how old does that make Pierrette?"

"You said Perrine was born in '86? That would put Pierrette's birth in 1904, so she's thirty-one."

Shirley nodded.

"Isn't it grim to have a niece of thirty-one?"

Anthony's jaw fell.

"Of course—she's your niece! Good lord, darling—what a family!"

"Isn't it! It depresses me frightfully when I think that for all I know she's been married for years and I'm a great-aunt. If she got married at seventeen like her mother, I could have ten or eleven great-nephews and nieces. It makes me feel about three hundred and fifty. I don't see how you can possibly marry a great-aunt, darling. Do you? Especially a great-aunt who is trembling on the verge of a prison cell."

Anthony put his arms round her again.

"You're not to talk like that—I don't like it."

"Shall talk any way I want to," said Shirley in rather a submerged voice, because she was being kissed. "Shan't marry you at all if you're going to be a trampler. What's the good of being a great-aunt if you're not respected?"

Anthony rubbed his cheek against hers.

"Do you want to be respected?"

"*Frightfully.*"

"Well, you won't be. Anyhow I'm not marrying you because you're a great-aunt."

"Perhaps you're not marrying me at all."

"Oh yes, I am."

"Why?"

If Shirley was fishing, she fished in vain. Anthony said firmly,

"For the Merewether millions of course."

Chapter Twenty-Six

Miss Maltby was not on her way to the police-station. Her thoughts were still in a state of agitated confusion, and she was, as Shirley had surmised, pattering, but she had nevertheless quite a definite idea of where she was going and what she was going to do when she got there. She was going to see Alfred Phillips at his hotel, and she was going to tell him quite plainly, *and* firmly, *and* decidedly that what he was offering her was not enough. It was not enough. It was not nearly, nearly, nearly enough.

She turned another corner and pattered on, her head poking forward in its shabby black hat with the faded bunch of heliotrope on one side of it. Jane had had the heliotrope on a summer hat five, no six, years ago—1929, a very fine summer. Jane had thrown the flowers away. Wasteful, because they were perfectly good. Always a little inclined to be wasteful, Jane Rigg. And here were the flowers, still perfectly serviceable, perfectly good.

She pattered on.

Alfred Phillips must be made to see reason. It had come to her as she walked up and down in Helena's studio that nothing less than a half share was her right, her absolute Legal Right. If Jane had lived Jane would have had half, and she was Jane's Residuary Legatee. Executrix and Residuary Legatee. What a pleasant sound—what an extremely pleasant sound that had. But it wasn't what it ought to have been if Jane had done her duty and lived for another six months.

She went on thinking of all the things she was going to say to Alfred Phillips when she reached the hotel. She hoped he wouldn't be out. It would really be very awkward if he were out, because she wanted to make it quite clear to him at once that the half share was her Legal Right. And then there was something about that young Wrenn. That was important too. She had distrusted him from the very beginning, and Alfred Phillips ought to know what he was up to. It would be another proof that they couldn't get on without her, and that she had earned her share—though of course she didn't have to earn it, because it was her Legal Right. But all the same Alfred Phillips ought to be very, very grateful to her.

If Al Phillips had any feelings of gratitude towards Miss Maltby, they were not in evidence when she looked round the door into the small over-heated room where he and Ettie Miller were sitting over the gas fire. If he managed to conceal a sharp annoyance, it was as much as he had time for, since Miss Maltby had preceded the hotel servant and appeared without any warning. She must certainly be aware that he had been sitting on the arm of Ettie's chair. Those pale darting eyes of hers missed nothing. And what brought her here when it was of all things in the world most important that none of them should be seen together? Women were the very devil when it came to business. Take Ettie—it was all very well for her to be fond of him, but they oughtn't to be here together like this—not now, not at this juncture. And could he get her to see it? No, he couldn't. Never had she been fonder of him or more clinging. And now this old Maltby, who was more than half crazy and about as safe to handle as gunpowder, she must needs come butting in too. He'd had to use her—why, with her Grievance, she was practically asking to be used—but all the same if he'd known how cranky she was, he wasn't so sure that he wouldn't have given her a miss.

He came a step to meet her, and saw her eyes go darting past him. As he had supposed, they missed nothing. Ettie Miller had taken off her hat, and that dark hair of hers was rumpled, decidedly rumpled. The arm of her chair had a pressed-down sort of look. Goings on—that's what there'd been, and they needn't think they could throw dust in her eyes, because they couldn't. A pretty fool Ettie Miller looked with her flushed cheeks and her untidy hair, and a pretty fool she'd be if she let Alfred Phillips get round her for the sake of the money, because that was what he was up to, and you didn't need half an eye to see it unless you were a silly vain fool like Ettie.

Miss Maltby's eyes glittered with contempt as she minced forward and shook hands. Men. What did any woman want with them? Noisy. Inconvenient. Domineering. And up to no good the minute you took your eye off them. As Ettie would find out. Oh yes, quick enough. If she was such a fool as to let Alfred Phillips get his fingers into her purse. She knew his sort. He needn't think she didn't. Or that he could frighten her by frowning, and looking down his nose, and telling her she oughtn't to have come. For that was what he was actually doing. No gratitude. Not a bit. Not even the offer of a chair. Nothing but a sharp "Look here, Miss Maltby, this won't do at all, it really won't. You mustn't come here."

If they didn't offer her a chair, she would take one. She sat herself down by the fire, laid her umbrella on the floor, settled herself comfortably, and said,

"I oughtn't to have come? That's all you know about it. I'd a very good reason for coming."

Al Phillips did not sit down. He stood with his hands in his pockets jingling his money and looking put out.

"Well, let's have it—because you mustn't stay."

Miss Maltby unbuttoned her coat. The fire was hot, and she had no intention of being hurried. She was aware that Ettie was suppressing a laugh, and set it down against her.

"I'll go when I've finished," she said. "Not before. Not one moment before, Mr Phillips. Not one single moment."

Al Phillips took his hands out of his pockets. It was no good, he'd have to humour her. He said in a would-be pleasant manner,

"Well, what's it all about, Miss Maltby?"

She sat up straight, her black-gloved fingers on the clasp of the shabby suède bag. She spoke in a sharp, thin voice.

"I hope I'm business-like, Mr Phillips. Men always think that women are not business-like, but I hope I can be as business-like as any man. In my opinion women have a greater aptitude for business than men."

"And your business?" He managed to keep his tone smooth.

"There are two points. The first is about my Share. I am not satisfied. Oh, not at all. Very far from satisfied. If I had been a man, you would not have tried to put me off with less than my Legal Share."

Miss Ettie Miller rolled her fine dark eyes in an expressive manner. They said quite plainly, "Here's a pretty kettle of fish!"

"Your legal share?" inquired Mr Phillips. "What are you talking about? You haven't got one."

Miss Maltby began to snap the clasp of her bag. Her fingers were bony but very strong. They clicked the bag open, and they clicked it shut—click, click, click, and click, click, click again.

"No?" she said.

"Certainly not," said Al Phillips.

"Perhaps the police will say I have."

"Nobody could possibly say you had."

Miss Maltby went on clicking. If Jane Rigg had lived, she would have had half. And no risk.

"I am Jane Rigg's Residuary Legatee. And Executrix. *And* Executrix. I have a Legal Right to Jane's share."

Ettie Miller leaned forward. She said in a soothing voice,

"We haven't any of us got anything yet, Miss Maltby. You'll get your share all right when it comes to shelling out."

Miss Maltby darted suspicion and dislike at her.

"My Legal Share?"

"Of course. Why, Mr Phillips is in a law firm—you know that. He'll have it all as legal as can be. But it's no use going into it now, because we haven't got the money yet, and if you were to do anything silly like going to the police, we shouldn't get it. And then what would happen to your Share as you call it?"

Miss Maltby stopped clicking for a minute. Her eyes became feed upon Ettie's. A cunning look passed over her face.

"That is a point. That is certainly a point. A woman's business sense is more acute than a man's. If I go to the police, there will be no Share. Because, though of course it is my *Legal* Share, the whole transaction is not quite as legal as it might be. I take your meaning. Or perhaps I don't." She frowned a little. The cunning look was succeeded by a vague one. The fingers relaxed, slipping away from the bag into her lap. "I don't know. It's all very confusing when you put it like that. I must think it over."

"That's right," said Al Phillips. "You go down to that cottage of yours at Emshot and think it over. I thought you were going there yesterday. Why didn't you?"

The vague look passed.

"Oh, but I did. I went down last night."

"Then why didn't you stay there?"

Miss Maltby pulled herself up.

"Really, Mr Phillips!" Then, offence swept away by what she had to tell, "I went down. And she was there. That girl was there."

"What girl?" said Al Phillips coldly.

"Shirley Dale." Miss Maltby's whisper was piercingly distinct.

"Miss Maltby—you don't mean that!"

She nodded triumphantly.

"There. In my house. In my kitchen. And I thought it was Mrs Ward who does for me. And she ran away out of the back door. And she left her bag and her hat. More like a cap than a hat. Such things as girls wear! Anything to get themselves noticed!"

Her manner shook Mr Phillips. If she wasn't raving—if it was true—

"How do you know the things were hers?" he said.

Miss Maltby gave a thin laugh.

"Men don't notice these things. Women do. Every day for months that cap's gone past my door. On that girl's head. Of course I know it. And the bag. There was a letter in it." She clicked open her own bag, picked out an envelope by one corner, and held it out. "It was in the bag. Miss Shirley Dale. From her old Aunt Emily's cook. To say she hoped her dear Miss Shirley is well." She laughed again. "Seeing is believing, Mr Phillips."

Mr Phillips believed. But he didn't see what sense there was in Miss Maltby coming along here to tell him about something which happened yesterday. Anything that could have been done about it should have been done then. He said so. He said with acerbity,

"What's the good of coming out with all this now? You ought to have rung up the police last night."

Miss Maltby bridled.

"And how do you know I didn't?"

"Did you?" There was a gleam of hope in his eye. If she had—

"No telephone," said Miss Maltby brightly.

It would have given Mr Phillips a great deal of pleasure to shake her. He said with great restraint,

"What *did* you do?"

"Nothing," she said. "Nothing at all. Why should I? There wasn't anything to do. Not till to-day. Then I came back to town. To see you."

It wasn't any good being angry with her. She could go to the police with her story now. It oughtn't to be so difficult to trace Shirley Dale from Emshot. She wouldn't have enough money to go very far afield. He said,

"Well, you'd better go along to the police now. Take the bag and the cap with you and say where you found them. I suppose you've had them round at Findon Road making inquiries?"

"Oh yes. Yes. Certainly. They searched her room. A pity they found nothing. It would have been better that way. I said so all along. Women have more finesse than men. Much more."

"Better be getting along," said Mr Phillips coldly.

"Not yet," said Miss Maltby with composure. "Not just yet. Not till I've told you about that young Wrenn. And the suit-case."

"What suit-case?"

"Shirley Dale's."

"Who the devil's Wrenn?"

"Language!" said Miss Maltby. "You interrupt. I'm telling you. Helena Pocklington's cousin. Room opposite mine. Rude, scowling young man. Infatuated with Shirley Dale."

"What's all this got to do with her suit-case?"

Ettie was leaning back in her chair between boredom and amusement. The old Maltby woman provided the boredom, but it amused her to see Al baited and afraid to let his temper go.

Miss Maltby was very bright in her manner—like a governess with a pettish child.

"I'm telling you. If you will listen. I heard him go upstairs into her room. It is over mine. I heard him distinctly. Moving about. Then I heard him come down. Right down. To the front door. When I looked over the banisters, there he was. Going out of the door with that girl's suit-case in his hand."

She had them both interested now. They couldn't do without her. No, no—not at all.

"Did you follow him?" said Al Phillips.

"No hat," said Miss Maltby with regret. "No coat. No gloves. Too much attention would have been attracted. A woman thinks of these things. By the time I had dressed no sign of him. No sign at all. But I am convinced he has gone to meet that girl."

"Sounds like it," said Ettie Miller. She yawned. "I don't see what we can do about it."

Miss Maltby darted a look of contempt at her.

"I shall inform the police. The young man must be called to account. As soon as I was dressed I went round to Helena Pocklington's. She lives at Pattenham Mews and is at present abroad."

"Why on earth?"

"He goes there to feed the canary. He has a key. It occurred to me that the girl might be there. A woman's intuition."

"Well?"

Miss Maltby coughed.

"The house appeared to be empty. If you can call it a house. Most inconvenient, and such a steep stair. I came away."

"Because there wasn't anyone there?"

The vague look passed over Miss Maltby's face again.

"No. No. Not exactly. It came over me that I was not satisfied. About my Share, you know. My Legal Share."

"Al, for *mercy's* sake!" said Ettie. Her eyes rolled in protest.

Mr Phillips rose to the occasion. He produced a notebook and an air of cold efficiency.

"Thanks, Miss Maltby," he said. "What Mews did you say? I'll just take down the address, and then you'd better go straight to the police-station. You don't want the girl to get away—do you?"

The vague look passed. Miss Maltby picked up her umbrella and began to button her coat.

"I shall have to go home. To get the bag and cap."

"Yes, yes—you'd better hurry."

He came back after seeing her out, to find Ettie turning down the fire.

"If I have to see much of that woman, Al, you'll have to put me in an asylum," she said.

"I wish she was in one," said Mr Phillips gloomily.

Chapter Twenty-Seven

JASPER WRENN RETRIEVED Anthony's suit-case without difficulty. Put like that, there is nothing in it, but to Jasper the affair was by no means a simple one. First of all there was a state of homicidal jealousy to be reckoned with. What sort of right had Anthony to send him off to fetch suit-cases whilst he went to Shirley? It wasn't Jasper's suit-case. It wasn't even Shirley's suit-case. It was Mr Anthony Leigh's suit-case. And Mr Anthony Leigh couldn't do his own fetching and carrying. In the calmest manner in the world he sent other people on his errands— people who had a great deal more right to be with Shirley than he had. Well, that was where the point went sharply home. Had they? Had they more right? No, not they—he. Had he any right at all? Did Shirley want him, or did she want this damned fellow who sent him fagging across London as if he were a schoolboy? Jasper's blood boiled. The worst part of the whole thing was that when Anthony said, "Go!" he had gone. He hadn't said, "Fetch your own suit-case and be damned to you!" He hadn't said anything at all, and whilst he was still thinking of something to say, Anthony had hung up at the other end of the line and he had been left. If the suit-case hadn't been in some sort Shirley's, and if it hadn't been she herself who had entrusted him with the ticket, he would have turned back half way. As it was, he went on.

But from the moment he entered the station a most unwelcome change came over his feelings. It is, no doubt, exceedingly unpleasant to feel like the hunted criminal upon whose shoulder the hand of the law may at any moment come crashing down. The stolen emeralds were in the suit-case. He was here for the express purpose of receiving stolen property. Suppose Shirley had been traced. Suppose a detective was watching the left-luggage office. Suppose they let him claim it and then arrested him ... "Jasper Wrenn, author"—even at this awful moment it gave him a thrill to think of being so described in print—"of 14 Findon Road, was charged with being in unlawful possession of the historic emeralds recently stolen from Mrs Huddleston—" Not well put—not at all well put. "The property of Mrs Huddleston" was better. Not that it mattered how it was put. He would be done for, branded. And as he couldn't possibly explain how the emeralds came to be in his possession he would certainly be convicted and sent to prison. He wondered what the sentence would be, and what Helena Pocklington would say. But it did not now occur to him to go back and tell Anthony Leigh to do his own dirty work.

In the neighbourhood of the left-luggage office he began to feel extremely sick. As if it had not already tormented him enough, his imagination now presented him with the sordid picture of Jasper Wrenn, author, being violently sick at the moment of his arrest. Fortunately for those who have to contend with this kind of imagination, what really happens however bad comes more or less as a relief. Nothing is in reality quite as unpleasant as fancy paints it. In this instance the reality was most blessedly tame and prosaic. A green and quaking Jasper produced Shirley's ticket, said in a tense undertone, "A suit-case. Initials A.L." and after quite a brief delay received the said suit-case and walked away with it.

If the bag had concealed a corpse, Jasper would not have felt guiltier. A momentary relief was succeeded by new visions of doom. Somebody was probably trailing him. They had let him get away with the case because they had wanted to see where he would go with it. In books it was always quite easy to find out whether you were being trailed or not. You nipped round a corner, lurked in a doorway, and then watched to see who went by.

Jasper proceeded to put this simple plan into practice. He found quite a suitable doorway, lurked there with a chilly tremor inside him, and waited to see what would happen. A man in a bowler hat went by, then a woman in a brown coat, then a pert-looking girl with an aggressively scarlet mouth. None of these people looked like sleuths, but of course if sleuths did look like sleuths they wouldn't be much use. The only one of the three who appeared to notice Jasper at all was the girl, but he didn't think she was noticing him as a person. She had the kind of eye that rolls automatically when a young man comes in sight. He thought he was just a young man, not a criminal fleeing from justice.

No one else turned the corner. He was just going to pick up the suit-case and go on, when he made a most frightful discovery. His nose had begun to bleed. From childhood agitation had had this effect upon him. There had been times when he had found it extremely-useful. Slight attacks could be induced at will, and had been instrumental in delivering him from sermons, family gatherings, and other undesired entertainments. A genuine attack had once saved him from a flogging. This was a genuine attack—a violent and most uncontrollable attack.

He turned his back on the road, pressed his pocket-handkerchief firmly to his nose, and waited for the affliction to pass. He hoped that anyone who happened to go by would imagine that he was merely blowing it.

By the time that the attack was over his handkerchief was in no state to be seen. Impossible to go on to the Mews like this. Impossible to confront Anthony Leigh in Shirley's presence with a smeared and pallid countenance and a sanguinary rag in one's pocket. He must return to Findon Road, wash his face, and provide himself with another handkerchief—several other handkerchiefs.

Miss Maltby saw him come in. She had visited the police-station, and now sat at her window peering down the street and awaiting developments. Would that young Wrenn return? If he did not return, it would most undoubtedly mean that he was with that girl. It would be her duty to write to Helena Pocklington and tell her so. She saw Jasper turn the corner and come up the road carrying a suit-case, and at this point surprise and curiosity became almost unbearable. He had gone out of the house with a suit-case after lunch, and he was coming back to the house with a suit-case now. But it wasn't the same suit-case. Oh no. Oh dear no. You couldn't deceive her. You couldn't possibly deceive her. It wasn't the same suit-case. Not at all. The first suit-case was that girl's suit-case. A cheap affair. Shabby. One corner damaged. This was a much better case. Larger. Newer. Quite a different affair altogether. Her eyes darted questions at Jasper until they lost him at the front door.

She was just going to turn away from the window and go tiptoe to the door for a closer view, when someone else turned into Findon Road right down at the far end, a mere speck in the distance. But a speck would have to be very small indeed to escape Miss Maltby. Especially when it wore a policeman's uniform. At the far end of Findon Road a policeman had just turned the corner. And he was most undoubtedly coming this way. He wasn't hurrying, but he was most undoubtedly approaching No 14.

With a sigh of rapture Miss Maltby tore herself from the window and set the door of her room ajar in order to be in a position to hear and see what happened when the policeman rang the bell and asked, as he certainly would ask, to speak to Jasper Wrenn.

Jasper was feeling better. Nobody was trailing him. He had got the suit-case. And he had been able to wash his face, change his collar—it had suffered considerable damage—and provide himself with several handkerchiefs. His nose had quite stopped bleeding and, if the past was any guide, could now be trusted to behave itself. He stepped forth blithely from his room with Anthony's suit-case in his hand, and heard in the hall below a heavy, authoritative voice say,

"Good afternoon. I'd like a word with one of your lodgers—Mr Jasper Wrenn."

It was a policeman's voice—unmistakeably and most terrifyingly a policeman's voice. The Law, with heavy boots and a Surrey accent. The Law, with a note-book ready to take down anything he might say and use it against him.

Miss Maltby's eye, at the crack of her door, saw "that young Wrenn" come to a standstill and stiffen there, just at the top of the stairs. He didn't just look guilty, he looked like a petrified image of guilt, eyes bolting, and—the only part of him that moved—hands closing and unclosing. From the unclosing hand on his right the suit-case fell with a bang, bumped on the top step, and went glissading down towards the hall. Four steps down both catches sprang. The smothering folds of Anthony's dressing-gown interrupted the glissade. The blue and white pyjamas sprawled between the fifth step and the tenth. Jasper paralysed with horror gazed down upon the wreck.

He heard Mrs Camber's fluttered answer. She came into view. The policeman came into view—a very large policeman with a face like an advertisement for some health food. Mrs Camber began to come upstairs. The policeman leaned against the newel.

And quite suddenly Jasper's imagination, which had up till now played so tiresome a part, swung about and cast him for the role of the cool, inscrutable hero. His knees still wobbled, but his mind was flooded with a delicious sense of being able to control the situation. He walked down as far as the fifth step, where he saw Mrs Huddleston's emerald headband lying in a casual heap. Two steps farther down there was an emerald brooch. He picked up the headband and put it in his trouser pocket. He then descended another two steps and collected the brooch. When he picked up the headband he retrieved the pyjama coat. As he stooped for the brooch, he also gathered up the pyjama legs.

Miss Maltby's eye, at the crack of her door, saw no more than Mrs Camber and the policeman did. The stair treads were hidden from all three of them, and in a court of law they would have had to swear that they had seen Mr Jasper Wrenn pick up a pair of pyjamas.

Jasper added Anthony's dressing-gown to the pyjamas and proceeded to cram them back into the suit-case. He was aware of Mrs Camber addressing him, still in that fluttered voice.

"Oh, Mr Wrenn, it's the police. He'd like to speak to you."

Jasper shut the case, hasped it, and came to the bottom of the stairs with dignity, as befitted one who is playing lead. The policeman towered above his head, and he found himself wishing that he had not come quite all the way down. However, inches are not everything. He said, "Good afternoon", and the policeman said, "If I might ask you a few questions, sir," and then produced a note-book and began to ask them.

"Information having been laid that you were seen leaving this house with a suit-case belonging to Miss Shirley Dale after packing same in her room, it is my duty to ask you whether you conveyed the said suit-case to Miss Dale, and if such was the case we should like to know where she is?"

"What do you mean by 'information having been laid'?" said Jasper haughtily.

Should he say that this was the suit-case he had taken out of the house, or should he deny having taken out a suit-case at all?

The policeman coughed.

"That's not for me to say."

Jasper made up his mind—or had it made up for him. He pushed Anthony's suit-case at the policeman and said,

"I don't know what all this is about. This is the only suit-case I've got. It certainly doesn't belong to Miss Dale. Look for yourself."

The policeman looked. A masculine hair-brush, dressing-gown, pyjamas. He coughed again.

"Our information is that you left the house with a suit-case after lunch, and you say it was this suit-case. Will you explain why you should take it out and then bring it back again?"

Mrs Camber chipped in in a flurried way.

"Oh, sir, I see him come back—not five minutes ago it wasn't, and the suit-case in his hand like he says."

Jasper frowned upon the policeman. His knees no longer shook.

"I don't mind explaining in the least. I went round to borrow these things from a friend. I took the suit-case to bring them back in."

The policeman stooped down and examined the case. Perhaps he did it to conceal a growing conviction that the balmy old girl had let them down. He looked a little brighter when he stood up again.

"Those aren't your initials on the case, Mr Wrenn, I take it?"

Jasper did not bat an eyelid. With superb calm he said,

"The suit-case is borrowed too. From the same friend. You can have his address if you like."

The policeman did not ask for the address, rather to Jasper's disappointment. It would have been agreeable to direct the attentions of the police to Anthony Leigh. Why shouldn't he come in for a spot of suspicion, and bully ragging, and having his answers taken down in a note-book.

The policeman dropped the subject of the suit-case, dropped Mr Jasper Wrenn, and retired in good order. Mrs Camber wiped her brow as she returned from letting him out.

"Never had the police in my house before. And poor Miss Dale, as nice a young lady as I ever see and no trouble in the house—not like some I could mention but wouldn't demean myself, spying out of windows and looking through cracks till you don't know when you've got an eye on you and when you haven't, which it gives me the creeps and I don't mind saying so. And did I hear you say you were going away, Mr Wrenn?"

Jasper blushed very slightly.

"No, I don't think I am—not now."

He let Mrs Camber get well away to the basement, and then walked out of the house with Anthony's suit-case in his hand and Mrs Huddleston's emeralds in his pocket.

Miss Maltby's blind was down. Miss Maltby's eye watched him from behind it.

Chapter Twenty-Eight

ANTHONY AND SHIRLEY were still sitting on Miss Pocklington's steep and dusty stair. This was partly because they had a great deal to say to one another, and partly because there was nowhere else to sit. There didn't seem to be a single chair on the premises. After ranging over their past lives they had returned to Miss Maltby. Shirley was doing her best to remember exactly what the muttering voice had said whilst she crouched behind the Potato Field and clutched her nose against the impending sneeze—"And you don't know how difficult it is to be interested enough to remember anything when a sneeze is just going to go off like a bomb and land you in the deepest dungeon below the castle moat."

"I want you to try all the same. What sort of things was she saying? See if you can remember any of them. Shut your eyes and imagine you're back behind the picture and she is walking up and down muttering to herself. What is she saying? Keep quite still for a minute and see if you can't repeat any of it."

Shirley leaned back against the wall and shut her eyes. Presently she said in a sort of half voice,

"It was rather horrid really, Anthony. I think she's—not right in her head."

Anthony's voice was very low too. He said,

"Try and remember."

Shirley's hands took hold of one another in her lap—grubby little hands, with grimy nails from crawling on Helena Pocklington's grimy floor.

"She said things like, 'All that money', and, 'You shouldn't have let me down, Jane Rigg.' She said Jane could have lived if she'd wanted to, and if she'd lived another six months, Miss Maltby would have got her share. She seemed to think Jane had died just to spite her."

"Was that all?"

"*Darling*—of course it wasn't! She went on for hours—at least I suppose not really, but the sneeze was *slipping* and it felt like years. I got out a book from the Free Library once which said there wasn't any such thing as Time. I didn't read it all, because it made my head go round, but I did read that bit, and when I was lurking behind that awful picture and the Maltby was raving up and down on the other side of it I understood exactly what the man meant—not just then, you know, but looking back on it now, because it really did seem like *hours*. Practically everything *has* since six o'clock yesterday evening when I started to run away."

Anthony patted her.

"Go on telling me what Miss Maltby said."

"Well, it was all like that—round and round, like a gramophone record. I don't believe she knew what she was saying half the time. There was a bit about 'All that money to Shirley Dale', and then, 'She shan't have it! She shan't have it! She shan't have it!' I remember that bit, because that was where I began to long passionately for a policeman and a nice safe prison cell, because honestly, darling, she sounded too horribly hating. And then there was something about her Share, and a Mr Phillips, and someone called Ettie. She seemed to think she could put them in prison, but I don't know why unless—unless—" She opened her eyes, jerked forward, and clutched at Anthony. "Oh! Do you suppose that Ettie could be Pierrette?"

Anthony submitted to being clutched. He put up a hand and covered hers.

"You're sure about those names?"

"Mr Phillips, and Ettie? Yes—she said them. *Anthony*—"

"Pierrette—Ettie ... It might be ... Only she was French—"

"They came to England—Perrine's widower and the child. Aunt Emily said so. It was just before the war. He was ill—not fit to serve when the war came. He was in some office. He wrote and told my mother he wanted to be naturalized. He wanted to bring Pierrette up in England. My mother wrote and told Aunt Emily. I believe he was naturalized. Then when the war was over my father and mother died, and I came home to Aunt Emily. And she never heard any more about the Meuniers, so I don't know what has become of them."

"You say he was naturalized?"

"Aunt Emily thought so. There was something about putting his name into English."

"What was the name—Meunier? That would be Miller. Pierrette Meunier—Ettie Miller. It seems to me we'd better look out for a Mr Phillips and a Miss Ettie Miller. It looks very much as if they were the people behind these attempts to get you into trouble. If you are disqualified for the Merewether money, Pierrette Meunier, who may be Miss Maltby's Ettie, scoops the lot."

"But who is Mr Phillips?"

Anthony laughed.

"Well, I should say at a guess that he's probably married to Pierrette, in which case, darling, you've got a very fine bargain of a nephew."

There was a short appalled silence. Shirley's hands dropped back into her lap. She drew as far away from Anthony as the width of the stair allowed and gazed at him with heartfelt reproach.

"That's the most disagreeable thing I've ever had said to me in all my life."

"I can do better than that," said Anthony cheerfully.

"And I suppose you think I'll marry someone who is going to throw odious middle-aged nephews and nieces in my teeth all the time!"

"Darling, you do look so funny being haughty with a smudge on your nose."

"I haven't got a smudge!"

"You've got six. Come here and I'll kiss them, and then you'll know just where they are."

Shirley opened her mouth to put him in his proper place, but she had got no farther than "If you *think*—" when a key scratched in the key-hole, the latch clicked back, and someone pushed unavailingly against the door. The word froze on her lips, and with an entire loss of dignity she grabbed at Anthony's arm and pinched it severely. Anthony froze too. If it was Miss Maltby whose key was scratching round in the lock, she would certainly want to know why the door wouldn't open. And when Miss Maltby wanted to know anything she made it her business to find out. Shirley's eyes asked a horrified question. Anthony's replied, "I don't know. Keep still!" and then the injured voice of Jasper Wrenn came to them from the other side of the door.

"It's me—Jasper. Let me in!"

He came in with the suit-case and the consciousness of having a very fine story to tell. Only why tell it on the stairs? To do it justice there must be room for a certain freedom of movement. He had a dramatic climax in view, and it demanded gesture. To gesticulate on Helena's stairs was to invite physical damage of one kind or another. He pressed an adjournment to the studio.

Anthony leaned past him and shot the bolt of the front door again. "Nowhere to sit," he said. And, "Why doesn't your Cousin Helena have any chairs?" said Shirley.

"She doesn't like furniture," said Jasper—"not real furniture. There are some canvas chairs behind the stove—you know, beastly folding things with stripes. They make me feel sea-sick, but I can get them out if you like."

They went up to the studio and got out three chairs. Miss Pocklington's taste in colour was extremely robust. The stripes were in the fiercer shades of emerald, orange, and magenta.

"If we sit on them we shan't see them," said Shirley helpfully. "Now, Jas, hand over the swag!"

Jasper did not sit down. He gave Anthony the suit-case and stood back. Shirley prattled on.

"The emeralds are in the pocket of your pyjamas. You'd better get them out. And then we must make a plan about getting them back to Mrs Huddleston, because as long as we've got them we're in simply frightful danger. I mean, I suppose—Darling, you *could* say you had snatched them from a burglar and were taking them back, and the police *might* believe you. That's why I put them in your pyjama pocket, just on the off chance of its going down with a nice believing sort of policeman. But if it didn't go down we should all be in a prison cell together, and it wouldn't be at all nice for you, being a barrister and all. Or do you think that would help you to wangle us out of it?"

"Not a wangle," said Anthony.

He opened the suit-case, tossed out the pyjama legs, and ran his hands over the jacket. He did this a second time, frowned, shook out the dressing-gown, and then went back to the pyjama legs. There were no emeralds anywhere.

Shirley made a faint sound of dismay. Jasper's moment had arrived. He plunged into his story. He had fetched the suit-case. Without his actually saying so, Shirley and Anthony received the impression that it was only by the exercise of considerable skill and presence of mind that he had managed to evade the vigilance of the police and reach Findon Road with his trophy. The nose-bleeding episode was lightly touched upon. If they inferred that it was the result of a hand-to-hand conflict, that could not be helped. Jasper had not in fact tried to help it. At break-neck speed he reached his room, changed his collar, and bathed the honourable wound. Thence to the dramatic moment on the stairs when the suit-case plunged from his hand and, bursting open, flung out the emeralds under the very gaze of Miss Maltby above and a police-constable below. Jasper found his moment very enjoyable.

Shirley's eyes were like saucers. Anthony Leigh stared at him in dismay.

"Don't tell me the police have got the emeralds! We're done if they have!"

Jasper drew himself up.

"No—I've got them," he said with modest pride, and fished them out of his trouser pocket.

"Oh, Jas—how clever! How *did* you do it?"

Jasper told her.

"And nobody saw you?"

"They only saw me picking up the pyjamas."

The moment lasted all too short a time. Then Anthony was packing the things back into the suit-case again and saying,

"Now we've got to make up our minds what we do next."

He clicked the catches home and held out a casual hand to Jasper.

"I'd better take charge of the gew-gaws."

Jasper handed them over with a relief just tinged with regret. They were romance and adventure, but they were also crime and the menace of the law. He felt that it was someone else's turn now, but he would have preferred that the someone else should not be Anthony Leigh.

Anthony took the brooch on his palm, and dangled the headband over his forefinger. The laurel-leaves caught the fading light. Shirley said quickly,

"I ought to hate them, but they're too lovely—I can't."

Anthony laughed softly.

"Napoleon—Italy. The laurels of Lodi, Arcola, and Rivoli. Josephine—Josephine who didn't want him back, but fancied the laurels—" He swung the headband to and fro. "Funny to think of her wearing this—and after her Lord knows who, and then great-grandmamma Robinson, whom I can just remember as a very fat old lady with about six chins. She kept peppermint lozenges in a bead bag and always gave me one when I was taken to see her. After her Aunt Agnes. And after *her*"—he laughed again and looked at Shirley—"I believe she's going to leave them to my wife. Perhaps she'll give them to us for a wedding present. Would you like to have them?"

Jasper's heart beat very hard and loud. They *were* engaged—Shirley was going to marry him. He had really known it, but it didn't hurt the less for that. He heard Shirley say,

"I don't know. They're lovely. Anyhow she wouldn't dream of it."

"She might," said Anthony. He picked up the brooch and turned it over to see the N on the back. "I say, darling, are you sure you cleared your coat out this time? Because oughtn't there to be more of these things? I seem to remember another brooch—and earrings."

"Yes, there are—I mean there ought to be. But they're not in my coat. I felt every bit of the hem."

"Well, I think we'll make sure. And we'd better have a light. Where's the switch?"

They put on the light, two bright unshaded bulbs in the ceiling. The windows had curtains which matched the blue of the paint. When they were drawn, Shirley took off her coat and she and Anthony felt it all over inch by inch, whilst Jasper gloomed at the Potato Field. The coat was innocent of any more emeralds, search they never so carefully.

"Well, where are they?" said Anthony. "Can't you see, there's no doubt they've all been taken. If the earrings and the other brooch had been left, Aunt Agnes would have said so, but it was just a long, loud wail about the emeralds being gone, and how unique they were, and what great-grandpapa Robinson paid for them, and all that sort of thing—not a single syllable about anything being saved from the wreck. So the whole lot had been pinched all right, there's no doubt about that. And whoever pinched them planted you with this brooch and the headband and kept the earrings and the other brooch. With any luck they've got them still, and if we can trace them, it proves your story and lets you out."

Jasper looked over a hunched shoulder and said, *"If."*

Anthony went on without taking any notice of him.

"Someone hid those things in the hem of your coat—first the diamond brooch, and then the emeralds. You said the catch of the brooch was damaged."

"Yes, it was."

"I've got an idea it had been tampered with. Someone wanted to make sure the brooch would be in the limelight. It came off, didn't it?"

"It came undone."

"Whilst you were there, and whilst Possett was out, so that it was a certainty that you would have the handling of it. I think that was all according to plan, but I don't know whether the emeralds were or not. Probably. Or they may have been suggested by the fact that you had helped Possett to put them away on Wednesday. In any case they make the theft a good deal more important—intrinsic value, historic associations, and all that—so I should think they were part of the plan all right. Well then, the plan was made to get you into trouble, and we're rather working on the assumption that it was made by Pierrette Meunier or by someone who is in with her—say the man Phillips. The plan might have been theirs, but it could only have been carried out by someone in the house, and that means Cook, Possett, or the new girl—what's her name?"

"Bessie," said Shirley—"Bessie Wood."

"Well, it lies between the three of them," said Anthony.

Shirley shook her head.

"Not Possett—she was in Ealing. She met her sister, and they went down to see their mother. Besides it couldn't possibly be Possett."

"Then it lies between Cook and Bessie. And *can* you see Cook heaving herself up those kitchen stairs and shoving diamonds and emeralds down into the hem of your coat?" He laughed shortly. "No, it was Bessie. Whoever did it had to go into the drawing-room and pinch

167 | HOLE AND CORNER

the diamond brooch off the mantelpiece. Aunt Agnes was asleep, but she might very easily have waked up. She probably would have waked if the person who came in had been someone who hadn't any business to be there. What excuse could poor old Cook have possibly given for rolling into the drawing-room in the middle of the afternoon? But Bessie would have had a dozen good reasons for being there—a note, a telephone call, the fire—" He shrugged his shoulders. "You see?"

Shirley put out a hand and rested it on his arm.

"*You* don't," she said. "That's all true, and I suppose it must have been Bessie. I don't know why, or how she could, but—Anthony, don't you see that everything you've been saying about her applies to me too? I wouldn't have needed an excuse for going back into the drawing-room. I wouldn't even have needed to go back. I could have brought the brooch away with me when I left Mrs Huddleston to have her sleep, and that's what Bessie will say. She's got a good character—I took it up myself. I've been accused of pilfering in the house where I lodge, and if it came to my being arrested, I shouldn't be at all surprised if someone didn't turn up who'd seen that business at the Luxe—someone who'd say I'd taken that glittering woman's purse and put it in my bag. It's no good *saying* it's Bessie—we've got to prove it."

Anthony nodded.

"That's quite true. We've got to prove it, and we're going to prove it. Now look here, don't laugh. Is it possible that this Bessie is Pierrette?"

Shirley did not laugh. She looked puzzled for a moment. Then her face cleared and she said, at first tentatively and then with more decision,

"No—oh no, I'm sure she's not. Darling, how horrid! What made you think of that?"

"Well, it just occurred to me. I thought they might be keeping the affair in the family so to speak. If they employ someone like Bessie, they take a big risk and expose themselves to blackmail afterwards—unless they've got some kind of hold on her, which is quite possible. All the same I'd like to know why you're so certain that she isn't Pierrette."

Shirley frowned.

"She isn't—I'm sure she isn't."

"But why?"

She said, "Oh!" in a breathless, startled way, and then, "Anthony—how queer! I was going to say 'I don't know', and all of a sudden something popped out of a door in my mind like a jack-in-the-box, and I know—I do know—I know quite well—because I believe I know who Pierrette is. She's the glittering woman. You just see if she isn't. You know—the one with the gingery man at the Luxe. And it would explain how her purse got into my bag, because of course she put it there to make me look like a thief."

"But why do you think she's Pierrette?"

"I don't think—I *know*. That's what Aunt Emily's cook used to say. She was a tremendously determined person, and that's what I am about the glittering woman—I *know* she's Pierrette."

"But why? You must have a reason."

Shirley stamped her foot.

"Yes, I have—and it's a horrid one—I hate it! She's Pierrette because of the way she looked that's like my mother. And I didn't see it at the time, because, you know, I don't remember my mother very well. I suppose I don't really remember her at all, only from photographs. But when I got down to Acacia Cottage there was her picture hanging in the drawing-room—the one that was painted when she married Augustus Rigg, so Jane had it, and that was quite all right because she was the eldest daughter and I suppose Augustus paid for it. But I do think it's abominable for it to be left to the Maltby—don't you?"

Anthony put his arm round her, half laughing, half serious.

"You'd make a most awful witness," he said. "You started out to tell me something about a likeness—"

"Well, I am telling you," said Shirley indignantly. She twisted herself free. "When I was looking at the picture something kept teasing me—in the back of my mind. *You* know, like a dog scratching at a door, and you're not quite sure whether you're hearing it or not. But just now it got the door open and popped right out, and I saw the glittering woman's face quite plain, and my mother's face in the picture, and there was just the sort of look that makes you say, 'Those two people belong to the same family.'"

"You don't think you're imagining it?" said Anthony.

Shirley stamped again.

"You don't suppose I *want* that horrible woman to be like my mother! But she *is*. Because she's her granddaughter—she's Pierrette Meunier. And I expect she's Miss Maltby's Ettie too. It all fits in."

Anthony nodded.

"It'll bear looking into anyhow. The devil of it is that here we are at—what is it?—just about four o'clock on Sunday afternoon, and we've got till ten o'clock tomorrow morning and no more."

Jasper looked over his shoulder again.

"Why ten o'clock to-morrow morning?"

"That's the time Shirley's due at my aunt's. It is ten, isn't it? Anyhow it's nobody's business what she did with her week-end. It can't really be brought up against her that she went down to Emshot on the spur of the moment after her work was over on Saturday, but if she doesn't turn up at her usual time on Monday morning, it's going to look very bad indeed. We've got to keep her from being arrested to-day and clear things up so that she can walk in on Monday with what William calls 'a shining morning face'." He grinned at Shirley and added, "So you've got just about eighteen hours to work up the polish."

Shirley sketched a Woggy Doodle at him.

"When my face shines I powder it," she said. "Only I haven't been able to since yesterday because of leaving my bag at Acacia Cottage and Jas forgetting to pack my powder though I told him most specially about it."

She missed an awful glance of reproach because she was trying to look sideways at her nose to see how shiny it really was.

"Well, that being that," said Anthony, "we'd better get on with it. I'll get back to Revelston Crescent and have a heart-to-heart with Aunt Agnes. I've got a card or two up my sleeve, and I think I can make it all right as far as she is concerned. You'd better stay here, and I'll come back and report progress as soon as I can."

At this point they both cast a fleeting glance at Jasper. His hands were in his pockets, and with a sulky back towards them he still brooded over the Potato Field. Anthony's eyebrows took an upward quirk. He came a step nearer, tipped up Shirley's chin, dallied for a pleasant moment over the ensuing kiss, and then went whistling down the stair. From half way he stopped and called back over one shoulder, "Better bolt the door again," and then was gone.

Chapter Twenty-Nine

WHEN THE DOOR BANGED Jasper went down, bolted it, and returned moodily to the studio. He walked past Shirley as if he did not see her, turned at the end of the room with a jerk, and came back.

"Are you going to marry him?" he said in a choked sort of voice.

Shirley nodded.

The choke merged into a sob. He said,

"Do you care for him—a lot?"

She nodded again. If she tried to speak she would cry, and if they both cried—help!

"Why?" said Jasper with a despairing break in his voice. "He doesn't love you like I do—he can't—nobody could."

She said, "It's no use, Jas." And then, "I'm so fond of you—I'm so sorry—"

"If you say you'll be a sister to me, I think I shall kill you!" He felt a sudden raw passion which frightened him.

He stood there for a moment, his hands clenching and unclenching, his face working. Then he jerked round and went to the row of curtained windows which looked out at the back of the Mews, kicking over two of Helena Pocklington's canvases as he went. He tugged at the curtains, pushed a window open roughly, and leaned out.

Shirley drew a long shaky breath. Poor darling Jas! But what a frightful moment to have a scene like this—it really *was*. And perhaps she'd better not say anything for fear of making it worse. Perhaps it would be better if he went away. She didn't *want* to be left all by herself in this beastly Mew and perhaps have the police or Miss Maltby come hammering at the door, and no one to look out of the window and say, 'Fly for your life!', or, 'It's all right—stay where you are,' in case of its being Anthony, but it was going to be too awful if Jas was going to go on like this all the time that Mrs Huddleston was being brought to see reason. Because, knowing Mrs Huddleston, she thought it was likely to take a good *long* time. Anthony might be hours.

She went to the window on the opposite side, pulled back a little bit of the curtain, and looked out. This was the window from which she had seen Miss Maltby's skirt whisk round the corner. It had been light then, but it was very nearly dark now—the deep dusk of a January day, with a rather bright lamp shining down from the garage opposite. Shirley watched the glow thrown by the lamp, and then suddenly she dropped her corner of the curtain, ran across to the switch, and turned out both the studio lights. Then she went back to the window again. If she looked out now she wouldn't be seen.

She looked out. Two people were crossing the lighted space over the way, a man and a woman. Shirley looked at them very hard and then shrank back because they had turned and were staring up at this very window. They couldn't see her of course. The light fell on the man and the woman, and the minute she saw them she knew where she had seen them before. They were the people who had had the next table at the Luxe—the sandy man, and the large glittering woman. And all in a flash she knew why they were there, and she was sure, quite sure, that the man was Mr Phillips, and that the woman was the Ettie of Miss Maltby's rambling talk. Mr Phillips and Ettie—Mr Phillips and Ettie.... And Ettie was Pierrette—Pierrette Meunier....

She hadn't the slightest doubt that she was looking at Pierrette Meunier, her mother's grand-daughter by that second, French, marriage. Her—own—niece. It was outrageous, and comic, and—yes, rather horrible, to be the aunt of a large, glittering female who was much older and much, much heavier than yourself. But the likeness was there—in the arch of the brow, in the setting of the eyes, and in something more elusive and more convincing.... She couldn't get it into words, or even into coherent thought, but it made her catch her breath and say, "It's Pierrette."

Well, what about it? She didn't know. Why had they come here? She thought she knew the answer to that. To spy, to find out if she was here—to set the police on her. But if they suspected she was here, it meant that they had seen Miss Maltby, and it meant that Miss Maltby had suspected something after all.

A hand touched her shoulder, and she very nearly screamed. Then Jasper's voice said in her ear,

"What's the matter? Why have you put the light out?"

She dropped the curtain, stepped back until she stood level with him, and whispered,

"Ssh! They're outside."

172 | HOLE AND CORNER

"Who?"

"The Phillips man, and Pierrette—she *is* Pierrette."

"Where?"

She was just going to say "Over the way," when the knocker fell against the door with a hard rat-tat. She said "Oh!" instead, and after her usual way when startled clutched at the nearest arm and pinched it hard.

In some odd way Jasper found this consoling. She was pinching him, not Anthony. He began to feel better.

Still pinching, she whispered quite unnecessarily,

"They're knocking at the door."

They continued to knock.

"If we don't do anything they'll go away. They can't get in."

Shirley shook the arm she had been pinching.

"I don't want them to go away—not yet. Listen—I've got a plan."

"Well?"

"A lovely plan. You give me two seconds to get out at the back, and then you go down and open the door. They'll ask questions. You've got to keep them long enough to give me time to get round from the back. There's a footpath, isn't there? Well, there's my plan. When they're sure I'm not here they'll go away, and when they go away I'm going to follow them."

"And what do I do?"

"You stay here and wait for Anthony. I must fly. You can take them all over the Mew and let them see I'm not hiding in the gas oven." She snatched up her coat, slipped it on, and felt her way down the stairs.

The knocking on the door went on. She could hear it as she picked her way through the small back yard and found the footpath. She came out upon the street, and saw the Mews entrance on her right. She had only to lurk until Pierrette and Mr Phillips came away from the Mews and then follow them.

She lurked, and the time seemed long. Jasper must have opened the door by now. They must be talking. She wondered what excuse she would make if she were Pierrette. She thought she would ask for Miss Pocklington and then pretend to recognize Jas and say, "Aren't you her nephew?" and, "We should so love to see over the Mews, because if we could persuade her to let—" Yes, something on those lines. She began to feel that she would do it very well, and that Pierrette was probably not making nearly such a good job of it.

And then with horrifying suddenness she remembered her suit-case. Not Anthony's suit-case—that didn't matter, because Jas could go on saying he had borrowed it—but her own—the one which Jas had packed and brought here, the one she had shoved behind a picture just before her dive for the Potato Field. She had only just got herself and the suit-case hidden before Miss Maltby came up through the hole in the studio floor, and from that minute to this she had forgotten all about the suit-case. But suppose *they* started moving the pictures and found it. That Phillips man had a frightfully gimlet eye. She had noticed it at the Luxe—one of those pale, sharp, persistent eyes. She felt it would be quite capable of seeing tight through Helena Pocklington's revolting picture of a girl with a dislocated neck and two badly broken arms to the initials on the suit-case. What a ghastly thought.

Well, if that was what was happening, it just *was* happening. Even if they did find her suit-case, it didn't really matter. She needn't go back there, she could just go on lurking till Anthony came. Only first of all she meant to find out where Pierrette was staying. Because that was the important thing. They had got *to* find out about Pierrette and the Phillips man, and they had got to find out quickly.

Yes, it didn't matter about the suit-case. But she did wish they would come. It was growing darker every minute, and she felt quite sure of being able to follow them without being seen. There was a lamp at the entrance to the Mews. She watched the lighted space about it, and waited for Ettie and Mr Phillips to come out.

Chapter Thirty

ANTHONY SAT by his aunt's sofa and listened.

He had had one stroke of luck, because he had arrived to find the drawing-room empty, and had therefore been able to retrieve the diamond brooch. It was still where he had pushed it down between the back and seat of the sofa. He put it in the same pocket as the emeralds, rammed a handkerchief down on top to keep them from tattling, and had time to assume the right expression of sympathetic melancholy before Mrs Huddleston came in supported by Possett with the usual array of shawls, coverlets, pillows, and smelling-salts. She embraced him—"My dear boy," sank down upon the sofa, and whilst Possett ministered informed him that she had been so agitated, so terribly agitated, that after consulting Dr Monsell on the telephone she had by his advice gone to bed, really to bed, for the afternoon.

"He most strongly advised me to lie quite flat in a darkened room—only one pillow. Thank you, Possett, that will do. You can leave us. Mr Anthony will ring if I need you. I suppose I ought not to have got up again, but as you know, I never give way. I remember Sir Sefton Carlisle saying to me, 'You never give way. It would be better if you did. You have too much courage, if I may say so. You force yourself when you should let nature have her way and *rest*'."

Anthony seized on the word, and hoped that his aunt felt rested. He received a mournful shake of the head.

"I did not expect it. I obeyed orders, but I did not expect any benefit. I know my own constitution too well." With this preamble she embarked on a very enjoyable dissertation upon her constitution, its peculiarities, its history from infancy onwards, together with the remarks, warnings, and observations uttered during that period by the most eminent members of the medical profession. All these gentlemen were quoted at great length. They had exhibited a most unusual unanimity in declaring Mrs Huddleston's case to be one of the most interesting that had ever come under their notice. With one voice they had urged her to take care of herself, to remember how fragile she was, and above all things to avoid the slightest worry or agitation.

"Perfect calm," said Mrs Huddleston. "I remember Dr Blanker saying that, I thought it such a beautiful expression. He had a very sympathetic voice too. But your uncle came in one day when he was holding my hand, and he wasn't quite pleased about it afterwards, though of course there was nothing in it. He used to hold my hand and tell me to relax and think of the green depths of the ocean. Such a very, very poetic idea, and most soothing. But your uncle was really quite unreasonable and made me have Dr Robertson instead—a very *clever* man, and Scotch, but I found his manner terribly abrupt, and I could never agree with your uncle that the improvement in my health which took place just then had anything to do with his treatment,

for he did not understand my case. Do you know, he once actually told me that if I had to scrub floors for a living I should find I was perfectly well. I don't know what I felt like, and I told your uncle...."

There was a good deal of what she had told Mr Huddleston. Anthony wondered whether any of it had really ever been said at the time. He remembered his uncle as an obstinate old gentleman with a singularly violent temper, very fond of his wife, very proud of her looks, but very much master in his own house. He thought his Aunt Agnes was saying what she would have liked to have said twenty years ago if she had dared. It was obvious that she very much enjoyed saying it now. He let her talk, because nothing pleased her so much. He really had very little idea of how he was going to pull Shirley's chestnuts out of the fire, but it would be a whole lot easier if Mrs Huddleston was in a pleased instead of a fretful frame of mind.

"But you mustn't think that we quarrelled—I shouldn't like you to think that. I don't believe your uncle and I ever had a real quarrel, and that is the reason why I should be so glad to see you married. Because, you know, if you've been happily married yourself, you feel you would like other people to be happily married too, especially if they are people you are fond of—and I am very fond of you, my dear boy."

Anthony felt touched. He really had an affection for the silly lady who had never been anything but exceedingly kind to him. He put his hand on hers for a moment and said,

"I know you are, Aunt Agnes."

Tears sprang into her eyes. The lace-edged handkerchief came into play.

"And that is why I am so terribly upset about the emeralds, because I have always planned to give them to your wife."

"That's most frightfully nice of you, Blessed Damozel," said Anthony.

She was gazing at him so soulfully and looking so exactly like Rossetti's picture that the name slipped out. He remembered his bet with Shirley—and had the grace to blush.

"I—I'm awfully sorry—it slipped out. I always think of you like that."

A soft, pleased colour came into Mrs Huddleston's cheeks.

"Do you really? My dear boy—how charming of you! I won't say people haven't said it before. Dr Blanker—but that's all past and gone—"

"Aunt Agnes," said Anthony, "I want to talk to you very seriously."

"Oh, my dear boy—what about? You're not in any trouble?"

"No. You said just now you wanted to see me married. Well, I've been thinking of getting married."

Mrs Huddleston sat up and clutched the sofa back.

"My dear boy! Who is she? Tell me all about her! Oh, I do hope you have been *wise*!"

"Well, she will probably have rather a lot of money."

"But you're not marrying for money? I couldn't *bear* that!"

Anthony laughed.

"Nor could I. I really wish she wasn't going to have quite so much, but she hasn't got it yet, so I'm not worrying. But it is a great deal of money." He said the last words in a slow, measured way which fixed Mrs Huddleston's attention.

"What do you mean by a great deal?" she said, still sitting up and gazing at him.

"Well—a lot. I expect you've read about it in the paper to-day. It's William Ambrose Merewether's money."

"What?" said Mrs Huddleston with a gasp.

"As far as I can make out she scoops the lot," said Anthony.

Mrs Huddleston blinked twice rapidly. She began to feel confused and giddy. She went on clutching at the back of the sofa and said,

"Who is she?"

"The only surviving daughter of Jane Lorimer to whom old Merewether left his money."

"She must be fifty!" said Mrs Huddleston, appalled.

"She's twenty-one," Anthony's look was very gay and challenging.

"Who *is* she?"

"Shirley Dale," said Anthony.

Mrs Huddleston let go of the sofa and fell back against her cushions in a perfectly genuine swoon.

Chapter Thirty-One

POSSETT, REPROACHFUL AND COMPETENT, turned Anthony out of the drawing-room.

"Quiet—that's what she wants—and nothing to upset her, not any more than can be helped. But really it seems as if it was one thing after another. And for goodness sake, sir, don't go and leave the house, because ever since last night it's been nothing but 'Where's Mr Anthony?' And I don't know what sent her off like this, but it's you she'll be asking for as soon as she comes round. So if you'd wait in the study—" All this whilst she held smelling-salts to Mrs Huddleston's nose.

Anthony waited in the study. He was sorry that the news of his engagement had sent the Blessed Damozel off into a swoon, but Possett didn't seem at all alarmed, and perhaps it wasn't a bad thing that there should be a break in the conversation at this point. He was rather pleased at the way he had presented Shirley as an heiress. Once get Aunt Agnes to see her in this light, and she would—at least he hoped she would—find it too absurd to imagine that she had stolen the emeralds. When she had been sufficiently revived by Possett's ministrations, he hoped to continue the conversation on these lines.

Meanwhile the emeralds were burning a hole in his pocket. He wanted to get rid of them in some place where they could afterwards be discovered with a reasonable probability of their having been there all the time. To let Shirley out it must look as if they had been in the house all the time. Well, where could they have been? His aunt's bedroom would be the most convincing place. Danton's motto came into his mind: *"De l'audace, de l'audace, et toujours de l'audace."* If he went straight up now while Possett was still fussing with smelling-salts and hand-slappings, he would with any luck at all be able to find a likely place.

He had the study door open, and had taken a step into the hall, when it came to him forcibly and unpleasantly that the plan was a wash-out because he only had half the emeralds. The whole set had been taken—Mrs Huddleston's lamentations left no doubt on this point—but he had in his pocket only the headband and one brooch. Someone, somewhere, had the other brooch and the earrings. Shirley would not be cleared by the discovery of half the set. He wondered very much where the other half was, and why it had been kept back.

Yes, why?... His mind stayed at this point, as his body stayed just clear of the study. Why had half the emeralds been kept back? He thought Bessie Wood had taken them under orders to plant them on

Shirley. Well, she had only planted half of them—and kept the rest? Was that in her instructions? He thought not. He thought that Pierrette, or Mr Phillips, or whoever it was who had given her those instructions was playing for much too big a stake to take any risk over a common or garden theft. They were out for the Merewether millions and not for Mrs Huddleston's emeralds. But Bessie, with the emeralds in her hand, might have been tempted to keep half of them back. If that was the way of it, what had she done with them?

What would she be likely to do? Get them out of the house as quickly as possible. But she wouldn't have been able to get away with them last night, or for that matter to-day, because she was on duty. He had seen her here in the morning, and she had let him in just now. To ask leave to go out would be to invite suspicion, and to go out without asking leave would be to make certain that the invitation was accepted. No, the only way she could get rid of them was through the post. She could post them to a confederate, but that meant a good deal of arrangement and a confederate she could trust. She might have done it, but he somehow didn't think she had. Thieves don't trust each other much, and his theory rather rested on the idea of a sudden temptation.

These thoughts were in his mind like quick pictures. He stood for perhaps half a minute and then turned to go back into the study. But he did not cross the threshold, for as he turned he looked down towards the front door and an impression already in his mind became apparent.

He turned back again, looking down the hall and considering this impression. It concerned the hall table and the fern which stood there in a hideous ornamental pot, a really horrible piece of majolica. But the impression did not concern the pot. It was the fern, something about the fern, which he had noticed without noticing when he came in. That is to say, his eye had seen it, but his mind had not regarded it—till now. He now regarded it with a fixed attention rather out of keeping with what might have been considered a trifle. The fern had a drooped and fading look. It had never been a very robust specimen, but it now looked very bad indeed. Anthony gave himself a shake. Ferns wanted a lot of water. If they were not watered they drooped at once. The fern had not been watered—that was all. The house was upset, and the person who ought to have watered the fern hadn't watered it.

Something went click in Anthony's mind. It would be Bessie's job to water the fern. If she hadn't watered it, why hadn't she watered it? Not because of being all upset and flustered. If he had ever seen a cold, apathetic fish of a girl in his life it was Bessie Wood. Efficient and methodical withal. Shirley had said so, Aunt Agnes had said so. Then why was the fern denied its daily drink? He thought he would go and see.

He walked over to the hall table, lifted out the fern in its earthenware pot, and looked down into the ornamental abomination. Something had clinked as he lifted the pot. Something sent up a green spark under the electric light. He put in his hand and pulled out Josephine's emerald earrings—and, for the matter of that, great-grandmamma Robinson's emerald earrings. The other brooch was down there too. He pricked his finger on it and dropped it back.

His thoughts tumbled over one another racing, laughing, triumphing. He was going to get Shirley clear, and Miss Bessie Wood was going to have the surprise of her life. Out of his trouser pocket came the diamond brooch and the rest of the emeralds. Into the ornamental pot they went, and back on top of them went the drooping fern.

Chapter Thirty-Two

IT WAS AT this moment that the telephone bell rang. Anthony crossed the hall, lifted the receiver, and heard Shirley's voice. She said "Hullo!" rather breathlessly, and he said,

"What is it?"

"Anthony, is that you?"

"It is. What's happened? Why are you ringing up?"

As he spoke, the door which led to the basement was pushed open. Bessie Wood looked out at him and was gone again. The door closed. It was Bessie's job to answer the telephone. The bell having rung, she arrived. Seeing Mr Leigh, she withdrew. The question was, how far had she withdrawn.

Anthony cursed inwardly. His Aunt Agnes belonged to the generation which invariably put the telephone in the most public place in the house. There was an extension in the drawing-room, but he couldn't very well ask to use it. Besides, extensions were traps—anyone could listen in on you at the main fixture.

Shirley said, "Anthony—are you there?"

He said, "Yes." What he would have liked to say was, "Yes—and I think Bessie Wood is on the back stairs with her ear to the crack of the door listening to every word I'm saying."

Shirley was excited, and exasperated.

"How funny you sound! Listen—things have been happening. Pierrette and the Phillips man came and banged at the door—"

"What door?" If Bessie was listening she couldn't make anything of that.

"The Mews door. So I told Jas to keep them talking—"

"How do you know it was them?" This wasn't so safe, but he had to chance it.

"Darling, I *told* you she was the glittering woman. Of course I knew her at once. Are you in a trance? *Do* wake up! Well, I left Jas to cope and got out the back way, and when they went, which wasn't for simply ages, I followed them. Shirley the Sleuth! I think they must have insisted on *searching* the Mew, they were so long. Or else the glittering female fell for Jas and couldn't be torn away. I thought they were never coming, but when they did I sleuthed, and I sleuthed them to a private hotel, 18 Mandell Street—rather grim but awfully respectable. He's staying there, registered as Alfred Phillips. I said I wasn't sure whether someone I knew had been there, so they let me look at the register."

"Where are you telephoning from?" said Anthony.

"Call-box in the hotel. I'd better ring off, because one of them might come by and see me. What's happening your end?"

If he had been sure that Bessie Wood hadn't got an ear at the crack of the door, he would have said, "I've been baiting a mouse-trap." As it was, Shirley was infuriated by a cool

"I'll see you later. Better go back. I can't get away just now—not for a bit."

"Who's going back?" she said. "I'm not!" and hung up the receiver with a bang.

Anthony hung up at his end, and as he did so, Possett came out of the drawing-room. She closed the door behind her and came to him with a deprecatory "If I might speak to you for a moment, sir—"

There was nothing he desired more. When he had shut the study door upon them, the astonished Possett found herself being led as far away from it as the room allowed. When they were up against the curtained windows, Anthony smiled at her and said,

"Can you watch a mouse-hole for a bit, Possett?"

"A mouse-hole, Mr Anthony?"

"No, as you were—a mouse-trap."

"A mouse-trap?"

He nodded, laughing a little.

"Yes. Do you know who took Mrs Huddleston's emeralds, Possett?"

"There's a diamond brooch gone too, sir."

"Do you know who took the lot?"

"Oh no, sir—and I can't believe—"

"Well?"

"I can't believe it was Miss Dale. Oh, sir, I really can't."

Anthony looked at her in a way that made her heart beat.

"Thank you, Possett," he said. And then, "Miss Dale and I are going to be married, you know."

"Oh, Mr Anthony! I do wish you happy—indeed I do!"

Anthony patted her on the shoulder.

"You mustn't cry now—there isn't time. You shall bring six pocket-handkerchiefs to our wedding, but just now—brace up, Possett—just now I want you to get inside the hall cupboard and watch the hall table."

Possett's little pink nose pointed up at him. Her eyes, suffused with emotion, gazed bewildered into his.

"The hall cupboard, sir? The hall table?"

"Only till I can get someone else to do it. Someone—*someone*, Possett, has hidden Mrs Huddleston's emeralds under the fern on the hall table."

"Oh, Mr Anthony!"

"Bit of a facer—isn't it? I want you to watch the pot like a lynx. If anyone comes to collect what they've hidden, lie low and let them collect it. Then yell if you like, or come for me. She mustn't leave the house."

Possett gulped helplessly.

"She, Mr Anthony? Who?"

"Wait and see," said Anthony.

She gulped again.

"She's asking for you, sir, Mrs Huddleston is."

"All right. Get along into that cupboard, and if her bell rings let it ring. The worst *she* can do is to give you the sack, but if you come out before I tell you, *I* shall murder you, so be very careful."

"Oh, Mr Anthony!" said Possett with a flutter of pink eyelids.

"With a blunt instrument," said Anthony in a bloodcurdling whisper.

He made sure the back stairs were clear, and saw the cupboard door shut on Possett before he went back into the drawing-room. If she knelt down she could keep her eye to the keyhole, and the keyhole commanded a very good view of the hall table.

He found Mrs Huddleston pale and inclined to tears. When she had cried for a time and dabbed her eyes, she showed a good deal of curiosity about William Ambrose Merewether, and assured him, at first faintly, but with growing conviction, that she had always considered Shirley a very sweet girl—"And I wouldn't have wished you to marry for money, dear boy—you know me too well for that, I'm sure—I mean, you couldn't think for a moment that I should wish such a thing, but a charming girl is not less charming because she has a little money of her own. Not, as I say, that you need consider that unduly, because of course poor Edward and Louisa left you very comfortably off, and whatever your uncle left me will go to you when I die. But still, money never comes amiss—does it? And even without it you would, I am sure, be happy with such a sweet girl as Miss Dale."

Anthony maintained a perfect gravity.

"But you'll call her Shirley now—won't you?"

"Dear Shirley!" said Mrs Huddleston, and dabbed her eyes.

Upon this there entered Bessie to make up the fire. Anthony withdrew the hand which his aunt had been holding, wandered away from the sofa, and made a brisk diversion.

"That fern of yours in the hall is looking very droopy Aunt Agnes."

Bessie put a lump of coal on the fire with a steady hand.

"Droopy?" said Mrs Huddleston vaguely. "Have you noticed it, Bessie?"

Bessie dealt with a second lump of coal.

"It's been watered every day, but I can give it an extra lot to-night, Madam." She had a neat, precise way of speech.

"I expect it wants re-potting," said Anthony. "I'm a dab at re-potting things. I expect I could scratch some decent earth out of your cat-run if Cook will lend me the kitchen shovel."

Bessie went on putting coal on the fire.

"I don't know, I'm sure," said Mrs Huddleston. "Perhaps it would be a good thing. Did you mean now? Poor Clara Nicholson gave me the fern, and I shouldn't like to lose it."

Bessie stood up, stood waiting. Anthony wondered what she would say if he said "Yes, I'll do it now." He felt sure that the cook would be busy, or the shovel not forthcoming just for the moment. He came back to his seat with a casual,

"I'll do it before I go. We'll have our talk first."

Bessie went out of the room as quietly as she had come in—no haste, no sign of fluttered nerves, a well trained maid going unobtrusively about her lawful occasions.

Anthony, with his ear cocked and his attention straining, thanked heaven for the Blessed Damozel's flow of speech. An attentive look and an occasional smile were all that were required of him. In his mind he followed Bessie into the hall. Had he got away with the tale of the drooping fern, or had he not? If she suspected anything, she wouldn't go near the pot. If she didn't, she would be across the hall by now, out of sight of the drawing-room door, looking over her shoulder to make sure that there was no one on the stairs, and then—lifting the pot—snatching the emeralds—

"... and so a rich wife may prove to be a very great blessing."

Mrs Huddleston was concluding some anecdote of which he had heard nothing. He smiled vaguely, and in the same moment there was a confused noise in the hall, Possett screamed, and something fell with a loud crash.

Anthony leapt up, flung back the door, and raced into the hall. He saw Possett getting up from her knees, and the earth and sherds of the broken pot, and the emeralds scattered. He did not see Bessie Wood, but the cold of the January night blew in at the open door. Possett held by the corner of the table, and shook and sobbed.

"She hit me! She's gone! Oh, sir—oh, Mr Anthony!"

Anthony ran out into the street and down to the left where a gleam of white looked like Bessie's apron-strings. He saw her at the next lamp, and then she was round the corner. When he reached the corner she wasn't anywhere. There was a narrow cut between the houses—she might have gone down that. He could see no sign of her there or anywhere else. She might have a friend in one of the houses and have run down the area steps to the kitchen door. Or she might have boldly rung a bell and pretended a message—she had the nerve for it.

He felt a certain relief as he went back to the house. He had had to give chase, but he hadn't very much wanted to catch her. She had left the emeralds, and Shirley was clear. The thought of haling a dough-faced young woman through the streets was a singularly unpleasant one. He was not, after all, a policeman.

He found Possett having a very fine fit of hysterics in the hall, whilst the Blessed Damozel, for the moment played quite off the stage, was down on her hands and knees collecting the emeralds.

"Oh, Mr Anthony!" gasped Possett as he came in. "Oh, the wickedness—the double-facedness! Right in the mouth she hit me—and who'd have thought she'd be so strong? And out of the door and down the steps before I could get my breath to scream!"

"You screamed very well," said Anthony, patting a trembling shoulder.

He helped his aunt to her feet, when she promptly dropped the emeralds and he had to pick them up again. After which he shepherded her and Possett into the drawing-room and shut the door.

"Now, Possett, that's enough—you can cry afterwards. I want you to tell us just what happened. Come along!"

Possett gave a rending sniff.

"Oh, sir—I was in the cupboard like you put me—"

Mrs Huddleston had actually forgotten that she could not stand. She stood now, looking at Anthony with a dazed expression and repeated in an incredulous tone,

"The cupboard—where you put her?"

Anthony slipped his arm round her.

"Yes, the hall cupboard. It's all right. I wanted someone to watch what Bessie would do."

"And I did!" said Possett. "Oh, sir, I *did*—like you told me! And what did I see? Oh, *sir!*"

"That's just what we want you to tell us."

Possett sniffed again.

"There I was, all in the dark and my eye to the keyhole like you said, which is what I've never done in my life, Mother having brought us all up most strict not to be tale-tellers nor eaves-droppers nor nothing of the sort, and I wouldn't have done it, not for anyone else, not if it had been ever so—I wouldn't indeed, sir!"

Mrs Huddleston looked completely bewildered. Anthony said soothingly,

"I'm sure you wouldn't. You behaved like a heroine. Now come along and tell us what you saw. You had your eye to the keyhole—"

"And I heard the drawing-room door open, and I saw that Bessie come over to the hall table and stand there, and I thought to myself, 'She's going to water that fern, and not before it wants it neither.' But she *wasn't*. Oh, ma'am, I don't know what I felt like—she took hold of the fern by its leaves as rough as rough and pulled it out pot and all. And then she puts her hand down into the china pot and brings up something and crams it into the pocket of her dress. And she puts her hand back into the pot and brings it up, and starts, and looks at it as if there was an adder fastened on it. And I see what she'd got hold of, and it was Madam's emerald hairband, and I took and pushed open the door and screamed, and she threw it in my face and hit me and out of the front door before I could stop her, the wicked thieving hussy!"

"What about the things in her pocket? Is anything missing, Aunt Agnes?"

"She took and threw them down," said Possett, trembling violently—"as if they was so many pebbles—and hit me right in the mouth and ran! And everything's all there, sir, if you'll look—two brooches, and a hairband, and earrings, and Madam's diamond brooch—they're all there."

At this point Mrs Huddleston remembered her spine, her palpitations, and her nerves. She closed her eyes and swayed a little, gracefully.

"My dear boy—I feel—so strange—perhaps—Possett, my smelling-salts—"

Anthony put her on the sofa and went to telephone to the police.

Shirley stood in the telephone-box and hung up the receiver, as already recorded, with a bang. Her temper did a short, sharp flare, her

foot did a short, sharp stamp. The constant efforts of old Aunt Emily
had achieved very little success in eliminating either the temper or the
tendency to stamp. Even being teased about it at school had not broken
her of a habit which she found a great relief in moments of stress. She
felt exceedingly angry with Anthony, who had just been talking to her
as if she was a policeman, or a registry office, or someone who had
written him a begging letter. "I'll see you later—" Perhaps he would,
and perhaps he wouldn't. "Better go back—" Well, she just wasn't
going to. What with Jas wanting to make love to her and morbing
because she didn't want him to, and Maltbys and people turning up
every five minutes or so, she had had as much as she wanted of Helena
Pocklington's Mew. Helena could have it, Jas could have it, anybody
could have it, and Anthony could say "You'd better go back" until he
was blue in the face. *Nothing* would induce her to go near the place
again. If Anthony couldn't get away when she wanted him, he could
stay where he was. Of course she knew very well that he was talking
from the hall, and probably everyone in the house was eavesdropping.
That only made it worse for Anthony, because it was his idiotic aunt's
idiotic obstinate fad to have her blighted telephone in her blighted hall,
and if you don't bring an aunt up better than that, whose fault *is* it? So
much for Anthony Leigh.

What about Shirley Dale? If she wasn't going back, what *was* she
going to do?

She really hadn't any idea. The only thing she felt quite sure about
was that nothing on earth would induce her to go back to Helena
Pocklington's Mew and a damp, despairing Jasper. It seemed hard on
Jas to leave him to it, but there it was—her toes were dug in and she
wasn't going back.

You can't stay in a telephone-box for ever without attracting
attention. She emerged cautiously, found the hall empty, and reached
the street. Fortunately 18 Mandell Street was not the sort of hotel that
has more than one entrance. If she walked up and down out here she
could make a plan, and at the same time feel sure that Pierrette and Mr
Phillips were not eluding her. She really did want a little time to sort
things out.

First of all there was Anthony. She would certainly have to have a
quarrel with Anthony. She spent a pleasant ten minutes or so planning

it in every detail, from the first blow-up to the final embrace. It was all very stimulating and amusing, the only drawback being that by the time she had finished with it she wasn't really feeling angry enough to quarrel with Anthony at all. However, that could probably be managed when the time came.

The next point to be decided was, what about Shirley Dale? Well, what *about* her? Was she going to wait meekly in a cold, draughty street until Anthony had quite finished talking to his aunt and could spare the time to come and look for her? No, she wasn't. The street was getting colder and draughtier every minute. She began to think of the warm fuggy hall of the hotel with affection.

She walked up and down, and made a plan. It came to her in a shining flash. Not a prudent, sensible, temporising plan, but a plan sudden, indiscreet, and fairly palpitating with excitement—a cap-over-the-windmill, jump-in-off-the-deep-end kind of plan. She was sick of running away, and hiding, and behaving as if she had a guilty conscience and a murky past when she hadn't. What's the good of conscious innocence if you can't confront your accusers? She felt an urge to confront somebody—or, to come from the general to the particular, to confront Pierrette. She didn't want to go to prison, but she felt a comfortable conviction that Anthony wouldn't let her go to prison. Men were exasperating but competent. They knew how to cope with policemen. She felt quite sure that Anthony was coping, and that she would not be arrested. But she wasn't quite so sure about Pierrette. The Maltby had said things about getting Ettie and Mr Phillips sent to prison, and if Ettie was Pierrette, Shirley felt very wobbly about this. However odious the behaviour of your near relations, you do not really want to see them in the dock. Shirley's imagination showed her Pierrette in a dock, her eyes bunged up with crying and every sign of glitter departed, whilst she herself stood up in a witness-box and took an oath, and kissed a Book, and deposed that the prisoner was her niece. Her mind reacted violently and her foot stamped—"I *won't*—I simply *won't!*" She fairly whisked into the hall, where she fell upon a page child and demanded Mr Phillips.

Conducted up a half flight of stairs, she stopped outside the door, pressed a shilling into a not unwilling hand, dismissed her escort with a nod, and after listening for a moment went in.

Her entrance produced a most gratifying sensation—gratifying, that is, to Shirley Dale, who after receiving a series of pulverizing shocks during the last twenty-four hours found it an uncommonly pleasant change to be in the position of shocking somebody else. She shut the door behind her, leaned lightly against it, and looked about her. She saw two very much startled people. A dog who has chased a cat into a tree not uncommonly runs away if the cat jumps down. Alfred Phillips, in the act of lighting a cigarette, stared fixedly, burnt his fingers, dropped the match, got to his feet. Ettie sat forward in her chair, her eyes bulging.

An extraordinary exhilaration possessed Shirley. She leaned against the door and said politely,

"How do you do, Pierrette?"

Mr Phillips recovered himself. He said, as if he were speaking to an intruding stranger,

"I think you have made a mistake. This is a private room."

Shirley nodded.

"I don't think there's any mistake. Your name is Phillips—but I haven't come here to speak to you, I've come here to speak to Pierrette."

Alfred Phillips raised his sandy eyebrows and turned to Ettie.

"Do you know this lady?"

"I'm quite sure she does," said Shirley. "I'm Jane Lorimer's daughter Shirley Dale, and she's Jane Lorimer's grand-daughter Pierrette Meunier—only you've turned it into English, haven't you, Pierrette? What is it now? Anthony guessed it would be Ettie Miller. Is that right?"

Ettie stared, and went on staring. She caught a choked breath, threw out her hands, caught her breath again, and said,

"What do you want?"

She had no French accent. She held her voice steady. Her hands moved, catching at one another, at the chair.

"I want to talk to you," said Shirley, still with that feeling of exhilaration.

Alfred Phillips advanced a seat.

"Won't you sit down?"

"No, I don't think so. I just want to talk to Pierrette. You do call yourself Ettie Miller, don't you, and not Pierrette Meunier?"

Ettie blundered. Like most large women she was timid at heart. Frightened and taken by surprise, she jumped out of the frying-pan into the fire.

She said, "I'm Mrs Phillips," and looked at Alfred, to be doubly frightened by the cold repressed fury in his face.

Shirley nodded again.

"Anthony guessed he would marry you," she said. "I think it was very clever of him. But of course he *is* very clever—you have to be to be a barrister."

Alfred Phillips came a step nearer.

"I don't know what you're talking about," he said. "This is a private sitting-room, and I must ask you to leave it."

Shirley stood her ground. Her eyes danced as she looked away from him to Ettie.

"He's not very polite, is he, when I've come to pay a nice call? There are quite a lot of things I think we ought to talk about, Pierrette."

Ettie recovered herself a little. She shrugged her shoulders, looked fleetingly at her husband, and said,

"I don't know what it's all about, I'm sure."

Shirley laughed.

"Come off it! What's the good of pretending you don't know who I am? Of course it's rather embarrassing—I quite see that—because you've been trying to get me into trouble. But you'll be very silly if you won't talk things over, because I haven't got any nasty vindictive feelings, and all I want is to avoid doing the family wash in public."

Alfred Phillips came across, pulled Shirley roughly away from the door, and opened it.

"Out you go!" he said. "We don't know what you're talking about, and we don't want to!" He had read uncertainty in Ettie's face, and he was most sharply afraid of what she might say or do.

Shirley twisted angrily away from him. Why wasn't Anthony here instead of talking to his aunt? And then, just as she was going to tell Mr Phillips what she thought about his manners, the page child came running up the stair in a state of shrill excitement.

"Telephone call—for you, sir! Long distance, sir! New York, sir!"

Mr Phillips without a word pushed past and was gone helter-skelter down the stairs to the box below. Shirley stepped back into the room and shut the door. She would have liked to lock it, but there wasn't any key.

"That's better," she said, "Now, Pierrette—what's the stupid game? Anthony says you can be run in for conspiracy. He knows, because he's a barrister. Oh, don't go on saying you don't know what I mean, because I'm sick to death of it! You know perfectly well you've tried to get me into prison because that old William Ambrose Merewether made a silly, idiotic will. I think people who make wills like that ought to be shut up in asylums, and if there was any sense in the law they would be, instead of being allowed to make mischief in families like he has. And anyhow if there *are* all those millions, there must be plenty for both of us, and I'm sure I don't mind dividing, because a lot of money is just a lot of bother, I think, and anyhow it wouldn't be fair for me to have it all—I should feel a perfect pig. But if I were you, Pierrette, I'd get my share tied up very tight and safe, because I don't think very much of your husband, not when it comes to honesty—and if that sounds rude, well, he's just been most frightfully rude to me."

The door opened behind Shirley and hit her in the back. She turned indignantly, to see Anthony coming into the room, whereupon she forgot that she had planned a quarrel and caught him joyfully by the arm.

"Come in, darling! You nearly broke my back just now, but it doesn't matter. Come in, and let's get into the corner, because everyone seems to burst this door open, and my spine won't stand another blow like that. And now I'd like to introduce you to Mrs Alfred Phillips, who is Pierrette Meunier, who is Ettie Miller—at least she didn't answer when I asked her about that. Are you Ettie Miller, Pierrette? Oh, and this is my *fiancé*, Anthony Leigh."

Ettie got up out of her chair. She looked angry, she looked frightened. The anger and the fear were in conflict. The colour rose in her cheeks, her fine eyes flashed. And then once more, before she could say anything, the door opened and Alfred Phillips appeared. He looked like a man who has had a shock, and he moved stiffly. He went over to the mantelpiece and took hold of it, staring down into the glow of the gas fire. Ettie turned a terrified face upon him and put out a shaking hand to touch him.

"Al—what is it? Al—what's happened?"

Without moving, he said in a low muttering voice,

"He made another will."

"Al! What do you mean—what are you saying?"

"He made another will."

Shirley did not think he had noticed her, or seen Anthony. Ettie's shaking hand shook his arm.

"Who did? Who made another will?"

He said, "Old Merewether," on a dropped note that was like a groan.

"No—no!" said Ettie. "He couldn't! He didn't!"

"He did. They've just found it."

"Who told you?"

"Schuyler Van Leiten. Said he hoped no false hopes had been raised." Ettie's hand fell from his arm.

"The new will—what's in it?"

He turned round on her in a spasm of fury.

"You're not! She's not either, if that's any comfort! Everything to charities! Every darned cent! It's in his own writing, and there isn't a hole in it anywhere!"

Anthony's voice cut in clear and cool.

"In fact, Mr Phillips, you've had a good deal of trouble for nothing." Then as Alfred Phillips started round and stared at him, he went on, "Trouble—and expense. I should be interested to know what you were going to pay Bessie Wood, and whether you had to give her anything on account. Miss Maltby, I gather, was to get a share when you had actually got away with the swag."

Alfred Phillips looked ghastly. He clenched and unclenched his hands, took a step forward, and managed to speak. He said,

"I don't know what you're talking about." He touched his tongue to his dry lips and forced his voice to a kind of steadiness. "I think you're under a mistake of some kind. I shouldn't like you to get a mistaken notion, Mr Leigh. I am employed by the firm of Van Leiten of New York, a very well known firm. They—" he stumbled for a moment—"they have done all Mr Merewether's business for years. When he went down with a stroke only twenty-four hours after signing what Mr Van Leiten naturally took to be his last will, the firm—" He stopped, groped for his handkerchief, and wiped his forehead. He wiped it twice, breathed deeply, and went on again. "The firm took advantage of my coming over here on a holiday. I was instructed to trace the beneficiaries under Mr Merewether's will—in an unobtrusive manner. He was not expected to recover, and his death might have taken place at any time. I have been engaged on my firm's business—in a perfectly regular and proper manner—" His voice stopped suddenly. It was as if a gramophone record had been running and had been suddenly arrested.

Anthony said, "Was it in the interests of your firm that you induced one of the possible beneficiaries to marry you?"

"And what's that got to do with you?" said Ettie in a loud angry voice. "What's it got to do with you who I marry or who I don't marry? I haven't got to ask your leave! I'm of age, aren't I?"

Anthony smiled agreeably.

"Oh, without any shadow of doubt," he said.

And what Ettie would have said to that is unknown, since the door was once again flung open and into the room, white and panting, ran Bessie Wood. She had got rid of her cap and apron. She was bareheaded in her dark red uniform dress. She had run nearly all the way from Revelston Crescent, and she now saw no one but Alfred Phillips whom she had come to find—Alfred Phillips who was her one chance of getting clear of the police. Ettie meant nothing to her. The open door hid Anthony and Shirley.

She said, "Al—they're after me!" and ran to him.

Anthony stepped behind her, shut the door, and stood against it.

"Al," said Bessie—"Al! You've got to help me—I've got to have money! They found me with the stuff! I chucked it down and ran—just as I was! You've got to help me!"

"Go away!" said Alfred Phillips. "You're mad! Go away!" His voice was hoarse and weak. Then suddenly he rallied. "You needn't try and blackmail me!" he said in such a tone of fury that Bessie went back a step.

"I haven't got a penny! I haven't got a dog's chance—like this—with no money! You promised me a hundred—"

Shirley was pulling at Anthony's sleeve, whispering in his ear, but when he answered her he spoke loud enough to be heard by everyone in the room. He said,

"Not my job, my dear. I think Mr Phillips can pay for his own dirty work." Then he looked at him directly. "She would be a very inconvenient witness. I really think you'd, better pay up, Phillips."

Shirley whispered again, tickling his ear, his neck, with a flood of soft, urgent words.

"What happened? Tell me what happened. Where are the emeralds?"

"My aunt has got them back."

"Then, Anthony, please, *please*, you'll let her go. Oh, darling, *yes*! If Mrs Huddleston's got her things back—oh, Anthony, I don't want to send her to prison! She—she's frightened."

"She tried to send *you* there," said Anthony.

Shirley pinched him very hard.

"Please, *please*—I don't want her to go to prison for that."

She ran up to Bessie.

"You can't go through the streets like this—they'd get you at once. And it's much too cold. Here, take my coat." She slipped it off and held it out.

Bessie threw her a pale, sharp look.

"And have you describe it to the police as soon as I'm out of the door?" she said. "Not much! Say I'd stolen it, as likely as not!"

Bright tears sprang to Shirley's eyes, and the outraged colour to her cheeks.

"Oh, I *wouldn't*! I'm giving it to you. I want you to have it, and it will cover your dress. How much money do you want?"

"A tenner," said Bessie. She snatched the coat and put it on.

Shirley turned briskly to Mr Phillips.

"How frightfully slow you are! Don't you see she wants to get away quickly? Where's your pocket-book? How much have you got?" She leant forward and whispered, "If you don't pay up, I'll let Anthony send for the police. He *wants* to."

Alfred Phillips paid up. It was a matter of considerable regret to him afterwards, but at the moment he was not feeling equal to an interview with the police. He would, in fact, have paid a good deal more than ten pounds to avoid one.

Shirley watched the notes pass with satisfaction. Then she moved, to see Anthony still with his back to the door. She pulled reproachfully at an arm which resisted her, but when she looked up there was the glint of a smile in his eyes.

"You want me to compound a felony," he said.

"Pouf!" said Shirley. She pulled again, and this time the arm had stopped resisting.

Bessie made a dart for the door and was gone. They heard her running feet upon the stairs.

"And now," said Shirley, "you'll have to take me somewhere in a taxi, darling."

Chapter Thirty-Three

IN THE TAXI she said, snuggling up,

"I don't know where we're going. Do you? It feels like eloping—rather nice."

"Women are definitely anti-social," said Anthony. "They have no moral sense, and they are not fit to be citizens. They ate not really civilised."

Shirley said "Pouf!" again. Then she snuggled a little closer. "All that because I'm not a horrid vindictive woman who gloats over people being punished! If you want to marry a gloating woman you can go away and do it—but you won't like it, darling, so I shouldn't *really*."

"Shall I like being married to you?"

"'Um—I expect so. I'm very, very nice. I think you are a very fortunate person."

They picked up Shirley's suit-case at the Mew, endeavoured rather unsuccessfully to placate the injured Jasper, and drove off again.

"You haven't told me where we're going," said Shirley.

"You can't go back to Mrs Camber's, because I simply won't have you under the same roof as that Maltby woman."

"You needn't say *you* won't—I won't either," said Shirley with spirit. "She might say I'd stolen her family diamonds next. Perhaps she's got some that belonged to Queen Elizabeth. I'm not taking any risks. Where *are* we going?"

"I think you had better stay with the Blessed Damozel until we can be married, then there won't be any talk."

"Oh—" Shirley sounded rather doubtful. "Will she like that?"

"She'll love it," said Anthony, laughing. "You are already the blue-eyed child. She will tell everyone she made the match, and what's more, she'll believe it. That's the way her mind works, if you can call it a mind—I don't think women have them really,"

Shirley pinched him so sharply that he jumped.

"Here, I say—don't do that! It hurts!"

"It was meant to, darling. Anthony—"

"Yes? You're not going to pinch me again, are you?"

"Not unless you deserve it. No, I was going to say—"

"All right, say it."

Shirley put her chin in the air.

"You say women haven't got any minds, but *I* think I was cleverer than you—about Bessie—because I *was* sorry for her, and I *would* have let her go anyhow, but I couldn't help seeing quite dreadfully distinctly that if the police arrested her she was just the kind of person who would give everyone else away to try and save herself. If she'd been charged with taking the emeralds she'd have said Mr Phillips put her up to it, and Pierrette would have got dragged in, and I should have had to stand up in a witness-box and say that large glittering female was my niece and that odious gingery ferret of a Phillips was my nephew-in-law—and *honestly* I'd rather die. So I thought, 'Why not make everyone happy and let Bessie go?'"

"No moral sense," said Anthony—"absolutely none. No, look here, Shirley—if you pinch me again I'll break off our engagement, and then you won't have anyone to go and stay with."

Shirley made an impudent face.

"And everyone will say it's because you found out I wasn't going to be an heiress after all!"

He said, "Don't rub it in—I'll have to marry you," and put his arms round her and kissed her very hard behind the taxi-driver's back.

Mrs Huddleston took the news of William Ambrose Merewether's latest will with perfect calm and a flow of anecdote. There was one about a marriage that turned out *most* unhappily because the wife had more money than the husband and was always reminding him of the fact.

"Not that dear Shirley would do such a thing as that, I'm sure," said the Blessed Damozel with a Pre-Raphaelite smile. She sniffed delicately at the new bottle of smelling-salts and continued. "I had nothing when I married your dear uncle, and no marriage could have been happier, although I cannot say I think it is right to raise false hopes and make wills, and then make other wills and disappoint everybody. I don't think Mr Merewether should have done it. The money was his own—he could have left it to charity or he could have left it to Shirley, but not first to one and then to the other, because it is very confusing and apt to lead to bad feeling in a family. And now we won't talk about wills any more. My dear boy's engagement is a much pleasanter subject, and I wish to mark my pleasure and—and the occasion by giving dear Shirley the Napoleon emeralds."

Shirley gasped.

Anthony said, "How very, very nice of you, Aunt Agnes."

Mrs Huddleston produced the emeralds from a pale blue satin bag—earrings, hairband, and two brooches.

"Come here, my dear," she said. "I should like to see how you look in them."

At any other time Shirley would have giggled. She was dusty, and she was dishevelled—her hair was wild—and she was invited to try on Josephine's *parure*—But the emeralds had taken away her breath. She had none left for laughter. She knelt beside the couch, felt a cold circle touch her brow, and the dangle of the earrings against her neck. Mrs Huddleston pinned the two brooches on to the grey jumper. A solemn embrace followed.

"And now, my dear, go and look at yourself in the glass."

Shirley went round to the back of the sofa. The ornate mirror which hung above the piano reflected her, reflected the emeralds. The laurels were undimmed by all the years which had passed since Lodi. They had clasped Josephine's smoothly ordered curls. They rested on Shirley's ruffled hair with the dust of Helena Pocklington's studio clinging to it. There was even a cobweb. The earrings fell gracefully beside two rosy cheeks with a good many smudges on them. The brooches winked scornfully from the front of the grey jumper.

Shirley felt a desire to laugh and a desire to cry. It had been horrid, but the horridness was over. It had been fun, and it was going to be more fun. She made the most superb Woggy Doodle of her life and turned it upon Anthony—eyes squinting inwards, eyeballs glaring, lips curved into the true Cheshire cat grin.

Anthony gazed—struck dumb. The emeralds shone under the light.

"Most becoming, I'm sure," said the unconscious Mrs Huddleston.

THE END

. . . .

Made in the USA
Middletown, DE
28 June 2021

43283202R00116